Code Name:
ORION'S EYE

Best Wishes
To my Friend, Sy — Oct9,2020

A Novel by

TOM GAUTHIER

Code Name:
ORION'S EYE

By Tom Gauthier

Published by
ToMar Associates Publishing, Reno, NV
United States of America

Third Edition Printed 2017
Copyright © 2010 by Tom Gauthier
All rights reserved.

ISBN-13: 978-1542934558

Cover Art: Created by Tyler Silkwood and Owen Johnston, edited by Dr. Ray White

Earlier Editions of Code Name: ORION'S EYE
ISBN 978-0-9846638-5-9 Published by Patriot Media, Inc., Florida
ISBN 978-1-4327-2713-0 Published by Outskirts Press, Colorado

DEDICATION

Dedicated to the Soldiers of the 855th Engineer Battalion (Aviation), the 1st Fighter Control Squadron, and the 253rd Ordnance Company (Aviation) who faced the enemy and the elements aboard USAT Cape San Juan in 1943, then prevailed.

And to their comrades who did not survive.

You are all remembered and honored still for your bravery and service in World War II.

"All warfare is based on deception. Hence, when able to attack, we must seem unable; when using our forces, we must seem inactive; when we are near, we must make the enemy believe we are far away; when far away, we must make him believe we are near. Hold out baits to entice the enemy. Feign disorder, and crush him."

Sun Tzu, the Art of War

FORWARD

Reading historical fiction provides a unique blend of entertainment and education. When well written, fictional characters provide the needle and history the thread that weaves a tapestry of pleasurable learning for the reader. *Code Name: ORION'S EYE* is just such a story, taking a plot that challenges the characters and setting it in little known locations and events from World War II history. Learning about German submarines operating in the South Pacific, Nazi spies and the government's fear of Japanese incursions in Mexico, and the dramatic event of the largest troopship sinking in the Pacific war are examples of 'below the fold news' that makes an entertaining backdrop for the story.

Tom Gauthier shows us his passion for accurate detail and his skill in putting it into a fast moving, enlightening and entertaining tale. I'll be watching for more of our antagonist Amos Mead and his intrepid band of OSS spy chasers in future stories.

> *Dr. Douglas B. Houston, Ed.D.*
> *Chancellor, Yuba Community College District*

Dr. Houston is a combat veteran, U.S. Army Engineers. He received his Master's Degree in Physics and Army Commission from the University of Florida. During his military service he commanded various military units and served as a Professor of Physics at West Point. After leaving active military service, he earned his Doctorate in Educational Leadership from the Pepperdine University.

INTRODUCTION

World War II (1941-1945), with all of its destruction, slaughter and human displacement, proved to be a crucible of new technologies that would provide significant breakpoints in human progress — breakpoints that define changes from which there would be no return: aviation, electronics, atomic weapons among them.

One such technology is radar. From the giant radio-ranging installations on the Cliffs of Dover, to the Germans' countering science, to the final miniaturization that placed the device in the nose of an aircraft, the warfighters ability to see his enemy first became critical to victory — on land, sea and air.

In 1943 Nazi Germany paid a high price for the sins of Adolph Hitler. The British bombed German cities by night and the Americans bombed by day. New long-range U.S. fighter planes protected the bombers deep into Germany, and the Luftwaffe lost many its best and brightest pilots.

Two of the most senior Nazis, *Reichsführer* Heinrich Himmler, head of the infamous SS, and *Reichsmarschall* Hermann Goering, head of the Luftwaffe, were competing to survive. Each had fallen out of favor with Hitler as his paranoia grew in the latter days of the war.

Himmler and Goering knew that they had a potentially deadly plight. They grasped at straws that might keep them afloat in the flood of Allied assaults.

A small event in the U.S. loomed large in their twisted mental state. They may have found a way to save the day — and themselves.

CAST OF CHARACTERS

AMERICANS and BRITISH:

Mead, Amos Nathan, Major, U.S. Marine Corps
Morse, Chandler, British Officer, SIRA, OSS R&D and BSI
Alexander, Jedburgh, OSS West Coast Training Center
Barrows, David P., General, Coordinator of Intel West Coast
Bruce, David K.E. Head of Mission, OSS London
Pearson, Norman Holmes, Yale Prof., Head of OSS X-2 London
Donovan, William 'Wild Bill', Brigadier General, Head of OSS
Murphy, James (Jim), OSS Chief of Counterespionage
Hyman, Maurice, OSS, South America Intel
Tweedy, George, OSS Deputy Director
St. James, Willie, Colonel, Liaison Officer, JCS, OSS
Wetmore, Harmon, CPO, OSS West Coast
Williamson, Betty Jean (BJ), House Mgr., OSS Safe House
Velasquez, Pedro, Cook, OSS Safe House, LA
Velasquez, Constantia, Maid, OSS Safe House, LA
Driest, Chester W., Tech Sgt, 1st Fighter Control Squadron
Gibbons, Harry A, 1st Lt. Training Officer for 1st Fighters
Dillon, Sam, LCDR, Naval Attaché, runs spook team for ONI
Layton, Edward, Rear Admiral, JICPOA
Nielsen, Manfield R. III, Major General, CO, 4th Interceptor Cmd., March Field

ABOARD USAT *CAPE SAN JUAN*:

Gochais, Donovan Ignatius (Don), OSS, LTJG, Third Mate, U.S. Maritime Service
Bonfoey, Edward M. (Ed), FBI, Captain, U.S. Army Air Corps
Dorcey, Bill, Second Mate
Harris, Graham, Navy Lieutenant, Communications Officer
Jeter, Arthur L., Tech. Sgt, 855th Engineer (Aviation) Battalion
Keefer, Harold, Lt Col, CO, 855th Engineer (Aviation) Battalion

Makowski, Thaddeus (Ted), P O, 2nd Class, Radio Operator
Manning, Earl, Chief Mate
McIntire, Manny, Corporal, U.S. Army, Radio Operator
Meuller, Rhinehart, Navy Lieutenant, Gunnery Officer
Strong, Walter, Captain, USAT *Cape San Juan*

NAZI GERMANS:

Himmler, Heinrich, Field Marshal, *Reichsfuhrer*-SS, GIS HQ
Goering, Hermann Wilhelm, *Reichmarschall*, Head of
Luftwaffe
Wolff, Karl, Himmler's Chief of Staff
Hauptmann, Otto, Colonel, Spy Master, Third Reich
Hauptmann, Heinrich, father of Otto Hauptmann
Nebe, Artur, Chief, GIS, SD, Berlin
Dönitz, Karl *Großadmiral* (Grand Admiral) and *Oberbefehlshaber
der Kriegsmarine* (Commander-in-Chief) of the German Navy
Gehlan, Reinhard, spy master, Third Reich
Kalbruener, Ernst, *Kapitän, Kreigsmarine* submarine *U-835*
Engels, Albrecht, Rio de Janiero, Brazil
Müeller, Adolph, (*Jaeger*–Hunter), mole for Nazi spy network
Nicolaus, George, Mexico City
Buchanan-Dineen, Grace, Fort Monmouth, Nazi spy.
Lehmitz, Ernest, Nazi spy implicated by Buchanan-Dineen

OTHER:

Byrnes, Margaret, Manager, Lennons Hotel, Brisbane,
Australia
Moss, William, Jr, (Bill), Pilot, Pan Am Martin Mariner

JAPANESE:

Inada, Commander, Imperial Japanese Navy, submarine *I-21*
Tanaka, Executive Officer, submarine *I-21*

 **CHAPTER 1**

New Jersey, USA
June 1943

The night watchman at the Monmouth Beach Bath and Tennis Club rose heavily from the broken-in chair that nearly filled his small office. He sighed and mumbled, "Time to make the rounds once more."

Retrieving his flashlight, he noted the beam had weakened a bit. He knew that batteries were hard to come by so he'd make do with what he had. His hourly patrol around the grounds consisted of routine, boring walks, made too chilly for his old bones by the night breeze off the Atlantic. Pushing eighty-years-old, a veteran of the Great War, the old man is one of the cadre of old timers covering the home front jobs for the boys fighting overseas.

No moon shown on the water this night, but the stars blinked bright in a clear sky as the low surf splashed onto the sand in a pleasant rhythm. The night air smelled of the sea with the not unpleasant hint of seaweed rotting at the hightide line.

Rounding the clubhouse building, following his own footprints from an hour before, the old man started along the stretch of beach that fronted the club. He clicked off his light so he could watch the starlight play off the small waves that foamed up onto the smooth sand. This part of the walk he really didn't mind.

A sound caught his attention.

Something ain't right, out of place ... a splash.

He stopped and peered up the beach. Squinting, he made out a shadowy figure moving up the beach toward the lawns. The old man tried to focus on whether this meant danger or not. Then he saw two other silhouettes emerge from the water—then another.

Now he felt danger.

Retracing his steps, being careful where he placed his unsteady feet, he reached his office and grabbed the telephone. Two rings connected him to the Monmouth Beach marshals' office.

"Marshal, this is Pete down at the beach club. Listen, I've got a group of strangers coming out of the ocean ... yup, you heard me. Straight out of the ocean. No, I don't think they saw me. You need to get over here. Better get a move on afore they get too far ... just in case."

Two miles away the town marshal had mixed feelings. Happy for a little action on the dull night shift, he also knew his shift ended in a few minutes. Seeing his relief pull up in front of the office, he went out to meet him and explained the phone call he's received.

"Probably just some kids playing whoopee in the beach. But the old man sounded a little shook up."

Finally choosing curiosity over going home to a cold house, he mounted his Harley Davidson, kicked the starter and roared off down Oceanside Drive alongside his partner and toward the beach club.

At the club, the old man snapped off the lights in his office and carefully emerged back into the night. He moved slowly across the grass toward the road, straining to adjust his eyes to the starlit scene. Unknown to him, the group of intruders, numbering four, had turned along the edge of the lawn and were approaching very near to where he now headed.

Suddenly, they met. Each surprising the other.

The old man fumbled to snap on his light, shining it into the eyes of his adversaries ... but the beam faded to a dull orange.

For an instant everyone froze ... then the first of the intruders moved menacingly toward the old man, his hand raised. The old man dropped his flashlight and stumbled backwards as he heard the roar of the Harley motorcycles coming down the road.

Berlin, Germany
Headquarters, *Sicherheitsdienst*
(German Intelligence Service) One week later

Reichsführer-SS Heinrich Himmler paced the room, fists clenched at his sides, his narrow set eyes fixed on the picture of Adolph Hitler on the far wall.

His voice rose with each word as he screamed, "Captured? They have been captured? When? How could this happen?"

Artur Nebe, Chief of the German Intelligence Service stood at rigid attention, barely able to breathe. He knew that those eyes—Himmler's stare— would soon pierce him.

In a voice barely above a whisper Nebe answered, "It is true, *mein Reichsführer*. We just received word.

They were captured near the beach. They never reached our contact in Fort Monmouth."

Himmler whirled to face him and hissed through clenched teeth, "*Sie sind imbeciles* (We have fools) ... *inkompetente dummköpfes* (incompetent dummies). Where is Otto Hauptmann? Get me Hauptmann!"

With the bile of fear welling in his throat, his voice quivering, Nebe responded, "Hauptmann is in Vienna, *mein Reichsführer*. His father is ill and—"

Red-faced, Himmler cut him off, "*Erhalten Sie Hauptmann hier jetzt*! (Get Hauptmann here now!)"

Himmler stormed from the room.

Nebe paled in terror at the furious anger in Himmler's voice. He stood frozen in place for an instant before rushing off to obey the order. Back in his own office at #8 Prinz Albrecht-Straße he sent the message to find Hauptmann. Waiting, he paced the floor, his third cigarette, one lit from the other, spreading ashes along his path. It wasn't only the waiting that strained his nerves. An unwelcome visitor sat behind Nebe's desk. Karl Wolff, Himmler's Chief of Staff, tapped out a cadence with his fingers that mocked the man's pacing.

keeping his back to Wolff, Nebe yelled through the open door to his aide, "Heinz, have you found him?"

The aide stepped into the doorway and said, "*Jawol mein Leiter* (Yes, my leader). Just now we heard he has gone to the Vienna hospital. They are going to find him. He will be on the radio in one moment."

Vienna, Austria

Otto Hauptmann stood in the cobbled square looking up at the great stone façade of the

9

Allgemeines Kranken Haus Der Stadt Wien, Vienna's famed hospital founded in the year 1686. His meticulously tailored black SS uniform, the gold embroidered oak leaves on the collars speaking of the cream of the Nazi Party, belied his very human and tender feelings at the moment. He is on his way to see his dying father—a man whom he had grown to love and admire after some hurtful first years.

Blond and blue eyed, with a muscular build, his mirror polished jackboots made him look taller than his five feet eight inches. Born in Austria and raised a Catholic by his mother, Otto Hauptmann had rejected his faith and followed the meso-pagan theology of Aryan race supremacy championed by Himmler. In the 1930's, with his father away in America advancing the Nazi ideas, he'd grown up in the Hitler Youth movement. Now the young SS *Standartenführer* (equivalent rank of Army Colonel) is the apple of his father's eye.

Otto Hauptmann graduated high in his class from the Reich School for SS Leaders that *Reichsführer* Himmler had established at Wewelsburg Castle. Here he received his *Totenkopfring*, a band of oak leaves engraved with Teutonic runes and the death's head skull—the infamous Death's Head Ring of an SS Officer.

Himmler recognized Otto Hauptmann's talents early and saw to his training and rapid rise in rank. He spoke English, French and Spanish fluently with no hint of an accent. It is rare to see him in uniform as he is today. His usual dress, civilian, blends into the places where he practices his trade. Otto Hauptmann is a Master Spy for the Third Reich.

But today, he is simply the son of a dying father.

He turned to the sound of the Mercedes sliding to a stop on the cobbled drive. A *Waffen* SS soldier emerged from the car, came to attention and asked, "*Herr* Hauptmann?"

Hauptmann nodded.

The soldier offered a stiffly raised arm in salute. "*Heil Hitler! "Gekommen mit mir, bitte* (Come with me, please). *Reichsführer* Himmler is searching for you. We have a radio."

Otto Hauptman turned to look up at the majestic hospital façade, then down to the stones at his feet. Slowly he turned back toward the soldier and returned the salute, his forearm raised palm forward. In a quiet voice he said, "*Danke.*" (Thank you)

He walked toward the waiting car,

Duty ... always duty first.

Sicherheitsdienst Headquarters
Berlin, Germany

"He is on the radio, sir. From Vienna."

Nebe pushed roughly past the aide and grabbed the microphone from the equally startled radioman. He toggled the switch and growled, "Hauptmann, *Können Sie nach Berlin wie bald kommen?* (Return to Berlin at once! It is urgent!)"

After listening to the reply, he thrust the microphone back to the radioman, his face stiff with contempt, as he slowly turned to Wolff and said, "You can tell Herr Himmler that Hauptmann is on his way."

Wolff calmly rose from behind Nebe's desk, a smile on his lips that hinted of his namesake, and replied, "You shall hope that he arrives in a hurry, Artur. You must know that this goes beyond

11

Himmler. This mission is very high on Goering's priority also. You above all know that failure is no option."

He took and slowly lit a cigarette from the silver case on the desk, blowing a wreath of smoke toward Nebe. Then he snapped to mock attention, clicking his boot heels, and raised his hand in stiff salute, *"Heil Hitler!"*

 **CHAPTER 2**

X-2 Operations Headquarters
Office of Strategic Services (OSS)
London, England

Major Amos Nathan Mead, USMC, sat at his desk, the proper English tea cup looked far too delicate in his hands as he mused a starting point for another long day. He thought, *this coffee is neither hot enough nor strong enough. At least it is coffee.*

Mead's desk, a ubiquitous Government Issue olive drab box, stood comically out of its element in the elegantly sculpted English town home parlor.

His gaze slowly circled the room as he thought, *Reminds me of Dad's study at home ... dark carved wood paneling, wool carpet with those woven roses and vines.* He leaned back, sipping from the cup. *That leather chair always creaked. Wonder if BJ's been in touch? BJ ... we'd sneak into that room for a stealthy teenage kiss. Seems long ago.*

Amos Mead grew up in a small Vermont town, the son of a prominent banker. The Depression had never really touched his life. There had been a short, turbulent marriage right out of college that didn't last long enough to even speak about. There hadn't been any real relationships since, as he focused on graduate studies and his law career.

London provided enough diversion for him. Mead did his best to live up to the Brits' description of American soldiers: 'over paid, over sexed, and over here!' But he didn't over-do it.

Why does BJ keep popping into my head?

BJ, Betty Jean Brown, his high school flame, had kept in touch for a while, but life seemed to intervene. Lately she had become a recurring vision for him.

Why?

Mead stood, stretched his five-eleven frame and ran a hand through his dark brush-cut hair. The tall heavy door creaked open with authority and his day began as he greeted his partner, "Good morning, Chandler."

Chandler Morse closed the door behind him with his heel and hefted the locked courier bag onto the desk, an effort for the slightly built man who looked the part of the research bookworm that he is. He answered, "Another batch of intercepts for you from good old Station X, Amos."

Mead produced his matching key. Together they opened the lock and retrieved more of what had become a growing mystery. Amos asked, "How's it look, Chandler?"

"Something's going on, Amos. Something big. The Jerrys are too steamed up about it. That *Auge Orions* phrase is all over it. What the hell could *Orion's Eye* be?"

"Don't know, my friend, let's keep digging. Solving these deep dark secrets is why we get the big bucks, you know."

Chandler Morse chuckled, "Big bucks ... another quaint American phrase for my collection."

Mead sorted through the work of the Bletchley Park production of German ULTRA intercepts. Station X, as Bletchley Park is known to the intelligence community, worked mathematical miracles with its code breaking mission.

Chandler sat over his stack of reports, running his fingers through his tousled and thinning hair. "These bits from *#8 Prinz Albrecht-Straße* are still tense. Two of the intercepts are worked from the *Lorenz Cipher*. That's only used by the bloody German High Command. Somebody's catching bloody hell from Herr Hitler himself it seems."

Mead said, mainly to himself, "We could only wish they'd kill each other off." Reaching for the open pack of American Camels he drew one out and tapped it on the desk. "Here's that *Auge Orions* again—"

He looked away to pick up the Zippo with the Globe and Anchor, thinking, *Auge Orions? And why are they so tight about finding Otto Hauptmann? Orion's Eye? Theirs or ours? Theirs or our* what?

The telephone rang. Mead fumbled for the receiver, "Major Mead here, how may I help you, sir? Yes, sir. One hour."

He re-cradled the telephone and snuffed out his cigarette. "Okay, Chandler, they got our report and we're on the hot seat in an hour."

Amos Mead, a lawyer by education, FBI Special Agent by trade and Marine Corp Officer by act of Congress, had been recruited from the Marines by the OSS and assigned to X-2 in London, working with British MI-6 to identify and track German Intelligence officers.

His partner, British officer Chandler Morse, is a member of the SIRA—the joint operation of American OSS Research and Development and British Strategic

Intelligence—known internally as the enemy objectives unit. He kept pace with Mead down the echoing hallway.

Mead paused at the door, rapped once and entered.

Inside, he directed his announcement at Norman Holmes Pearson, a Yale University professor and the head of X-2 in London. "Reporting as requested, sir."

"Take a seat, Major ... Mr. Morse. Do you know everyone?"

Mead glanced around the elegant mahogany table. "No, sir ... not everyone."

James Murphy, the new OSS Chief of Counterespionage, rose with outstretched hand. "Jim Murphy, Major. Sorry I haven't caught up to you yet. But I've sure seen your work."

"Thank you, sir, welcome to London."

Murphy nodded to Mead then turned to Morse and said, "Chandler, good to see you again."

"And you, sir."

From the far end of the table David K.E. Bruce, Head of Mission, OSS London, spoke, "Good morning, Major Mead, Mr. Morse."

Almost in unison they replied, "Morning, sir."

Nearly everyone in the room had been recruited personally by the head of the OSS, Brigadier General 'Wild Bill' Donovan. He recruited people who studied world affairs, often representing *the best and the brightest* at East Coast universities, businesses, and law firms. The OSS eventually drew such a high proportion of socially prominent men and women that witty pundits dubbed OSS to mean 'Oh So Social.'

Mead considered himself *second tier* in the recruit ranks as it had been the influence of his bank executive father in Vermont that got him—then a U.S. Marine captain—the tap on the shoulder and the fast promotion to major.

Bruce spoke first, "All right, gentlemen, let's get down to business. As you know Major Mead works for Pearson's X-2. They identify and track German intelligence officers ... and quite successfully, I might add."

Bruce rose from his chair, uncovered a chart set on an easel to his left, and continued, "Here's what Mead and Morse sent to me. They suspect a pattern of communications is forming that should be of concern to us. Major, would you please take us through this material?"

Mead moved to the easel and began, "Virtually all of this intelligence came from ULTRA (German military code broken by the Allies) intercepts, mostly to and from *Prinz Albrecht-Straße* in Berlin ... SS Headquarters. We began to see a curious pattern in these messages so I notified Mr. Pearson."

Pearson interjected, "And that's when I talked with most of you."

Mead looked around, then continued, "I was checking on the whereabouts of one Herr Heinrich Hauptmann. This guy's a repatriate from the U.S. and he's helping Himmler himself recruit U.S. dissidents. Then I lost him. Next thing I see is Otto Hauptmann, his son, being sought out from Berlin. The messages are mostly from Nebe and sound a bit frantic."

James Murphy asked, "*The* Nebe?"

Mead nodded and continued, "Yes, sir. Artur Nebe, the Chief of German Intelligence Service. Two of the messages contained the words *Auge Orion*. The English translation is *Orion's Eye*. We'd seen the words earlier in a transmission coming into SD Berlin. I'm told it originated somewhere on the east coast of the U.S. It's in code, but *Auge Orion* is in the clear."

David Bruce said, "So you got curious about this *Orion's Eye*."

"Yes, sir. But I was more curious about the increasing urgency and the frequency and tone of the messages." Mead paused and pointed to an underlined name on the chart. "Then we began to see Otto Hauptmann sending back to Nebe in Berlin. They had ordered him back from Vienna in a real rush."

He turned the chart over to an outline of South America. "Next we see Otto contacting Herr George Nicolaus in Mexico City, and then Albrecht Engels in Brazil ... Rio de Janiero. Both these guys are German intelligence, *Sicherheitsdienst*, the SD. They both work for Nebe and both of their messages mentioned *Auge Orion*—"

David Bruce again interrupted, "Gentlemen, Mead's report coincides with the report of the arrest of four Germans landed by submarine on the New Jersey coast."

Mead cast a quizzical look at Bruce. "Hadn't heard that, sir."

"Not surprising, Major. It didn't come together until yesterday. It seems that their mission to locate a certain piece of technology at Fort Monmouth went astray. Now they're guests of the OSS at Fort Hunt ... and they've coughed up more than seawater."

Pearson interjected, "So these guys planned to steal this technology?"

"Don't know for sure yet, Norman, but we do know that they had a contact who works at

Monmouth. A woman name of Grace Buchanan-Dineen. The FBI has her in custody."

A sharp rap on the door and an aide stepped in at attention. "Mr. Bruce, sir, excuse me, sir, but you asked to be informed immediately if we heard more on the FBI arrest." He handed a file marked TOP SECRET to David Bruce who acknowledged it, "Thank you, Lieutenant."

The aide continued, "Sir, there's more … E Street just confirmed that the technology the Germans are after has already left Fort Monmouth. It's going operational. The first stop for it is supposed to be Selfridge Army Air Corp Field in Michigan. There's a new special Fighter Control Squadron supposed to be taking custody of the stuff."

"Any more, Lieutenant?"

"No sir." Executing a sharp about face, the aide exited.

Bruce opened the file and quietly read the decoded wire. After a moment he looked up. "Gentlemen, this Buchanan-Dineen lady is singing along with her German spy heroes. FBI reports that she's turned another contact … a fellow named Ernest Lehmitz. The FBI picked him up too … in Mount Clemens, Michigan."

Chandler Morse sat up straight. "Sir, that's near to where Selfridge Field is located!"

Bruce nodded, then looked around the group. "Connections … conclusions, gentlemen?"

Mead spoke, "Sir, it seems obvious that this crew is either after or tracking the technology … or whatever it is. Do we know where it goes from Selfridge?"

"Only that it's deploying with the Army Air Corp to the Pacific. No details here."

Mead set the pointer on the easel's ledge, stepped toward the table and said, "The urgent messages to Mexico and Brazil from Berlin ... they track west ... and the Germans are jumping all over Hauptmann." He turned to Pearson. "Sir, Otto Hauptmann is one of their best, one of Himmler's personal spy dogs."

Pearson asked, "And ... how connected?"

Mead crossed his arms and looked up at the ceiling. "I'm curious about the frantic tone of those Berlin intercepts." He turned back to the group. "Tie that to this new information and I think when the New Jersey bunch blew their mission Otto Hauptmann got called in to pick it up ... only farther west. Somebody's going to have their hands full with him. He's smart ... and ruthless. This guy's a Nazi's Nazi."

Pearson stood and made eye contact with Bruce, who nodded a knowing assent. Pearson turned and put a hand on Mead's shoulder. "Somebody does have their hands full, Major Mead. Get your gear together and report back here at 0900 tomorrow. We'll have a package of all we know ready for you. Your flight leaves from Heathrow for Washington at 1100 hours."

Mead stammered, "Me, sir? Are you sure? I'm no spook."

Bruce smiled. "Don't need a spook, Major. Your qualifications fit the bill ... besides, you dug all this up. You'll learn more at E Street in DC from the OSS staff people. Chandler here will keep up the intercepts and stay in touch with you. You've both been cleared for use of MAGIC, so communication should stay timely."

Bruce sat down at the table and shuffled his papers into a neat pile as he continued, "One more piece of information, Major. The technology the Germans are after... it's got a name: Code Name: ORION'S EYE."

"*Auge Orions* ... I'll be damned."

Mead knows that the meeting is over—and that his future is now more uncertain than ever.

Major Amos Mead, USMC, climbed the rattling metal steps toward the open door of the aircraft, his military issue Valv-Pak bag in his right hand, the courier pouch joined to his left wrist by a chained handcuff.

Moments later, the C-75 StratoCruiser taxied to the end of the runway, ran up the four Wright R-1820 Cyclone radial engines, and began her takeoff roll. Mead felt the tail rise, followed shortly by the almost gentle sway that signaled wheels up. The sky bright blue, clouds placed for effect, the long Atlantic flight lay ahead.

Mead figured that one day he would be parachuting into Nazi Europe with other OSS operatives to support the French Maquis—maybe even blowing up a few things himself. This is why he wanted to be in the outfit, the OSS. *But now I'm headed in quite the opposite direction, West, to chase down phantom spies—or God knows what else.*

Unlocking the pouch, Mead slipped a sheaf of papers onto his lap. He scanned copies of *Saint Messages* (OSS indicator of counterespionage message content). They didn't tell him much more than he'd heard in the London meeting. A message from *Cassia,* the OSS underground contact in Austria, confirmed that the senior Hauptmann is ill and in hospital, and that Otto had been there and rushed back to Berlin.

His mind rushed, *Give me something new. Maybe this Army stuff ... Movement Orders Shipment 0445: Code Designation 0445-D, 1ˢᵗ Fighter Control Squadron moving from Selfridge Field to March Field in California ... ORION'S EYE on the move?* A note from Bruce:

```
Army unit is testing on west coast
before deploying to SWPA (South West
Pacific Area). Officer list attached.
Best we know, they embark on troopship
USAT Cape San Juan in October. Ship's
officers list included.
```

Mead ran a finger down the list. Out loud, he said, "I'll be damned." *I know this guy ... Donovan I. Gochais ... in the Merchant Marine... Third Mate.*

 **CHAPTER 3**

Los Angeles, California

It's a good sound—the shrill laughter of small boys. Elma Gochais sat on the shaded porch watching her two sons attack and retreat from the tickling attention of their father. The boys loved the romping sessions—all too few these days. The tiny, nearly five-feet tall 'with the right shoes' she liked to say, former Elma Palmer had married her sailor-boy in St. Vibiana's Cathedral in 1939 in Los Angeles. Since then the family had grown.

Lieutenant (JG) Donovan Ignatius Gochais, U.S. Maritime Service, had been home one day from his first voyage to the Pacific War Zone. Just a year ago the 5' 10" tall sandy-haired boy from Minnesota had finally settled into a promising career with the Los Angeles Police Department.

Pearl Harbor changed all that.

With his prior service in the Navy as a seaman on the battleship USS *West Virginia* before the war, Gochais was recruited by the Maritime Service, succeeded at the Academy in Alameda and was assigned to troop transport ships.

As he cradled a giggling boy in his arms, Donovan said to Elma, "Tommy's arm doesn't seem to bother him much."

Elma replied, "He's got good days and not-so-good days." She stroked the toddler's golden curls. "He's tough."

Three-year-old Tommy Gochais, injured during a difficult birth, suffered a withered arm. The doctors told Donovan and Elma that surgery may be needed if the shoulder joint did not become firm enough to support the arm—the cause of his pain.

Such an operation will be expensive. With money being tight, the family barely had enough to get by when Gochais is at sea.

Gregarious, self-confident, sometimes irreverent, Gochais never let his concern for his growing family peek through. He saw that as weakness. He also wasn't much for outwardly showing the deep love he had for them.

Donovan Ignatius Gochais grew up in depression ravaged Minnesota. His father, Jule Gochais, died of pneumonia when Don was only thirteen-years-old. Times were lean for a widowed mother with four children. He managed to finish school with jobs on the coal docks of Duluth filling the rest of his time and helping with the bills.

During this time his namesake grandfather, Ignatius McKinnon, who had not approved of his daughter's marriage to that *Frenchie*, was of little help. What he did provide he offered grudgingly and Donovan saw it as an insult to his mother. These feelings shaped his later life and his commitment to being the best father and husband he could be.

Elma went into the house and prepared a lunch of Spam sandwiches and fresh vegetables from the communal victory garden that stretched across three back yards of the little houses on Mayfield Place. The boys loved their veggies raw.

She carried the tray back to the front porch and called out, "Come and get it, you guys."

Reaching for a sandwich, Donovan asked, "Your mother and father are coming over this afternoon?"

"Yes. Father has some news about the Shriner's Hospital program."

"I'm not keen on charity, Elma. Not keen at all."

She replied, "If Tommy can get that arm fixed so he doesn't hurt anymore, I don't care how we do it."

Elma's tone said that this part of the conversation is over. She changed the subject. "You haven't told me anything about Australia. I know the war stuff is secret, but there must be something."

Donovan Gochais washed down a bite with a sip of the ice tea that had come on the tray. "Nothing much to tell, really ... but, hey, I did meet a guy from my home town! We were anchored off Espiritu Santo with about forty ships. I had the deck watch just after dawn and the deck officer on the ship next to us ... I think it was the USS *Denver* ... hailed me, just saying hello. Guy's name is Lightburn, Jack Lightburn, and he's from Duluth. A long way from home we were."

No more said, Elma led the boys off for their nap.

Donovan Ignatius Gochais, Lieutenant (JG), US Merchant Marine, sat on the porch step, arms around his knees, and stared off toward the Pacific Ocean.

International Airport
Los Angeles, California

Mead's stopover meetings at the OSS office on E Street, Washington, DC, had been brief—a whirlwind of information. One thing he did come away with—the highest powers in the U.S. government are keenly interested in his mission.

That to him is both good news and bad news.

The long flight to Los Angeles followed.

As he walked toward the terminal the stiffness in his back eased. Puffy fair weather clouds dotted a clear blue sky and the sun felt pleasantly warm on his head and shoulders. It reminded him that he much preferred California weather to the east coast—and certainly to dreary old London's.

As he reached for the Valv-Pak setting on the baggage rack, he thought, *Something to be said for dry air and an ocean breeze ... and the smell of real flowers,*

The Navy chief reached in front of Mead for the bag and said, "I'll take that, Major. Welcome to paradise, sir."

Broad-shouldered, bull-necked, and 5'9" tall, Chief Petty Officer Harmon Wetmore's sharply pressed khaki blouse carried ribbons that told a career story to other warriors.

Mead said, "Thanks, Chief." As he stepped back to allow the chief to pick up the bag, he asked, "And just what is the Navy doing greeting me?"

"We're on the same team, Major. They pegged me for OSS duty, too. Not sure what they need with an old Yangtze Station China-sailor, sir, but the hours ain't all bad and the chows better'n my last station. I'm to look out for you, sir."

"Look out for me, Chief? We'll see about that. You got a car or something? You seem to know where we're going and I need a long hot shower and a tall cold Scotch."

"Can do, Major. On both counts. This way, sir. Car's over here."

Chief Wetmore swung the Valv-Pak into the navy gray Plymouth's trunk. Mead noticed the bulge in the back of his khaki blouse. *He Packs a 1911 Colt .45. This guy's serious.*

The car pulled into the sparse traffic and headed downtown. Mead settled into the rear seat and starred at the back of the Navy driver's head. *This guy is nobody's fool. Gruff, tough sailor boy ... OSS? There's more.*

He leaned forward and tapped Wetmore's shoulder. "Okay, Chief, I know you don't run a taxi service ... so talk to me. You said we're on the same team. I've been traveling virtually non-stop since London. I didn't know I *had* a team. In fact there's a hell of a lot I don't know. So who the hell are you? And who the hell's *our* team? Talk to me, Chief."

A hearty laugh came from the front seat. "Okay, Major. Here's the scoop so far. I am what you see, sir, but my last billet was with Naval Intel in Pearl. I was an analyst with experience that I guess the OSS boys thought they might need. Spent a lot of time in the Far East, mostly China. Had some, shall we say, special missions before the Japs decided to take on the world. Anyway, I got pegged to come here and help set up OSS west. Frankly, sir ... tween you'n me ... I'm thinking Admiral Nimitz just wanted to be sure he had eyes and ears over here."

Mead leaned forward, arms folded on the back of the front seat, listening intently. *This is the first time I've heard anybody with specific things to say.*

Wetmore continued, "The operation here is less'n a year old. General Donovan set up Barrows, that's General David P. Barrows, as Coordinator of

Intelligence and Information on the West Coast. Damned if I can figure what he's coordinating. Not much going on 'til you popped up."

"Popped up?"

"Yah, popped up. Word came straight from E Street a few days ago to get ready for a counter-espionage operation ... and a gyrene. Oh, 'scuse me, sir ... a Marine from London."

Mead thought, *Son-of-a-bitch ... they had this thing moving before I was even asked.* "So what did they tell you, Chief?"

"Not much, sir. But then we heard from Pearson in London. By the way, Major, Chandler Morse sends his regards. He's linked up as our man for ULTRA intercepts. We're using MAGIC. OSS is authorized as needed, but I've been cleared since Pearl."

"Okay, Chief, that's the first good news ... and Chandler's got a nose for news. Who else?"

"Right now, Major, it's you and me. Oh, you got the usual staff weenies and go-fers at the office. But General Barrows thinks you'll want to build things your way."

Soon as I figure out what the hell to build. "He's right, Chief. Okay, my new friend, one more question ... where are we going?"

"Home, sir. We've got a nice little house not far from the Federal Building. Much simpler than hotels and stuff these days. With all due respect, Major, you do need a shower and a shave ... and that Scotch. This afternoon we can brainstorm, and get some dinner. Tomorrow it's to the office and the next chapter of our lives. All with your permission, of course, Major, sir."

Mead's reply came somewhat overemphasized and plainly facetious, "Permission granted."

The *nice little house* on Wilshire Boulevard is a spacious 1920's California pseudo-Spanish hacienda with lots of tile, spacious rooms, high dark wood beamed ceilings, and plenty of airy windows to let in the California sun and fresh air. Mead had his own bedroom, sharing a large bathroom with Chief Wetmore. So far they were the only two residents, except for the immigrant cook and maid, Pedro and Constantia Velasquez, a husband and wife team who live in the guest bungalow across the back lawn.

Freshly showered and shaved, Mead changed into cotton slacks and a sport shirt. He walked out onto the patio, surrounded by the house on three sides, noting the fragrant wisteria vine mingled with blood-red bougainvillea that formed an impenetrable ceiling above the space.

Wetmore, already seated at a large oak table that centered the polished clay tiled oasis, raised a glass of amber liquid over ice in his large hand. "Cheers, Major."

"Wonder how the poor people live, Chief?"

"Well, I'm as poor as you get … and this is how I'm living. Scotch?" Wetmore lifted his glass, displaying the dragon tattooed on his forearm. "We've got Chivas."

"Thought you'd never ask. Pour it neat. I think I'm going to survive. Let's get to work." Mead saw that a cord led to a telephone set on the patio table and said, "Nice to work in the great outdoors."

"Work comes after dinner, Major. Pedro's a magician with the local veggies and steaks on the grill. Blood rare?"

Dinner, served with a southwestern flair on colorful earthenware, eased both hunger and the tensions of a too long day. The Velasquez couple move

29

effortlessly to serve the two men, sharing timid smiles but no words, then quietly disappear into the kitchen.

Mead asked, "Where'd you find these two, Chief?"

"They came with the house, Major. Well, that is the real estate guy provided them for us. Nice touch. We never know when we'll get *guests*. You know, guys passing through on assignment and stuff like that. Pedro and Constantia keep everything just humming along. He even takes care of the grounds."

Mead asked, "Where are they from?"

"I assumed Mexico. They speak English pretty good... if you speak to 'em directly."

"Well they're damn good cooks. That steak with the crunchy salt rubbed into it is fabulous. Never had it prepared like that before. Great meal, Chief ... now let's get to work."

"Aye, aye, sir."

Constantia Velasquez immediately appeared to clear the remains of the meal.

Mead said, "Thank you, Constantia."

She replied, her dark eyes cast down respectfully, "*Mi gusto, Senores. Buenos noches.*" (My pleasure, gentlemen. Good night.) Then she added, "*Tengas ustedes café, senores?*" (Do you want coffee?)

Wetmore answered, "Thank you, Constantia. Black coffee good for you, Major?"

After retrieving the material that made up what they had worked on so far, Mead and Wetmore sorted it into a tabletop of official documents, charts and hand written notes. Mead set a clean tablet in front of him and uncapped his pen.

"What do we know? What do we *need* to know? That's where I want to start, Chief. You've got some of it ... I've got some ... so stay with me."

As they talked the list grew:

1. The Germans are intense about getting this Orion's Eye technology.
2. They knew about Fort Monmouth and sent people there. Amateurs. They screwed up. Got caught. Turned their contacts. Both at Monmouth and in Mount Clemens, Selfridge Field.

Wetmore said, "The Selfridge Field bit shows how amateur they were. Sure the 1st Fighter Control Squadron formed up there, but the Orion's Eye stuff shipped by air directly to March Field here in California. That's where the Squadron is headed now to mate up with their gear."

Constantia came in with a tray with two heavy ceramic Navy mugs of steaming black coffee. Wetmore cleared a spot on the table as they continued the list.

3. Otto Hauptmann is on the mission – envoy of Himmler himself.
4. Latest report has Hauptmann in South America.

"Wait a minute, Major. Who's this Hauptmann guy?"

"Sorry, Chief. Actually, there are two of them, father and son. I've been tracking them since I landed in London. Senior seems to be out of the play for now, but Otto boy is in … and he's one of Himmler's best spies. I got the South America stuff from my stop in DC."

Chandler had sent two more ULTRA intercepts— first, 'Hauptmann is in Bariloche, Argentina,' and then reports of an increase in radio traffic from Mexico. Mead set the pen down and folded his hands. He picked up the pen again, tapping it on the table. "Here's the one that worries me."

5. Military officer possibly or probably involved.

"Where'd that come from, Major?"

Mead took a cigarette from his shirt pocket and lit it. Setting his Marine Zippo on the table he answered, "Also from my short stop in DC, Chief. That guy at E Street, Maurice Hyman ... yeah, the South America Intel guy ... he told me an American, probably an American military officer, is somehow involved in the German's effort." He leaned back in the oaken chair, rubbing his temples. "Damn! If it's true, how do we check security with the Army? What if it's one of the officers with that radar squadron?"

He picked up his pen to add the next note, "What else do we know?"

6. Orion's Eye - going to war by ship.

Looking over at Mead's last note, Wetmore said, "But not for a while, Major. Before they ship out the 1st Fighter Control Squadron is supposed to come up to LA and train on the equipment for a few weeks."

Once again, Mead laid down the pen. "Okay, so we've got a little time until they ship out. If the Germans screwed up so bad back east, could Hauptmann have recovered enough to hit us stateside?" Through fingers again massaging his temples he added, "I'm thinking not. But we can't take anything for granted. In the meantime ... in meantime ... there's Gochais."

"Go chay?" parroted Chief Wetmore. "Go *what?*"

Mead chuckled as he sat back in his chair and crossed his arms. "Donovan Ignatius Gochais, a guy I used to know here in LA. Got to know him before the war when I was FBI and he was a young cop. He's a swell kid. Eager, rough, but smart. I found out he's now a Maritime Officer. And, his ship is the USAT Cape San Juan."

The Chief sat up. "That's our transport for Orion's-god-awful-Eye, Major."

"You've got it, Chief. And if our package makes it to sea we need eyes on board."

Mead stood and stretched, stifling a yawn. "First thing tomorrow we call him. Me thinks we've got our sea-legs. But for now, my friend, I'm done." He stretched his arms over his head. "Goodnight, Mr. Wetmore."

Mead set off down the hall as Constantia appeared to clear the coffee cups. In his room he opened the carved sash window above his bed. Stripping off his civilian togs he laid them neatly over the chair atop his uniform. He settled into the crisp linens, easing his head into the firm pillow. A mellow breeze wafted through the window. *The smell of California ... flowers. London has that coal-burning, wet wool aroma. Vermont has to be the sweet-wet earthy whiffs of leaves in the hardwoods ... That soap that B.J. used ... And California, flowers. BJ? Why the hell do you keep poking into my lonely life?*

Then sleep, blessed sleep.

 **CHAPTER 4**

Los Angeles, California

The chief petty officer had opened the rear door and saluted crisply. Lieutenant (jg) Donovan Ignatius Gochais, U. S. Maritime Service, returned the salute but declined the rear seat and climbed into the front. The gray Plymouth with **Navy** stenciled on the door pulled away from the neat compact bungalow on Mayfield Place.

As they drove toward the main boulevard, Gochais asked, "Do you know Major Mead, Chief?"

"Yes, sir, Lieutenant. He's my boss."

Gochais probed for more, "And...?"

The chief replied with an end-of-story inflection, "Sorry, sir. The Major will tell you what you need to know."

Three days home from his last deployment, Gochais had received a strange phone call from an old friend. Its urgent tone and clipped instructions, *'car coming for you. Get down here,'* were out of character for the man who had mentored him through his before-the-war-interrupted police career. He thought, *Whatever this is, if Amos Mead is involved*

I can count on some excitement, Don't know what he wants with me ... or how he knows where I am. Anyway, I ship out again in three weeks. Not much time to ... Just gotta wait and see.

Gochais remembered when, nearly two years earlier, he had been a uniformed police backup for an FBI raid on a suspected bank robber's house. FBI Special Agent Mead had been pinned down by an unsuspected fusillade of bullets from a side window. In position to see the shooter, Gochais sent six rounds of .38 police special lead into a tight pattern that settled the situation for good. A friendship flourished from that day.

The Plymouth turned off South Sepulveda onto Wilshire and then into the driveway of 11072, a neat Spanish style hacienda. The long driveway led to an expansive garage abutting a two unit guest house, all of the same style and decor. Alighting from the Plymouth at the same time, Gochais stepped back to allow the chief to lead the way toward the main house. They followed the slightly curving stone walk across the lawn to the vine covered patio.

Mead stood and extended his hand. "Don, my young buddy, how've you been?"

He added a firm pat on the shoulder to the offered hand.

Assuming a stance of semi-attention, Gochais answered, "Just fine, Amos ... it's good to see you. But you didn't run me down just to check on my health ... First, why don't you get to *what's up* ... and then we can *catch up* ... sir."

The 'sir' added when Gochais reflected, *Whoops, a little more polite, I'm still junior here.*

"Okay, Don. You're still a smart-ass, I see. Relax. I owe explanations and a lot more. Sit down."

Mead pointed to one of the sturdy carved chairs that flanked the table. Wetmore pulled out the chair for Gochais. Mead said, "You've met Chief Wetmore, Don? He's part of the team here."

Wetmore pulled up another chair and motioned to the maid for something to drink, as Mead leaned onto the table and continued, "I ran you down ... as you say, Don ... because, by a unique set of circumstances, you're the man I need for a critical assignment."

Gochais blurted out, "Assignment?"

"Yes, an assignment. Before I tell you anything more, Don, you need to know that you can turn us down. But, if you do you're still under mandate for silence. Should I go on?"

Amos Mead gave no hint of a smile or anything but deadly seriousness. Gochais turned a ruddy face up toward the vine covered beams and took an audible breath.

Turning back, his blue eyes brightened, then narrowed on Mead. "Amos, I trust you. You know me and you know that I can't turn down anything that smacks of intrigue ... and getting the bad guys. But you're not a cop, so who's the bad guy? And who the hell is this *we* you keep saying?"

Mead answered slowly, "Okay, Don. Last question first. The *we* is the OSS ... the Office of Strategic Services.

Moving to the edge of his seat, Gochais said, too quickly, "This is a spook outfit?"

"Not exactly, Don. We're in the counterespionage business. Catching the other guy's spooks, as you call them."

Gochais slid back into his chair and ran a hand through his full head of sandy hair. "So where do I fit in? What the hell can I do for the OSS?"

"I said it's a right place, right time thing, Don. You used to be a cop. Now you're a maritime officer. You're Third Mate on the USAT *Cape San Juan.*"

Mead continued to pace himself, emphasizing each point, "And, I know you personally ... which is both good news and bad news for me."

"Right on all counts, Amos. You seem to know a lot about me. I'm just back from Australia ... and you probably know all about that. But look, in three weeks I've got a coastwise cruise, and then it's back to the South Pacific. So, unless your OSS gets me some new orders pronto I'm not much use to you guys."

"On the contrary, my friend. Your assignment for me *is* the *Cape San Juan* ... and some critical cargo."

Mead leaned back in his chair. "But before we go on ... are you in, at least to this point?"

"Damn you! I mean damn you, *sir.* You know I'm in. I sure as hell don't know what *in* means, Amos. But you talk like you do ... and I can deal with that. Best of all worlds ... working with you again and—"

Mead interrupted, "I hoped you'd feel that way. But, before we get all the way into this thing, I want to know a little more. You've got a family. What about them? This might be, probably will be, a little dangerous."

"Holy crap, Amos, what do you think I do for a living now? Sailing in and out of a war ain't what you call safe work. Doesn't take a fancy Yale college boy lawyer like you to figure that out."

Mead looked down and shook his head. "Family, Don, family."

"Yeah, okay. You remember Elma? Well, we've got two kids. Boys. Oldest is three. That's Tommy. Bobby's just 13 months younger. Kinda close. Tough on Elma when I'm gone. But, hey, that's war ... tough on everybody. Her folks keep an eye out, even her grand folks. Not like when I was a kid. Different story. So what's up, Amos?"

Mead answered, "What's up, my boy, is the cargo you'll have on *Cape San Juan*'s next voyage to war. And the little fact the Germans are trying to steal it. That's not very nice manners and we've got to do something about it." He flashed a wry smile. "If things play out right, Elma won't have to know what you're doing. We'll get a plausible story together for her. Nothing much will change in her life ... except maybe the pay's a little better."

"Hey, Amos, I don't keep stuff from her."

"I appreciate that, Don. But here you're in a different game. There's a lot of need-to-know. A lot of new rules. For instance, you'll be away soon ... but not on a coastwise ship. Your next stop is Toyan Bay on Catalina Island. It's the west coast training center for OSS operations officers. You'll be working for Jedburgh Spencer Alexander for a few weeks. You've got things to learn."

"Holy shit. Wait'll Elma hears about ... Uh, I guess not, huh."

Wilmington, California
July 1943

The Pacific Electric Red Line Car swayed along the tracks nearing the port of Wilmington, California. The hypnotic rhythm of the metallic clicking had a relaxing effect on Gochais. He'd ridden this route many times before, but never on a mission like this.

The goodbyes with Elma had been as routine as any war-time goodbye could be. He'd avoided speaking about the voyage, allowing her assumptions to hold sway. He'd thought, *Maybe then it's not a lie.* He was, after all, boarding a ship.

It just wasn't USAT *Cape San Juan.*

His destination today was SS *Avalon* for the crossing of the San Pedro Channel to the small port of Avalon, Catalina Island, and ultimately, Toyan Bay and his rendezvous with his new career with the OSS.

As the expanse of the Los Angeles Harbor snuck into view between the strobing trees lining the boulevard, Gochais reflected on his connections to this inlet of Pacific waters. Three towns divided its seafaring commerce: Wilmington, Los Angeles and San Pedro. He knew them all.

The 22nd Street Landing at San Pedro defined his late teens as a battleship sailor aboard USS *West Virginia.* It also defined life and death for him.

Here he met, wooed and married Elma. Here he'd finished his Navy tour of duty. Here USS *West Virginia* and the navy's battleship fleet had set sail for their new home in Pearl Harbor, Hawaii. And here he'd seen the last of his friends and shipmates who met death under Jap bombs and torpedoes on 7 December, 1941.

He reflected, *It could'a been me ... could'a been me. God bless you guys.*

The memory tugged at his heart.

The jerking and squealing stop of the trolley snapped him back to the present. He stepped down from the red street car and the distinctive smell of an ocean port greeted him like an old friend. He shouldered his bag and joined the line of similarly burdened men moving toward the pier.

He could see the superstructure of USAT *Cape San Juan* across the harbor. Smoke from her stacks told him that she was firing up her boilers in preparation for the coastal voyage that Elma believed he'd be on. *What the hell am I doing? Is this the right thing? Shit, I don't even really know what this is.*

He crossed the gangway and stepped onto the deck.

The twenty-six mile voyage to Catalina proved uneventful for Gochais. The morning fog slowly broke up as the ship passed over the submarine nets at the mouth of the harbor and snaked its way through the sea mines that protected this part of the California coast.

This event is routine for Gochais, but obviously nerve-wracking for the *gleebs*—as new Merchant Marine recruits are called—who lined the rail jabbing one another as they spotted a mine, or thought they did.

Lots of people trained on Catalina—The Merchant Marine, the Army and the OSS. Gochais thought, *New jobs for these kids too.*

He tried to focus on what lay in store for him at the secretive OSS Toyan Bay, but nothing gelled clear in his mind. He knew what he knew. Battleship sailor, Los Angeles police officer, graduate of Alameda Maritime Academy, and one safe voyage to Australia and back.

Yes, he knew what he knew alright.

And it didn't include the OSS.

Or this deviation in his future.

OSS Safe House
Los Angeles, California.

Constantia poured Mead's first cup of coffee. He took it and turned to Wetmore. "What've we heard from Chandler Morse, Chief?"

Chief Wetmore hesitated answering until the maid left the room. "Chandler reports that Berlin is still hyped up with Hauptmann's mission. He says that Himmler is personally touching everything."

"And Hauptmann? We still got a track on him?"

"Yes, sir. Chandler's coordinating with a contact at E Street. They've linked up with the U.S. Naval Mission in Chile. The Naval Attaché there's a guy named Dillon ... Lieutenant Commander Sam Dillon. He's been running a little spook team on the side for the Office of Naval Intelligence."

Wetmore set his coffee cup aside and retrieved a notebook. "Last word is they had Otto Hauptmann getting on an Air Lati flight from San Carlos de Bariloche in Argentina. The flight's going to Puerto Montt ... Chile."

"I'll be damned, Chief. You can't get much further south without a penguin escort. Puerto Montt is in Patagonian Chile."

"Yes, sir, Major, I looked it up. How in hell is Hauptmann gonna be any kind of threat to our Orion's Eye target way the hell down there?"

"With what we've got so far, Chief, your guess is as good as mine. Tell Chandler and his gang to keep Hauptmann in the crosshairs and keep us posted. What I'm worried about right now is that suspicion of an American spy ... the military officer. If he actually exists I suspect he's close to our package."

"For God's sake, Major, what makes a man spy on his own country?"

"Good question, Chief. What makes a man a robber or a killer? There are all kinds of people spying. There always has been."

"Yeah, Major, but spying on your *own* country?"

"Look, Chief, sometimes it's immigrants with ties back home. You know, spying for the old country. Then you've got the out-and-out traitors. Some of these creeps work from greed, some from a warped sense of patriotic duty to another cause. I quit trying to figure them out, Chief. I just know they're out there ... and we need to catch as many as we can."

Wetmore shrugged and took a sip of his cold coffee and reached for the pot. "More coffee?"

"Hold the coffee, Chief. Gather this stuff up. Get down to the office and get those replies off to Chandler. Also, I want to know what assets we have in Mexico. And check any activity there. Hell, check for any increased German activity in all of South America. I've got a plane to catch."

"Someplace fun, Major?"

"Come on, Chief. All our work is fun. I'm going down to March Field. It's time we meet the Commanding Officer of the 4th Interceptor Command. And God save us if he's the spy."

Puerto Montt, Chile
Latitude 41°28' S—Longitude 72°56' W

Otto Hauptmann and Reinhard Gehlan walked slowly along Canal Tenglo toward the sea, their overcoats snugged and collars turned up against the penetrating cold. The wind-churned Pacific surged in and out of the canal. The smell of seaweed mixed with the effluent of the small town carried on the wet air. Both men are taller than most of the locals, but Gehlan is a gaunt one-hundred-twenty-five pounds to Hauptmann's more robust build. It didn't matter whether they stood out. Everyone in this town knew who they were—spy masters for the Third Reich.

Puerto Montt had been settled by Germans in the late nineteenth century. Sentiments ran high in favor of *der Vaterland* (the Fatherland).

Until this assignment, Gehlan spied on the Russians for Hitler and when the opportunity rose to move his operations to Argentina he saw his chance to survive the war. Now he aided in Hauptmann's mission.

Hauptmann broke the silence, quietly asking, "When will she arrive, Herr Gehlan?"

"It will be another two or three weeks at least, Otto. She sailed from Kristiansand for Penang. The High Command diverted her west for us." After a few more steps, he added, "You must have some great influence in Germany to move our U-Boats wherever you wish."

"It is not my influence, Reinhard. It is the panic of the *Reichfürers*. Those fawning sycophants of *der Führer* provide me the power."

"Panic, Otto? Do you believe we are losing badly enough for panic?"

"What I believe is of little concern, my friend. The fact is that the American and English bombers are overwhelming our defenses. And the Americans have the new long range fighter planes ... their P-51s ... and the Luftwaffe is stretched too thin."

"So, your mission, Otto? You are to capture some new magic machine from the Americans? And you are way down in this cold god-forsaken place alone to do it? *Was ist dieses?* (What is this?) *Wie tun Sie dies,* Otto? (How will you do this, Otto?)"

"*Gott weiß*, Reinhard. (God only knows.) But I am not exactly alone. I have some people already at work. I will tell you more later. Let us get in from this *Gott verdammt* (goddammed) bone-chilling cold. Perhaps we can find some schnapps, my friend."

 **CHAPTER 5**

4th Interceptor Command
March Field, California

The flight from Los Angeles to March Field took just under an hour from wheels up to engine shut down. The Army Air Corp C-47 and its canvas paratroop seats was not the most comfortable method of travel, but it provided the quickest and most direct for today's mission. The hot, grit-laden desert wind hit Mead like a slap as he walked to the waiting jeep.

The driver snapped to attention and saluted. "Major Mead? I'm to take you directly to General Nielsen's HQ."

Mead returned the salute and climbed into the jeep. They drove the few blocks from the flight line to the clutch of newly built wooden buildings that housed the 4th Interceptor Command.

Mead hopped from the jeep. "Thanks, Sergeant. Don't know how long I'll be. You be around?"

"You bet, Major. I'll check flight schedules and stand by for you."

Mead returned the sergeant's salute and strode up to and through the double doors. The duty officer obviously expected him and showed him directly into the office marked *Commanding Officer*. Two paces into the spacious room Mead halted and stood at attention.

By tradition, Army soldiers salute indoors, but Marines do not. Mead figured standing at attention will be a good compromise. The intricately carved and painted sign on the desk proclaimed *Major General Manfield R. Nielsen, III*. The man behind the desk did not look so pretentious—tie loose, collar unbuttoned and sleeves turned back on the wrist.

The commanding general of the 4th Interceptor Command rose, smiled and extended his hand. "Stand easy, Major, your mission precedes you. Take a seat."

"Thank you, General."

Mead moved to one of the leather chairs facing the desk.

General Nielsen continued, "I wondered when I'd be hearing from you, or at least from OSS or the FBI. I've been briefed about the so-called attempts on our prize possession … and that there's a special mission in place to see it doesn't happen again. Would that be you?"

"Yes, General. In a matter of speaking, sir, that would be me."

"So what are we looking at, Major? How's the *Hun* going to get at us?"

"That's what we're working on, sir. You said you were briefed, General. Were you told about a possible spy within the American military?"

"I was. And I think it's bullshit!"

The general slapped the leather topped desk. "Absolute unadulterated bullshit!"

"Sir?"

"No, I mean the fact that a soldier would spy on his own country is pure bullshit."

Smiling and sensing that he could relax a bit, Mead said, "Yes, sir, General, my sentiments exactly. Sir, you've done your homework on me and my assignment. Permission, sir, to ask the general some questions?"

General Nielsen sat back in his chair and swung his hands up behind his head. "Of course, Major, ask away. You know, the more I think about it the way they're going about this mission is a good idea. One man like yourself can move around a lot quicker than a Company of MP's ... or a damn bevy of FBI weenies. Sorry, Major, you had questions."

"Yes sir. My first question is an obvious one. Just what exactly is Orion's Eye ... and why are the Germans so focused on it?"

General Nielsen leaned forward, his elbows on his desk and peered intently at Mead. "Funny nobody's told you yet. I know you're cleared to know ... and your mission sure as hell gives you a need to know. *Orion's Eye* is the code name for our project. You're aware, Major, that these technical guys always try to get clever with their code names. In this case, though, the *Eye of the Hunter* ... you know, the Orion Constellation they call The Hunter ... well, it says it pretty good. This Orion's Eye project is a real leap in radar technology for us, Major. A goddam giant leap."

General Nielsen reached for the inter-com on his desk. "Hold on a minute, Major." He pushed the black lever. "Find Lieutenant Gibbons. Get him here on the double." The order acknowledged, General Nielsen turned back to Mead. "Lieutenant Gibbons is the training officer for the 1st Fighters. He's originally from Fort Monmouth and worked on the late development of this stuff. He's the go-to guy for Orion's Eye. You asked me why the Germans are so keen to get it. Well, son, they're getting the shit kicked out of themselves with the new P-51 Fighter and the combination of Brits bombing by night and our guys by day. Their radar is pretty good, especially the anti-aircraft control ... but they can't do tight coordination of fighters on target."

"And that's what Orion's Eye does, General?"

"Sure does ... but Gibbons' going to have to tell you how. By the way, the unit's being assigned to the Los Angeles Air Defense Wing for a final shake out and live training before shipping overseas."

Mead asked, "Then they're moving out?"

"Yeah, in a few weeks is my guess. The up-and-running tests for Orion's Eye will be in the South Flower Street facility and the troops will rotate in for fine-tuned live training. The others are scattered at regular radar sites from Santa Barbara to San Diego."

A rap on the door. The duty officer stepped in and announced the arrival of the 1st Fighter Control Squadron's training officer.

First Lieutenant Harry A. Gibbons, USAAC, entered the office, approached to within two steps of the desk, snapped to attention and saluted. "Reporting as requested, General."

"At ease, Harry. Meet Major Amos Mead. He's our bird dog on all this German threat stuff. He needs a briefing on Orion's Eye and you're the one to give it to him."

Mead rose from his chair and extended his hand. The grip and the square set of the shoulders told Mead that this slightly built officer is a serious soldier.

"Nice to meet you, Major," the lieutenant said. The two men settled back into their chairs as he added, "Anything particular, sir, you want to know?"

Mead leaned toward Gibbons. "Anything you can tell me, Lieutenant. I'm trying to get a feel for the possible motivation that's pushing the Germans to act in the unusual way they're acting."

"Okay, Major, let's start with a little history. You know about the Brits development of *radio ranging*, I'm sure."

Mead nodded.

Gibbons continued, "Well, we use the term *radar*. The Germans have also developed their version. Both the Brits and German systems are large and cumbersome. They're great for installations, like the coast of Dover … but they're no-way mobile."

Gibbons stood and clasped his hands behind his back. He paced slowly and continued the lecture he'd obviously delivered before. "The Germans have two primary systems. Their long-range radar, out to about one hundred miles, they call Freya. It measures azimuth and range with a wavelength of 2.4 meters. The German's use this radar to guide their anti-aircraft batteries. But they can't guide their fighters.

"The Brits developed a system they call Mandrel that easily jams Freya and causes a lot of confusion. Oh, yes, and Freya's only got about an eight kilowatt output." Gibbons stopped and turned toward Mead. "You with me so far, Major?"

Mead answered, "So far, Lieutenant … at least around the edges." He shifted in his chair. "But tell me. What's *different* about Orion's Eye?"

"Specifically, Major, its power and wavelength ... and we guide the fighters all the way to target. More generally, though, it's part of a total system."

"And that's important?"

"Extremely important, Major. I said the Germans operate at a wavelength of 2.4 meters. We operate in centimeters. They have eight kilowatt output ... we're in the one-hundred kilowatt range. We see more and we see it faster and farther."

Mead asked, "Why haven't the Germans done the same thing?"

"They're good enough, Major, and they may do it someday. But not now."

"Not now?"

"No, sir. Fact is, we got lucky. There've been four key breakthroughs in electronics for us ... and somebody recognized that they could converge to make our miracle." Gibbons returned to his chair. "The first is the invention of the magnetron by a guy named Hull at General Electric. The second is the klystron that serves as an oscillator in the receivers. It's these two things that give us the microwave radar—"

Mead interrupted, "And microwave is the difference with Orion's Eye?"

"Yes, sir, the big difference. But there's more. The third breakthrough has been developed in Bell Labs by a guy named Schockley. They call it a transistor. Short story is transistors replace all the tubes ... and we lose the size and heat problem. How we doing, Major?"

"I'm hanging on your every word ... by the skin of my teeth. What's the fourth miracle?"

"The fourth miracle is our air-to-ground radio communication. Thanks to a damn smart tinkerer named Al Gross we've got hand-held VHF/UHF spectrum above one-hundred megahertz radios."

General Nielsen rose from his desk, retrieved a large, partially smoked cigar from its tray, lit it and walked over to the two officers trailed by a plume of blue, fragrant smoke. "Bottom line, Major, we got ourselves a three foot by two foot by four foot box with the ability to find and track the enemy and vector in the Air Corps' finest to blow them to smithereens. We can do it in real time, even at night, then pull up stakes and move to a new neighborhood. We got eyes for our hunters that neither sleet, nor snow, nor dark of night will sway from its appointed rounds ... better'n the Post Office. 'Bout right, Lieutenant?"

"'Bout right, General."

Mead rose from his chair and stretched his back with a little shrug. "Orion's Eye. Incredible. No way can we let the Germans near this! Incredible ... just god-damned incredible!" He faced General Nielsen. "By your leave, General. I need to get back to LA. I'll be in touch soon on our spy."

Lieutenant Gibbons flashed to the word *spy* and asked, "Spy, sir?"

Nielsen raised his hand. "Later, Lieutenant." Then he turned to Mead. "We'll nail the son-of-bitch, whoever he is. Keep me posted, Major!"

Mead stood at attention. "Thank you, General. I will."

As the office door clicked shut behind Mead, General Nielsen turned to Lieutenant Gibbons and said, "Forget the *spy* comment, son. That's above your paygrade for the moment."

"Understood, sir. By the way, General, have we heard anything about the new commanding officer for the 1st Fighters?

"He's due in today, son. Thank you for the briefing. The more times I hear you give it the more I learn. Who knows, someday I might even understand the damn thing! You're dismissed, Lieutenant."

Gibbons rose, snapped to attention and saluted. "Thank you, sir."

As he watched Lieutenant Gibbons exit the office, General Nielsen leaned back in his chair. *Yeah, you're getting a new CO, son ... and I don't know shit about him.*

The intercom broke in, "Sir, there's a Captain Edward Bonfoey to see you."

Captain Edward M. Bonfoey, US Army Air Corp, presented his orders to Major General Manfield R. Nielsen, Commanding Officer of the 4th Interceptor Command, March Field, California. Standing at attention he saluted and said, "Captain Bonfoey paying respects to the General and reporting as ordered."

With a halfhearted return of the salute, General Nielsen said, "At ease, Captain. Take a seat. Now suppose you tell me why we're getting a change in command for the 1st Fighters so late in the game?"

"Respectfully, sir, I don't know."

His agitation growing, Nielsen thought, *Why would you know? This whole thing is strange.* "Okay, Captain, then tell me where the hell you come from."

Bonfoey spoke calmly, unruffled by the general's demeanor, "As my orders show, sir, I've been transferred here from the 364th Fighter Group in Van Nuys ... however, sir, I've only been there for three weeks. They told me that my orders to them were a foul up and that the correct orders are as I gave you."

"Captain, that needs a bit more explaining."

"Yes, sir. My last real assignment is England ... as executive officer of the 817th Aviation Engineering Battalion at AAF Station 169. That's near Stansted in Essex."

"I've no clue where that is, Captain. Is that 8th Air Force?"

"No, General, we were with the 9th. Anyway, my CO told me that if I wanted a career in the Army I needed to take a combat command. He made the arrangements ... and here I am. As I understand it, sir, the 1st Fighter Control Squadron is headed for the Pacific Theater."

"That it is, Captain, that it is. Leave a copy of your orders with the clerk and see the duty officer for quarters assignment. He'll get you a ride over to your new command. Lieutenant Gibbons is acting XO. He'll bring you up to snuff. You're dismissed."

Bonfoey assumed attention and saluted. "Thank you, General."

Nielsen returned Bonfoey's salute with a wave toward his forehead. He watched the door close behind the captain. *Strange, damn strange. Who is this guy?*

He reached for the black telephone on his desk and dialed Operator. As it rang he reviewed the Los Angeles number handwritten on the card he'd retrieved from his shirt pocket.

OSS Safe House
Los Angeles, California

Chief Wetmore picked up the telephone on the third ring. "Clinton 58873."

This phone number is not known to too many people. Protocols had not yet been established, but

53

he knew that being careful about revealing too much to unknown callers would be prudent.

"Major Mead is not at this number. I may be able to locate him. Who's calling?"

With a sweep of his arm Wetmore cleared a space on the table in front of him. He turned up a fresh page on a yellow tablet and wrote the number given.

"Thank you, General Nielsen. We expect the Major shortly. He will return your call, sir."

As Wetmore returned to his sorting of the day's messages from Chandler Morse in London the telephone rang again. "What the hell?" *This thing never rings, now twice* ... "Clinton 58873."

Surprised by the female voice, Wetmore nearly stammered. "No, ma'am, he's not at this number."

The voice remained pleasant, but insistent that she had the correct number and that it had been given to her by Major Mead's father. Wetmore relented and took the message. Re-cradling the phone, he entered it on the same yellow page. Within the hour, Mead turned his key in the front door and entered the large living room. As always, the transition from the heat of the day to the cool of the tiled expanse of the room is a pleasant experience.

He spied Wetmore through the high arched passage to the dining room. "Hi, Chief. Pretending to do real work, I see."

The chief replied as he offered the yellow sheet of paper to Mead, "Right, sir, covering for you is always fun. You've got messages ... and some good stuff from London."

Mead saw the first note.

URGENT, CALL GEN. NIELSEN.

He picked up the telephone, and then replaced it on the cradle as the second message registered.

MRS. BETTY JEAN WILLIAMSON — WEBSTER
73547 — AMOS KNEW HER AS B.J. — FATHER GAVE
HER THE NUMBER.

A tired Amos Mead sat fixated on the scrawled messages in his hand, not really thinking, just looking.

Wetmore broke the reverie. "Oh, forgot to tell yeah. We've got a couple of guests. Two new OSS guys. Marines, stopping over from Toyan Bay before shipping to the Pacific. They tell me Gochais' anxious to finish his spook training."

Mead looked up. "Oh? Bet he is. Guests? What've we got for quarters? Guess I've never really looked."

"We can handle six if they double up. Looks like we'll be a regular Inn of Choice. Constantia fixed 'em up ... Hey, Major, I didn't train to be no innkeeper!"

Without responding, Mead picked up the telephone and dialed. "Major Mead calling. Yes, returning General Nielsen's call. I'll hold. General ... Amos Mead here, sir."

Mead sat back in his chair and listened, acknowledging what he heard, "I understand, sir. It does sound strange. Frankly though, Bonfoey seems a bit too obvious to be our guy. No, no. We can't overlook anything, General. Thanks for keeping me informed. We'll be following up."

General Nielsen continued to talk. Mead closed his eyes and rubbed a temple with his free hand.

Tired and not a little anxious to avoid the general's predictable pontifications, he interjected, "What's that, General? The shipping out date? When?

Okay, we've got some time. And Bonfoey? Yes, sir, I know the location. 8th and South Flower Street here in L.A. Thank you, sir, I appreciate your help. Absolutely, sir, we'll get the son-of-a-bitch."

Whoever he is, he thought as he set the phone in its cradle.

"Chief, run down anything you can find on a Captain Edward M. Bonfoey, US Army Air Corp. Start with General Nielsen's staff. By the way, did B.J. say anything else?"

Wetmore nodded his head without speaking.

Mead picked up the phone, then hesitated and set it down, saying, "It's getting late and I'm starved ... what's Constantia got set up for dinner? And where are our guests? Come on, Chief, you're in charge ... help me out here."

"Right, Major. Come to think of it I haven't seen either of our Velasquez folks for a while."

 **CHAPTER 6**

Sicherheitsdienst Headquarters
Berlin, Germany

Heinrich Himmler watched the entourage arrive on the street below his office window, the large man in the long white uniform coat easily identifiable. *Reichsmarschall* Hermann Wilhelm Goering, second in command of the Third Reich and head of the Luftwaffe, is paying him a visit. Goering's visits are never social. Himmler cleared his desk, sat straight in his large chair, pulled his tunic to its best fit and waited for the knock.

But no knock came.

The door burst open and the ominous bulk of the *Reichsmarschall* filled the opening. "*Guten morgan*, Heinrich, *wie geht es Ihnen*? (Good morning, Heinrich, how are you?)

Himmler stood slowly to face his nemesis and replied, "I am quite fine, *Reichsmarschall* ... though I assume you are here to speak of the American Orion's Eye operation and not my health."

"No, Heinrich, not to speak ... but to listen. To listen to you tell me that we have obtained the secret devise. *Meine Geduld nähert sich einem Ende!*" (My patience is nearing an end!)

"For your sake, *Reichsmarschall*, I hope your *patience* has a bit longer to go before reaching that end you speak of. We have the best agent on the task and he has all of the resources of the Reich as his tools. The task is formidable, Herr Goering, thus will take what time it takes."

Himmler sat back into his chair, his contempt for this bloated effigy of what the Third Reich had become, seething beneath his forced deference to rank.

Hermann Goering posed a real danger. Since the failure of the Luftwaffe caused the abandonment of Hitler's planned invasion of England, Goering's political eclipse became more and more evident. Further failures of the Luftwaffe on the Russian front and its inability to defend Germany itself from Allied bombing attacks underscored Goering's gross incompetence. He had rapidly sunk into lethargy and a world of delusions, expressly forbidding the Luftwaffe's Commanding General to report to Berlin that enemy fighters were accompanying bomber squadrons deeper and deeper into German territory.

The Luftwaffe's technical research is run down completely, not surprisingly with Goering praising personal heroism above scientific know-how.

His idea of dignified combat is ramming enemy aircraft.

Discredited, isolated and increasingly despised, Goering is now blamed by Hitler for Germany's defeats. It is obvious, even to Goering himself, that he is being overtaken in influence by Himmler. Mentally humiliated by his servile dependence on the Fuhrer, Goering's personality has begun to disintegrate. He has become a dangerous foe for anyone he perceives as a block to his ultimate survival.

His single-minded fixation on quickly acquiring the American technology—Code Name: Orion's Eye—stems from what he sees as his last and best hope to regain Hitler's trust.

This power struggle between Himmler and Goering would be deadly to one of them.

Goering spoke, "It may take what time it takes, Herr Himmler, but that time must be short. For the sake of this war and for your personal sake the time must be short indeed."

Goering did not wait for a reply. Turning on his heel and pushing past his retinue, he exited the building.

Heinrich Himmler fumed. *You pompous ass. We will succeed—but not for your sake.*

He switched on his intercom. "Bring me the latest reports from Hauptmann!"

OSS Headquarters
Washington, DC
Same Time

The liaison officer from the Joint Chiefs of Staff to the OSS, Colonel William St. James, shifted from one foot to the other as he stood before General William Donovan's desk, reporting, "Army insists they can handle it, General."

George Tweedy looked from St. James to General Donovan and asked, "How does that sit with the President, General?"

"Just fine, George, just fine. Franklin loves to keep a little friction going between his teams. This suits him just fine."

Looking back to Colonel St. James he continued, "Sit down, Willie. You'll probably need to report back to the generals, eh? Well, you can tell them that they're responsible for getting Orion's Eye into combat ... and for keeping it out of German hands. But, they need to also know that others in this government are close to it, too. Very close indeed."

St. James nodded his understanding. "General, the Army sees this as a test of what could be a major breakthrough in radar capability. For security all of the operations related to it at Fort Monmouth have been shut down ... their missions to assemble the three units that are going into combat testing complete. Since then each of the merged technologies has receded to its respective organization for further development. If the Germans would ever penetrate one of them they would not have the whole story. Our only exposure is the three active units ... and they're under Army's tight control as you know."

Donovan reflected, "So that's where we are?"

George Tweedy added, "Our Intel from London says the Germans are in a rampage about Orion's Eye. Ultra intercepts have all been received in Lorenz Cipher ... all German High Command message traffic. This isn't over yet by a long shot."

Donovan nodded, "Get an update from Mead, George. We haven't heard from him since he recruited that sailor ... Gochais is it? One more thing, George. Clear Mead's team for access to SIGSALY encrypted radio ... London, California, Hawaii ... and that ship in Australia."

George Tweedy responded, his voice rising, "My God, General, as far as I know only Churchill has been using this system ... and he's talking to Roosevelt."

"Got it cleared by Franklin today. He thinks we've got to be quick and stealthy in tracking these Germans. The latest voice encryption should help."

OSS Training Site, Toyan Bay
Catalina Island, California

Donovan Gochais enjoyed the rare break from the constant rounds of training in weapons, martial arts, intelligence gathering and interpretation—and PT, always physical training in lieu of rest.

Gochais used this rare break to write a letter that he knew he couldn't send. He sat on a bluff over the Catalina beach, watching a group of sea lions lounging in the sun, now and then flinging sand onto a too warm back with a sweep of a flipper. Gochais dropped his gaze, moving his attention to the pad of paper in his lap, and began to write.

My Own Sweetheart,

You just can't imagine how it is out here without you and the boys. We're kept plenty busy, but when I get into bed and start thinking, that's when it gets to me. Am I doing the right thing? I think so, but not being able to talk with you about it, well....

But, Honey, there's an old saying that sort of fits in around here – you have to peel the orange before you can eat it, and I sort of feel it might fit our circumstances.

We have got a big fight to win here and until it's won our Tommy and Bobby ain't going to be really free Americans as you and I have been. So until this cloud is removed from over our head it's up to you and I to take whatever is in store for us with a smile.

I've met some swell guys here, but I don't suppose you'll ever get to meet them.

God only knows that I realize that you are carrying more than half of our load. But darling just grit your teeth and think of why we are doing it. And, Darling, take each of our 'proud possessions' and give them a big kiss for their Daddy, and tell Tommy that Daddy will be home just as soon as he can make it.

Well, Sweetheart, thanks for letting me talk to you for now. Someday you'll know all about this.

Gochais stripped the paper from the pad, folded it and drove it deep into his pocket. He stood and took one last look at the sea. *No need to close this. Can't send it anyway. Back to work.*

A Clandestine Location
Southern California

The man watched the hands of the clock reach the number. The radio, tuned to a prearranged frequency, flipped on at a prearranged time. Keying the microphone, he spoke in measured tones, "*Jäger ist auf Luft.* (Hunter is on air.) Over."

Almost at once the speaker crackled with static, then the words, "*Hallo Jäger. Wir bestätigen Position von Auge Orions.* (Hello Hunter, we confirm position of Orion's Eye.) At least one unit is in operation at South Flower Street headquarters of Air Defense. Do you read? Over."

"*Verstehen Sie.* (Yes I understand.) Over."

"Other possible units in Santa Barbara and San Diego. Over?"

"We will move. Over."

"We will be in contact with you ... *Folgendes Getriebe ist Geburtstag plus vier.* (Following messages will be at 'birthday plus four'.) *Heraus.* Out."

Anyone on the frequency had heard that the next message would go out at *birthday plus four.*

But only one who may have heard it understood.

Air Defense Wing Headquarters
Los Angeles, California
Later That Night

The P-51 Mustangs of the 383d Fighter Group flew in formation inbound to Los Angeles from Oxnard Field. Tonight they played *bad guys* for the exercise. The 1st Fighter Control Squadron, in the final stages of their training and shakedown for the new radar system, anxiously awaited the signal to begin.

The P-38's from the 364th Squadron, already scrambled from Van Nuys, orbited Los Angeles awaiting directions from the 1st Fighters—tonight they are the *hunters.*

The first call came from the radar operators, "Red Dog, Red Dog, this is LA Center. Squawk IFF (Identification Friend or Foe)."

The lead P-38 pilot responded, "Roger LA. Red Dog squawking."

"We have you at 20,000 feet Red Dog. Your bogies are 135 degrees from your position ... level at 10,000, heading 360, speed 300 knots. Suggest your heading 045 to intercept."

"Roger LA, Red Dog flight turning to 045 to intercept."

A few minutes elapsed as the radar operator sat quietly waiting for the next report.

His radio crackled, "LA, Red Dog. We have the bogie's exhaust fire in sight ... closing from their six for positive ID."

"Roger, Red Dog. We show your intercept in two minutes."

"LA, Red Dog. Bogies in sight. ID aircraft as friendly."

The 1st Fighter operators heard the expected results, but this never lessened their excitement about how effective they could be with this new gear.

"Roger that Red Dog. Good job once again. LA will be going on standard watch for the rest of tonight. Thanks for your help. LA Center out."

The intercept NCO turned to another frequency and spoke, "383 Flight, this is LA. Thanks for another good mission. The P-38's are returning to base. You're clear to head for home."

"LA, 383 Flight. Roger that. Good night. 383 out."

The training sergeant flipped switches and adjusted room lights. "That's it guys. Standard watch for the rest of the night. Nothing on the board. Should be quiet."

As he moved into the hallway he spoke to a soldier dressed in wool OD shirt and trousers and web belt with bayonet scabbard and ammo pouch—and a very sour look on his face. "Hey, Sarge, sorry you're goin' to miss the fun. We're goin' over to Lyman's Bar and roust a few more of those zoot-suiters."

Technical Sergeant Chester W. (Chet) Driest replied, "Yeah, yeah ... have your chuckles. One of these days one of those nuts is going to stick a switch blade into you ... then no more chuckles for you."

Laughter drifted off down the hall and echoed in the stairwell. Then it was quiet.

Sergeant Driest, a rosy-cheeked, average height and newly married soldier from Detroit, Michigan, is not a happy GI as he marched his guard post in a hallway of the South Flower & 8th Street building. After a full day's work, this is the second night straight for guard duty for this highly trained radar technician from the 1st Fighter Control Squadron.

With no one else in the deserted hallway, he muttered to himself, "Four hours to go. Gotta stay alert ... alert hell, I'll settle for awake."

Carrying his bayonet rigged M-1 Garand at right shoulder arms, the sergeant measured the distance from one end of his post to the other by counting his paces. Idly he thought, *Might as well look sharp ... Do I remember my General Orders? Let's see ... Walk my post in a military manner, being always on the alert and noticing all within my ... my ... oh, what the hell.*

He reached the end of his post where the hallway turned into some sort of fire escape alcove and smartly moved his rifle from his right shoulder to port arms, then to his side. He executed a precise about-face and had raised his rifle back to port arms when the garrote slipped around his neck from behind.

The shock yanked his head back as a knee hit him in the lower spine. The attacker grunted as he pulled the noose tight enough to cut into the larynx of his victim. Expecting this to be over quickly, the soldier's cry of "shit!" confused him reflexively he pulled the garrote ends tighter.

The wire stretched—and snapped, throwing him off balance.

The position of Sergeant Driest's rifle and bayonet at the moment of the attack had saved his life. The bayonet came between him and the deadly force of the garrote. As it snapped—freeing him—he lunged forward into a perfectly balanced port-arms defense stance. Infantry basic training kicked in as he spun on his forward foot to face his attacker. Driest drove the butt of the Garand up and into his assailant's face with a butt-stroke that broke a nose and received a cry of pain. The assailant flailed back into the wall, recovered and lunged toward the sergeant, spitting blood.

Driest feinted to his left and drove the rifle butt up into the man's groin with all his might, then slammed the barrel onto the back of his head as he fell forward with a sickening moan. Driest bounced against the wall and quickly regained his balance. The assailant down, moaning and pulling his knees up into almost a fetal position, Driest leaned over him and poised his bayonet.

THUD

Driest felt the rifle slip from his grasp in a blinding flash. With a ringing in his ears he thought, *I'll walk my post in a military manner*—a calm darkness overcame him as he slumped to the cold concrete floor.

The second man had arrived on the landing in time to slam a pistol into the sergeant's exposed neck. The time for a guard change approaching, the assailants knew escape must be now.

Outside, patrolling along South Flower Street in the early morning hour, a police cruiser saw two men crossing to a parking lot. One supporting the other, bent over in seeming distress.

The officer hailed them, "Your friend alright?"

Keeping his friend's back to the police car, the man replied, "Yes, sir, just too much to drink. He's pretty sick ... I'll get him home. His wife's gonna be real upset ... know what I mean Officer?"

"Sure do, fella, sure do. You be careful."

The police cruiser pulled away. The officer laughed to himself, thinking, *No crime ... no paperwork ... a good thing.*

Then he stepped on the brakes and looked back. *Wait a minute. The nearest bar is Lyman's ... and that's over 6 blocks away. Where in hell?*

But there is no one in sight.

OSS Safe House
Los Angeles, California.
Next Day

Mead and Wetmore rose early to work on all the new information forwarded by London from Bletchley Park's intercepts.

Wetmore informed Mead of the SIGSALY authority and the request by E Street for a report. Pouring his third mug of coffee, Wetmore said, "Talking directly with Morse on this SIGSALY net sure helps to speed things up. I'll get the material together for your report this morning."

"Thanks, Chief. You've got my notes from yesterday."

The maid stepped into the dining room. "May I set out the breakfast, senores?"

Mead replied, "Thank you, Constantia, and tell our other guests to join us ... but I have a phone call to make before I eat." He looked at the note.

MRS. BETTY JEAN WILLIAMSON — WEBSTER 73547 — AMOS KNEW HER AS B.J. — FATHER GAVE HER THE NUMBER.

Then he picked up the phone.

An Apartment House
Van Nuys, California

The telephone on the wall in the dingy hallway rang. A terry-cloth robed girl on her way to the shower shifted the towel and bottles in her hand and reached for the receiver. "Hello. ... You want Betty Jean? I'm her roommate. Let me see if she's available. Hang on."

The girl left the telephone to dangle at the end of its cord while she retraced her steps to the door of the room she shared with BJ. The paint-weary door creaked as she opened it a crack. "Betty, telephone for you. You still up?"

The weary reply, "Thanks, Jo, let me get a robe."

Back at the phone the girl said, "She'll be right along ... she just got in from the night shift, you know. Too early? Naw ... Here she is."

BJ took the receiver, hesitated a moment then spoke, "Hello."

A smile spread over her haggard face, still grimy from the nights work at Lockheed Aircraft. "Amos! Thank you for calling back. No, no, the time is fine. When I talked with my folks they said that you were in L.A. Then I called your dad ... yes, they're fine. He gave me your number."

She talked a little faster, energy coming back from somewhere. "I'd love to see you. I'm planning on moving back home soon, but—"

She listened, looking up to nod at a passing friend. "Today? Sure ... I can get a ride. Tell me the address. Yes, as soon as I can. Okay, Amos. This is swell."

She hung up and looked at the Wilshire address she's written on the grimy plaster wall with the string-suspended pencil stub. "Wow. Jo! I need a ride!"

OSS Safe House - Same Day
Los Angeles, California

Mead sat with the receiver still in his hand, *what the hell am I doing? I sounded like a school boy ... what's the damn hurry?*

He idly replaced the receiver onto the chrome cradle of the shiny black phone. Instantly it rang, causing him to jerk his hand back. "What the—"

Wetmore reached for the still warm receiver and said, "I've got it, Major. Clinton 58873. Yes, General, he's right here."

Mead took back the phone. "Good morning, General."

A wide-eyed pause followed. "Shit, when? Yes, sir. I'm on my way."

The receiver slammed back into place as Mead rose, slapping the table. "They tried to get to Orion's Eye, Chief ... actually attacked a guard. I'm headed over to South Flower."

Mead strode down the hall to his room. He slipped into his uniform blouse, then went to the bureau drawer and retrieved his 1911 Model Colt 45, slipping it into the waistband of his trousers. *Time for this thing. They're getting rough ... Oh, shit ... B.J.*

Barging back into the dining room, he yelled, "Chief. Call B.J. ... uh ... Mrs. Williamson. Tell her she can't ... that is ... I'm not... you handle it for me, Chief."

He moved straight out the door and headed for the Navy grey Plymouth in the driveway. Wetmore answered to no one in particular, "Okay, Major."

He picked up the phone and dialed.

It rang four times before a tired voice said, "Hello." And then answered the query with, "Nope, saw her and a couple others scoot outta here a few minutes ago."

A Clandestine Location - Same Day
Southern California

This transmission, not prearranged, broke protocol. But this was an emergency. The radio's speaker crackled with static, "*Hallo Jäger. Hereingekommen,* come in. *Antwort, verdammen.* Damn it, answer, over." (Hello, Hunter, Come in. Reply dammit.)

A voice, weak and shaken replied, "*Jäger here. Ja verstehen Sie, bin ich hier.* Yes I understand, I am here. Over."

"What went wrong? Herr Nicolaus will be furious. Over."

"I can explain. It is not my fault ... uh. Over."

"You do not explain to me. Are other teams in place? Time is short. Over."

"Ja we have others ... but, er—"

The radio clicked off. He now talked to thin air. The last words he thought he heard was in Spanish, "*Mierda muda. Ahora toda la paga.*"

Dumb shit. We will all pay now!

 # CHAPTER 7

OSS X-2 Operations Headquarters
London, England

Morse sat drumming his fingers on the oak table as the SIGSALY encoding system buzzed and crackled in its efforts to synchronize with Los Angeles, California.

Finally the sounds cleared. "Hello, Chief Wetmore. Chandler Morse here. How are you?"

From 5,456 miles to his west came the reply, "Swell, Chandler, just swell. We've had a little excitement out here."

"Excitement? What could possibly excite an old salt like you, Chief?"

"Not much usually, my English friend. But this is good enough to raise a twitter. Somebody tried to get to our favorite gizmo."

"Somebody tried to nip off with Orion's Eye? Need I ask ... Were they successful?"

"Nope, bungled this one too ... but it got a little hairy."

"Well, well, I think that explains the flurry of ULTRA intercepts we've had coded in the Lorenz Cipher. Those German High Command blokes are in a tizzy. Himmler's headquarters and Goering's mob at the Luftwaffe High Command are trading some rather nasty insults. It seems Goering has given orders directly to Nicolaus in Mexico. Herr Himmler is furious! It's quite jolly to watch them twist each other's knickers, don't you think?"

"Yah, knickers ... Hey, Chandler, any word on a location for our boy Otto Hauptmann?"

"Oh, Yes. Sorry, that's why I called you. We seem to have lost him, old chap."

"Lost him? What the hell do you mean, lost him?"

"Well, our Commander Dillon reported that Otto just dropped out of sight in Chile."

"Is Dillon on the hunt?"

"I'm sure he is. But you must remember, Chief, Dillon's only working for us on the side. He can't really press a search with anyone else in Naval Intelligence just yet."

"Okay, okay ... I've got it. We'll make the report from here and keep our sources mum. Good work, Chandler. Anything else?"

"That's it, Mr. Wetmore. Give my regards to the major. Oh, one more thing. We have an ULTRA intercept of a message from *Kriegsmarine* Headquarters to a submarine at sea. It mentioned Himmler and our Project. Decoding's not complete but it shouldn't be long. I'll let you know if it's anything interesting. Cheerio for now, old chap. London out."

Los Angeles, California
Same Time

Mead parked the Plymouth a block south of the eight story stone building that served as headquarters for all air defense operations on the southwest coast.

Civilian volunteers and military personnel scurried in and out of the large revolving doors that faced South Flower Street. They manned the labyrinth of offices and the rooftop observation posts twenty-four hours a day.

Mead only wanted a look around. He knew that the attack had not penetrated to Orion's Eye and he didn't want to disclose his role beyond the few who knew of his interest in it. Passing through the revolving door, he entered the elevator, indicating 5 with a spread of his fingers to the uniformed operator.

The scissoring safety gate slid shut and the cage lurched up as he thought, *Bonfoey can't be here yet. If it is him ... has he got friends?*

The car lurched to a stop and the gate opened. Mead exited, looking up and down the corridor where the 1st Fighter Control Squadron had set up its training and test operation. A uniformed Los Angeles policeman slouched against the wall near an office door about twenty feet away.

Mead approached him. "Good morning, Officer. May I go in?"

The policeman responded, "Sorry, sir, they're still talking with that guard in there." He slowly straightened up and shrugged his shoulders. "Gonna be awhile, I reckon."

"Is he with the LAPD or Military Police?"

"Both, Major."

"Thank you, Officer."

Mead turned down the hall toward a sign that announced *HQ 1st Fighter Control Squadron.* Entering through the frosted glass door he responded to the duty sergeant's call for attention, "At ease ... as you were. Sergeant, I need a phone."

"Right this way, sir."

Led into a small office with a bare desk, a typewriter and the telephone, his first call went to Chief Wetmore. "Any background stuff on Bonfoey, Chief?"

Wetmore's replied in the negative. No one seemed to have a record of the captain. At least not that he could find yet.

"Okay, keep digging, Chief."

With just a second's delay, he added, "Oh, Chief, has B—?"

But the call was already disconnected.

Retrieving a crumbled note from his tunic pocket he dialed the number it contained. "General Nielsen, please ... Major Mead calling."

Nielsen came on the phone, "Mead, what in hell's going on? Nobody's telling me shit!"

"Not much, General. I'm here at the 1st Fighter HQ. They're still talking with the guard. Nothing's missing. Looks like they botched it up, but these people are serious. Damn it, this could have been deadly. But I'm not sure your soldiers realize it's a try at stealing Orion's Eye. What I'm hearing is that they think it's some kind of two-bit robbery attempt. By the way, General, is Bonfoey still out there at March Field?"

"Far as I know, Mead. I just put out a call for him to get over to my office."

"General, I don't want anyone else to know my connection to this thing. Just you and Lieutenant Gibbons. Okay?"

"Whatever you say, son. Makes sense to me. God damn it, boy ... keep me posted!"

74

Mead hung up the black phone, idly straightening its stiff cord as he pondered events. *Things are happening, but I'll be damned if I can find anything to act on. Just keep on watching until we get this thing out to sea.*

4230 Mayfield Place
Los Angeles, California

Elma Gochais sat on the oak wood floor with her two boys. The toddler, Bobby, squirmed in a walker seat, trying gamely to reach the wooden toy train that three-year-old Tommy maneuvered around deftly with his left hand. His withered right hand trailed behind, but never seemed to get in the way of whatever he wanted to do.

Elma's father, Harvey Palmer, sat on the sofa, perched on the edge of the cushion with his hands in his lap. He said, "The hospital bill will all be paid by the Shriners, but we still don't know about the doctor's bill." He pursed his lips as he always did when he was thinking.

Her mother called from the kitchen where she busily cleaned up the lunch dishes, "Elma, have you heard from Donny?"

"No, mother. I expected a call by now from San Francisco."

Reatha Palmer said, "Doesn't he know we have to take care of Tommy's situation?" She slammed a handful of silverware onto the wooden counter.

Elma replied, "Yes, mother, of course."

She knew no other answer would suffice. "Thanks for your help, dad. I know Donny will be happy to hear all this too."

Tommy fended off one more attempt by his little brother, moving the wooden train just out of reach.

"You too little for train."

OSS Safe House
Los Angeles, California.

The long black hood of the 1940 Packard convertible nosed in by the curb and stopped.

The four women in the car stared in awe at the beautiful Spanish style house and its manicured grounds.

Jo broke the silence. "Betty, are you sure you want to go in alone?"

"Are you kidding? That's the only way I'm going in. Besides, you've got to get your father's car back to him."

"If this is your friend's house, Miss Betty, I've got just one question for you ... does he have a brother?"

Giggling sentiments echoed from the back seat riders. Betty Jean Williamson opened the car door. She hesitated a moment before stepping out. "Down, girls. I'll let you know. Jo, thanks so much for the ride. You're a dear."

"Should I wait?"

"No, I'll be fine."

As the car drove away, the slender, honey-blonde haired woman walked slowly toward the house. Her tired face, a beautiful face even now, showed little emotion. But inside churned a confused mix of trepidation and anxious anticipation. *I feel like a damn schoolgirl. Straighten up, BJ ... he's just an old friend.*

The rap of the large wrought iron knocker seemed to echo. The door slowly opened and the face of a

Spanish women appeared around its massive carved edge. "Si, Senorita, may I help you?"

"Yes, I'm here to see Mr. Amos Mead. He gave me this address."

"He is not here."

A man's voice boomed from inside the house, "Who's there, Constantia?"

"It is a senorita asking for Señor Mead."

A large hand took hold of the door well above the Spanish woman's head and opened it enough to the see the petite visitor. "I've got it, Constantia. You may go. You must be BJ ... come in!"

The man pulled the door to full open and gestured the way into the large living room. "My name is Harmon Wetmore. With a flourish, he added, "At your service, ma'am ... Amos got called away on urgent business right after he talked to you."

BJ quickly said, "Oh, I can come back another time."

"Nonsense, you come right in. He'll be along. Can I get you some coffee?"

Her anxiety melted away. "That would be nice, Mr. Wetmore."

"Not 'Mr.', ma'am ... Call me Chief ... as in U.S. Navy."

"Okay, Chief ... My husband was ... I mean *is* in the Navy. He's a fighter pilot."

She took the cup of coffee and added a bit of cream from the pitcher offered. She stirred and gazed into the browning swirl. "He's been shot down. Somewhere in the Solomon Islands, I believe. My dad thinks it might have been Bougainville, but he doesn't really know. We haven't heard anymore."

Her voice trailed off as the rollercoaster effects of working all night, getting an exciting call from a dear old friend, finding him not at home, then feeling strangely welcome and safe with this grizzled Navy Chief bore down on her.

"I'm sorry to hear that. It must be tough ... not knowing and all."

"It surely is, Chief. But working at the aircraft plant and making a lot of friends with the girls there has helped. A lot of their guys are overseas. My folks back in Vermont have been real sweet. They keep in regular touch. That's how I found out about Amos being in Los Angeles. My Dad and Mr. Mead are great friends, you know."

She shifted in her chair, finally sipping the cooling coffee. "I'm babbling, Chief. You must have things to do. I'm sorry to be such a bother."

"You're nothing of the sort, ma'am. It's a pleasure to make your acquaintance. I can sure see why Amos is taken with you ... 'course that's none of my business."

BJ smiled into her coffee cup. *Amos taken with me? It's been a long time, but —*

Wetmore laughed. "I'm talking too much! You got plans, BJ? Like keepin' on working at the plant?"

"I don't really know, Chief. I've been thinking about going back to Vermont. My folks would really like that. It's hard to keep my mind clear, waiting for word and all."

"Ma'am, I'm going out on a limb here, but I've had an idea brewing and I think this is the time to act on it. Please, will you excuse me while I make a phone call."

"Of course, Chief."

Wetmore freshened her coffee and stepped out of the room. Betty Jean could hear his muffled voice on the phone, but paid no attention. She started when the Spanish lady moved through the room and on into the kitchen. *I'm getting jumpy, too tired.*

Wetmore stepped back into the room. He wore a conspiratorial smile. "Okay, Mrs. Williamson, er, B J ... I'm sorry. It's okay to call you B J?"

He didn't wait for a reply. "I've been talking with General David Barrows ... he's the big boss around here ... about needing somebody to take over running this house. I'm no innkeeper and that's a fact. He's good with the idea. So I just called him with a candidate. I've gotta ask you. B.J., would you be interested in the job?"

"My goodness, Chief, I don't know—"

"Please, just think about it. I'm sorry this is so sudden ... but doggonit sometimes you just got to act. You can meet with the general tomorrow and get all the details ... and he'll get a look at you. No guarantees, B.J., but it looks good. Before you say no, think about it. You'll be a darn sight closer to information from the Pacific."

The conversation continued as B.J. warmed to the idea. Chief Wetmore could be charming in his own gruff way and B.J. saw the sense of trusting him.

Wetmore closed. "We're going to get you home, young lady. I don't know how long Amos is going to be and you need to make whatever arrangements you need to meet with General Barrows."

"Thank you, Chief. I am really tired. Where do I go tomorrow?"

"I'll give you the address. It's not far from here. Let's get you home. I'll drive."

Puerto Montt, Chile
Same Time

The *Lati Air* flight from San Carlos de Bariloche, Argentina, taxied up to the lean-to building that served as an air terminal for Puerto Montt.

The messenger blended in with the other deplaning passengers, until Reinhard Gehlan spotted the briefcase secured to his wrist.

He approached the man and said quietly, "*Usted está buscando a un amigo*? (You are looking for a friend?)

The man responded, "Pardon me?"

Gehlan switched to German. "*Sie suchen einen Freund?*" (You are looking for a friend?)

"Oh, ja."

"His name is Otto?"

"Ja."

"Come with me. My name is Gehlan ... Reinhard Gehlan. I am his associate."

The messenger recognized the name and followed Gehlan to the waiting Mercedes Benz. The short drive wound down toward the town. The car stopped in front of a small brick house that overlooked Canal Tenglo. Gehlan climbed out of the car and motioned the messenger to follow him into the house where a wood-fired stove warmed a comfortable room and held off the bitter Patagonian cold. Something cooking, and a table set for two, reminded the visitor that a hot meal is but a distant memory.

The only indication that the house is an active branch of the Nazi SS is the military radio set up in the corner. On the wall were a map of the Chilean coast and a large scale sea chart of the Pacific Ocean.

Gehlan said, "Sit down, my friend. We shall eat, and then you can tell me what you've brought."

"But, sir, my message is for Herr Hauptmann."

"Herr Hauptmann is not here. He has moved down the coast to prepare for his rendezvous. I cannot say more as I'm sure you understand."

"I understand full well, Herr Gehlan. And you must understand that my superior is Johannes Becker in Argentina and that he has sent me with information that impacts Herr Hauptmann's mission. We are in contact with Berlin ... but Herr Becker thought it too dangerous to transmit the message to you here in Chile. Others are listening."

"You have not told me your name. I suspect you are more than a messenger."

"Ah, I have heard that your observation skills are well honed, Herr Gehlan. My name is Ludwig von Bohlen. I escaped from Brazil with Albrecht Engels when the Americans convinced that government that we are spies ... Imagine that. Also, as you have guessed, I am well versed in Hauptmann's mission."

"Well, Herr von Bohlen, since we have satisfied our suspicions let us get down to business. My housekeeper prepared this fine stew which we must not let go to waste. We can eat and talk."

The steaming bowls were joined by chunks of freshly baked bread. There was no talk for a few moments.

Gehlan sipped a fresh glass of schnapps and set it on the table. He broke the quiet, "Ludwig, you said that others are listening. What did you mean?"

"Berlin, Reinhard, Berlin. There is more fighting between Goering and Himmler than on the Russian front. Each of them thinks that obtaining this new American technology will turn the tide of war around

... and make them the darling of der Fuhrer. Goering has gone quite mad in my opinion. I trust I'm safe in saying that aloud in this place."

"Of course, Ludwig. In our business we must be pragmatic ... not stupid."

Herr von Bohlen dipped a crust of bread into the remnants of his stew and savored the dripping morsel. He looked up and said, "Stupid is a good word for the game George Nicolaus is playing in Mexico. He sided with Goering and is now trying to steal this Orion's Eye for him." He paused a moment, then added, "Is Hauptmann aware of all this dangerous foolishness?"

Gehlan answered, "Otto may or may not know, my friend. But for sure he does not care. He has his own reasons for defeating the Americans. He seeks revenge for his father. Orion's Eye is the mission that gives him his opportunity ... Himmler and Goering be damned."

"We all have our reasons don't we, Reinhard? When do you expect Hauptmann to return? I must pass along a warning to him."

"A warning? I do not expect him to return. He is meeting his submarine—and possibly his fate."

Gehlan rose and began to clear the table. "What is your warning?"

Ludwig von Bohlen reached for his briefcase, turned a key in the lock and retrieved a photograph. He handed it to Gehlan and said, "This is HMS *Achilles* ... a New Zealand Destroyer. She has been tracking the U-835. She patrols these waters, careful to not violate any neutrality protocols with Chile or Peru. We believe she awaits his submarine off this coast."

Gehlan shook his head and laughed. "You underestimate Herr Hauptmann. Why do you think he moved down the coast for his rendezvous? Hauptmann has been tracking *Achilles* for a week. Maybe we should warn the New Zealanders that they are in danger of receiving a torpedo for their troubles. May I pour a schnapps for you, Ludwig? You've had a long day."

"Danke. I would like some schnapps. It will have more value than my message, it seems."

The Mouth of Aisén Fjord
Latitude 45°24' S - Longitude 72°42' W
4 Km from Puerto Aisén, Chile

The U-835 arrived off Puerto Montt on schedule. The pre-arranged radio communication from Otto Hauptmann produced a warning about the New Zealand ship, and he relayed his change of plans to the *Kapitän.*

Hauptmann's sail from Puerto Montt to the mouth of the Aisén Fjord had been as smooth as these waters allowed. His hired fishing sloop is manned by a Chilean crew, descendants of Germans émigrés and loyal to the Third Reich.

Skillfully they sailed one kilometer up the entrance to the fjord, then seeing no other boats they tacked about and returned to the rendezvous line arriving at the agreed time.

At the same time the U-835 arrived underwater, spotted the sailing vessel through their raised periscope, and moved in its direction. Hauptmann sighted the periscope off the starboard bow of his small sloop. At the same time he spotted a Chilean trawler headed in from the open sea and coolly ordered the captain of his sloop to lay on a westerly coarse, favorable to the offshore breeze that blew cold from the mountains.

Ernst Kalbruener, *Kapitän* (captain) of the *Kriegsmarine* submarine U-835, watched through his periscope as the sloop that he believed to be his target took up the westerly course, swinging the mainsail outboard to catch the offshore wind. It bore down on his periscope and passed a few yards to the north. As they passed the periscope to seaward Hauptmann immediately showed a small red flag, keeping it behind the sail so that the trawler could not see it.

Per instructions to confirm their identity the sloop dipped its main sail three times.

Fifty yards away toward the shore the U-835 broke the surface, appearing where only moments before had been vacant sea. Pacific blue water poured from her partially surfaced superstructure as the two vessels closed. At the precise time agreed upon, Hauptmann sprang aboard and entered the opened hatch on the side of the conning tower.

The U-835 slipped below the waves, never seen by the trawler, and set a course north by west.

The *Eye of the Hunter* had become the prey.

 **CHAPTER 8**

**4230 Mayfield Place
Los Angeles, California**

Gochais stepped from the taxi and retrieved his military Valv-Pak bag. He handed the driver a bill and told him to keep the change.

Before arriving home, Gochais had gone straight from Catalina Island to the OSS house on Wilshire to complete his initiation into his new role. Wetmore briefed him on what had transpired and gave him $500 in cash as his initial OSS paycheck. Gochais received instructions to report back to the house on his way to meeting his ship. He also met a charming lady at the house who seemed to share some secret with the chief that he didn't bother to probe.

Glad to be home, but still uncomfortable with his own secrets, Gochais walked to the familiar front door and turned the knob. "Anybody want to see a sailor coming home?"

"Donny!" Elma ran from the back room where she had just put the boys down for their afternoon nap. "You didn't call. I was worried."

The kiss stifled further words for the moment.

"Daddy!" Gochais felt little Tommy's grip around his leg. The boy called to his brother, "Come on, Bobby, daddy's home!" Donovan Gochais reveled in the hugs and horseplay from his treasured sons.

Later, after some lunch, and the boys finally succumbing to their naps, Donovan and Elma had the first chance to talk. She told him of the Shriner Hospital's providing free services for Tommy's surgery and about her father trying to help out with the surgeon's fees.

Elma said, "The surgery is scheduled for next week. I'm so happy that it worked out for you to be here."

She slumped back on the sofa, her hands in her lap. Donovan produced the nearly $500 dollars he had left and said, I can pay the doctor ... I won this money in a poker game on the ship."

Another lie joined the others that weighed heavily on Donovan Gochais.

OSS Safe House
Los Angeles, California.
Late the Same Day

Mead arrived at the house to find Wetmore and two Marine officers finishing dinner. "Could have waited for me, Chief ... I'm starved!"

Wetmore answered, "Work better hours, sir, and you'll get a meal now and then." Then with a final morsel of steak on the way to his mouth, he added, "Mmmm ... good."

"Shut up. Where's the Scotch? How are you guys doing?"

A guest replied, "Great, Major."

A nod from the other Marine agreed. "Bottle's here on the table, sir."

Wetmore pushed back from the remnants of his meal as Constantia moved quietly in to clear his plate. "You missed a couple of folks today, Major. Gochais came through on his way home. And BJ ... I mean, Mrs. Williamson."

"Was she angry?"

"No sir. Disappointed, but not angry."

"How's Gochais?"

"He's gonna be fine, Major. Still concerned with the spy bit, but he's ready to go. I got him some pay. He said it'll help with his boy. Oh, I talked with Chandler this morning, he's—"

"Save it, Chief."

Mead's eyes surveyed the room, indicating an end to any more reports for now.

Constantia finished clearing the table.

Wetmore hesitated to be sure Mead would let him continue, then said, "Major, about Mrs. Williamson ... She'll be back tomorrow to meet with General Barrows."

Mead looked down into the last of his Scotch, his glass held with both hands, then realized what he'd heard. "Barrows? What the hell for?"

"Well, sir, looks like she's going to take over running this place for us. You know I ain't no innkeeper, and—"

"She's going to do what?" *BJ, here?*

Wetmore moved quickly to explain, "If it all goes okay she'll be moving into the quarters out back next to the Velasquez's ... and she'll be in charge of running the place. She had planned to go back home to Vermont. But, hell, we need her here. And besides, she can keep better watch for news of her husband.

We're getting busier, what with more Marines going through Toyan Bay and all. Also we—"

"Okay, okay. I got it. We got some more ice? I need another one of these."

Mead slid his empty glass toward Wetmore. *Why have I been thinking about her? She's married ... can't worry about it now ...* "What's that about BJ's husband, Chief?"

Los Angeles Air Defense Wing Headquarters
Los Angeles, California
Next Day

The Duty Officer for the 1st Fighter Control Squadron sat stiffly, facing the telephone he held to his ear. His head bobbed up and down to the cadence of the voice on the other end. "Yes, sir. Yes, sir. I understand, sir. I'll get the word out, sir. Thank you, sir."

Before the receiver hit the cradle he called out, "Sergeant, we're moving out! The captain just got the word. Notify all stations to pack up and prepare for transport to March Field."

His hand still on the receiver, it rang again. He answered, "O.D., Lieutenant O'Sullivan, sir."

He listened, his eyes scrunched tightly shut and head moving side to side in slow denial. "We don't need this shit, Sergeant. We're packing up right now to move out ... you'll get the word. Just turn it over to the local cops and pack up the rest. Everybody okay? Good. Hey, second thought ... you're gonna have to report this to CID ... then let them work with the locals."

Lieutenant O'Sullivan set the phone down once again. "Judas Priest Almighty … what's goin' on here? I don't need this shit."

The phone back to his ear, he dialed, "Hi, Shorty. Is the 'old man' in? … Captain Bonfoey, this is Lieutenant O'Sullivan. Yes sir, L.A. Flower Street. Captain, I just got a report from Santa Barbara that somebody broke into the remote sight, tied up the guy on watch and took off with an SCR 582 … No, sir. That's the old Selsyn-Amplidyne System. No, sir … nobody's hurt. Yes, sir they're filing with CID and the local authorities … Thank You, sir."

Seventy miles south, Captain Bonfoey set the phone down and leaned back in his chair. *Okay, it's happening.*

4th Interceptor Command
March Field, California

General Nielsen leaned forward, his elbows on the desk, his telephone held firmly to his right ear, and the unlit cigar he chewed down to a tattered nub.

He continued to work it with nervous vigor as he spoke, "Mead, 1st Fighters have Shipment Orders. Their pulling back here to March Field from all stations … and the L.A. bunch are bringing the Project with them. What? … No, no, Bonfoey's been here all along. What's next? What's next is they'll be getting a call from the Port Commander with a final embark date. Your sailor boy should know about that before we do. They'll be going up to 'Frisco by train … actually, they'll go to Camp Stoneman first. That's it, Major. Good luck!"

General Nielsen spat the cigar remnants into the butt-can next to his desk and replaced the warm telephone receiver on its cradle. *Wish to hell I could go along on this one.*

His phone rang again. "Yes. What? What the effing? When?"

Pacific Ocean – At Sea
German U-835 Underway

The U-835 preceded west by north at *schnorchel* depth, keeping a sharp eye out for Allied patrols. Technically, she could keep this up for twenty hours a day before having to surface.

At two-hundred-ninety-four feet in length and displacing sixteen-hundred-fifty tons, the German submarine U-835 originally served as a minelayer. Like many in its class she had been converted to a Japan-Transporter.

She has made this run from Kristiansand, Norway, to Penang, Malaysia, and on to Japan three times before—but this time is different.

Very different.

Kriegsmarine Kapitän Ernst Kalbruener received new orders two days out of Kristiansand to put his boat into Lorient, France, for re-outfitting for a special mission. His Japan-bound cargo was off loaded and replaced with three motorized whaleboats. Each of these boats carries a 105mm gun, a high powered searchlight, and other rigging that the captain found odd. He received no explanation. He did receive a set of sailing orders that sent him across the Atlantic, through the Straits of Magellan, and up the coast of Chile to Latitude 41°28' S - Longitude 72°56' W—near Puerto Montt, Chile.

Here he is to listen for a contact and arrange to pick up an agent of the German SS.

Kalbruener is not happy, but his new orders were signed by Admiral Dönitz, so his personal happiness is not a factor.

The voyage across the Atlantic is tedious ... except for a close call off the Falkland Islands. An allied Destroyer tracked them, but no attack came.

And now his passenger is aboard, carrying orders from Himmler himself. The *Kapitän* is not used to anyone giving orders on his boat but himself. Especially the order to run on the *schnorchel* for this extended time.

Kalbruener knew this to be dangerous.

The *schnorchel*, a device that provides them air while underwater, could sometimes be detected by radar or keen-eyed lookouts in calm weather. It is virtually impossible to spot in rougher conditions, but these same conditions can cause problems of their own. The float valve which closed the *schnorchel* if its intake became submerged often caused a sharp fall in air pressure in the U-boat as air is sucked into the diesels. Breathing difficulties and injury such as perforated eardrums can result, and crews had actually suffocated.

Kalbruener always avoided extended use, but this passenger, Otto Hauptmann, is in a hurry.

The U-boat officers assembled in the cramped wardroom.

Hauptmann addressed them, "We will proceed on this course to Latitude 22°01' South. We will be listening on frequencies that I will give you as we approach that position. Are there any questions?"

With obvious tension, *Kapitän* Kalbruener asked. "How long must we remain on the *schnorchel*?"

"Speed, *mein Kapitän,* is most important. If you feel you can maintain our way without it … you may proceed as you see fit."

Kalbruener replied, "That is so kind of you, Herr Hauptmann." His mocking tone evident, then rolling his eyes toward the low overhead, he added, "Are we to learn of your mission soon?"

The others leaned in, curious but unable to speak.

Hauptmann replied, "Soon enough, *Kapitän.* Though you may rest assured it is important. Now, sir, I wish to inspect our cargo. Later we all shall train for a very special rendezvous."

The *Kapitän* rose and pulled back the curtain to the passageway. "Follow me, Herr Hauptmann. We shall visit your toys."

Federal Building
Los Angeles, California
Next Day

Once again the SIGSALY voice radio encryption system buzzed and crackled in its efforts to synchronize with the receiving unit. This time it is Los Angeles, California, sending to Honolulu, Hawaii.

After the requisite fifteen minutes the Signals Sergeant called out, "Chief, I've got Hawaii for you."

Wetmore moved to the radiophone from his usual station in the basement of the Federal Building in Los Angeles. "Chief Petty Officer Harmon Wetmore calling for Admiral Ed Layton … Yes, I'll wait."

The OSS front office is on the sixth floor of the Federal Building, shared with General Barrows and his staff. Wetmore and the Orion's Eye team had opted to be nearer to SIGSALY and out of sight of the usual comings and goings. With time growing short until their Project sailed to war, Wetmore felt it time to reconnect solidly with his mentor on Admiral Nimitz's intelligence staff. In fact, his mentor, Rear Admiral Edward Layton, is now head of the JICPOA (Joint Intelligence Center, Pacific Ocean Area).

Layton, with the blessing of Nimitz, had been the one who placed Wetmore with the OSS in Los Angeles as *eyes and ears* for Nimitz and the Navy's Pacific Operations.

In late 1937, Layton, then a lieutenant commander attached to the Office of Naval Intelligence, served as acting Naval Attaché in Peiping, China. He met Wetmore after the chief evaded capture by the Japanese at the battle of the Marco Polo Bridge and the subsequent guerilla action fought with the Chinese Army. Survivors of Wetmore's China-sailor detail made it the one-hundred-seventy-five miles northeast to Peiping and reported in to the American Legation.

Chief Wetmore's detailed after-action report and his intelligence analysis impressed Layton so much that he arranged Wetmore's assignment to ONI (Office of Naval Intelligence), and finally to his staff in Pearl Harbor.

A familiar voice came on the line, "Harmon Wetmore ... how are you, my old friend?"

"Fine, Admiral. I'm calling to bring you up to date on project Code Name: Orion's Eye. It'll be on its way to you ... that is, to the South Pacific ... shortly. The Germans have been working hard at getting ahold of this technology, but, so far, no luck for them. Frankly, sir, it's hard to fathom how they'd make a play in the Pacific Ocean."

"Don't kid yourself, Chief. They're very active in supporting the Japs down there … mostly with supply submarines running to Penang. We sink 'em, but they keep coming."

"Roger that, Admiral. I'm sending all the details we have to you on MAGIC. Hope things are well with you, sir."

"All's well indeed, Harmon. But, tell me, how in hell are you cleared to be on SIGSALY? We've only had it for a couple of weeks and only Nimitz has used it so far."

"Friends in high places, Admiral. Friends who think Orion's Eye is important."

"Well keep up the good work, Chief. When this thing's over we need to sit down for a stiff drink and some really deep reminiscing."

"Aye, aye to that, Admiral. Oh, Admiral, one more thing … I need a favor."

"A favor, Chief?"

"Aye, sir. Can you have someone run down whatever the Navy knows about a pilot named Williamson, Phillip J.? He's Navy Air … a JG, I think. He's MIA, Admiral, shot down somewhere over the Solomons … that's all I've got.

"I'll look into it, Chief. Why the interest?"

"He's the husband of our new house manager at the OSS Safe House in L.A. He's kinda like family, you know, sir."

"Okay, Chief. I'll get people on it. Stay well. Hawaii out."

"Stay well, yourself, Admiral. Los Angeles out."

Wetmore threw the switches to terminate the connection and gave his seat back to the Signals Sergeant on duty.

As he started through the door the Sergeant called after him, "Oh, Chief, you got a call from General Barrow's office to go up to 6th and pick up a passenger."

"Okay, Sarge ... So we got our new housekeeper."

OSS Safe House
Los Angeles, California

Turning off Wilshire Boulevard, the gray Plymouth drove all the way down the driveway and parked near the quarters in the rear.

Wetmore pointed to the little duplex cottage that spanned the rear of the property. With red tiled roof and covered with bougainvillea in full flower it mimicked the main house in the front. "There you are, B.J., home sweet home. Yours is the one on the right. Here's the key. Go on in and see what you're going to need."

"It's lovely, Chief."

B.J. turned in her seat toward Wetmore. "Thanks for everything. I think this is going to be a good move for me." She put a hand on the door handle, then turned back. "I hope this is alright with Amos."

"Leave the major to me, BJ. Come on over to the house when you're finished with your list. I'll take you over to Van Nuys later today for your gear."

As she stepped carefully along the manicured tile walk, BJ noted the curtains pulled shut on the first cottage, the Velasquez quarters. Slipping her key into the wrought iron latch she thumbed the lever down until the solid click released the round top oaken door. She stepped into the nearly empty room and saw it also to be a mini version of the big house up front. A leather divan sat flanked by oak tables and a small but sturdy kitchen table nestled in the eating alcove. *This is going to be very nice. A little dusting and airing out will help.*

She peered down the short hall that led to the rear and made her way slowly to the bedroom door. The heavy door opened without effort on large silent hinges. As she stepped around the dust-sheet covered bed, focused on the curtained window that looked into a tangle of old trees, she heard it ... muffled and indistinct ... not from outside.

From where? A voice?

She looked at the wall that separated the two dwellings and pressed her ear to the cool plaster.

Two voices? One mechanical. What language? Strange.

Then all went quiet.

A door slammed. BJ walked back down the hall. As she opened the front door she spied a woman nearing the big house, striding with purpose along the flagstone walk that crossed the manicured lawn. *That Spanish woman. Constantia.*

BJ quietly closed the heavy door and stepped back into the room. She didn't know why, but she waited before following.

 # CHAPTER 9

Air Defense Wing Headquarters
Los Angeles, California

The Army Air Corps captain entered the door marked HQ 1st Fighter Control Squadron. Lean and fit, the 5'9" officer had closely cropped dark hair and piercing dark eyes. He is unknown to the soldiers in the room. The duty sergeant rose to call attention, but the captain held up his hand palm forward and said, "At ease, gentlemen. Where's Sergeant Driest?"

A voice came from the adjoining room, "In here ... who wants to know?"

The captain strode across the small office and entered the control room of project Code Name: Orion's Eye.

When they spotted the silver railroad tracks on their visitor's collar, Sergeant Driest and the other technicians rose to attention.

"At ease ... continue your work. Sergeant, how're you feeling?"

"Fine and dandy, Captain. They only got one lick at me and that didn't break the skin. Rung my bell for sure, but no blood. Not so for the sonabitch that attacked me, I'm told."

"Well done, Sergeant. Training or luck, you got the job done. How's the packing coming?"

Driest answered, "It's coming along fine, sir." Then he added, "If you please, sir, may I ask who you are?"

The captain gave a nervous laugh. "Sorry, Sergeant. My protocol's a little rusty. I'm your new CO ... Bonfoey. Ed Bonfoey."

Everyone heard the introduction and a tech sergeant from the other side of the equipment array spoke up, "What's the poop, Cap'n? We really gonna get to use this stuff in a shootin' war?"

"That you are, Sergeant. All this stuff ... and you ... are headed for March Field to get your final outfitting and join up with your support troops. Then it's off to Frisco for a boat ride."

The sergeant replied, "Roger that, sir!" He looked beyond the captain to another officer entering the room. "Hey, Lieutenant, you come up to help us pack our babies?"

First Lieutenant Harry Gibbons, the Training Officer for the 1st Fighter Control Squadron answered, "Sure, Sarge, sure ... In your dreams."

He reached out his hand to Bonfoey. "Sorry, Captain, I expected to get here first and shape this sorry lot up for your visit, er ... your introduction."

"No harm, no foul, Harry. Let's get out of these folks' way and let them get the real work done. We've got a load of paper to create over at Wing HQ."

"I'm right behind you, sir. I've got a quick phone call to make."

Lieutenant Gibbons stepped to the empty desk and picked up the phone. His back to the room, he quietly dialed Clinton 58873. A pause. The ring. He said, "This is Gibbons. Our guy's here at Wing. We're packing up."

OSS Safe House
Los Angeles, California

Mead hung up the phone. "Okay, Chief, 1st Fighters are packing up. And Bonfoey's at Wing in L.A. A lot of information ... and no information. Damn, when are..."

His voice trailed off as he looked beyond where Wetmore sat. Wetmore turned to follow his gaze.

She stopped in the doorway and looked around. Mrs. Betty Jean Williamson then moved through the open door and walked up to the table. "Hello, Amos. It's so good to see you."

Mead rose from his chair. "You, too, BJ."

He couldn't explain why he found it hard to take a breath.

Wetmore leaned back in his chair and grinned. "Well, here we are, folks. Got your list, BJ?"

Mead moved around the table with his hands extended in greeting. His eyes never left the gaze of the petite blond vision from so long ago. "Hi, kiddo."

She said, "Can't an old friend get a hug around here?" The hug melted the awkwardness that had hung in the air. Finally, she asked, "So, Amos, you're okay with my new job?"

"Sure, BJ. I think it's swell ... and believe me the Chief can use all the help he can get."

Constantia came into the room. "Will the lady be having lunch with us?"

Wetmore said, "She sure will, Constantia. Sit down BJ, take a load off."

The maid nodded and turned back to the kitchen. BJ followed her with her eyes. Wetmore noticed the stare and asked, "You okay, BJ?"

"Yes, fine. Just fine. Guess I'm just hungry."

She turned to Mead, slid forward in her chair and reached out for his hand. "Well, Amos. Everybody back home sends their best." She frowned in a mock scowl. "And we all want to know what the hell you've been doing!"

All he could get out in reply, "You look swell, BJ."

Across the room Constantia opened the front door in answer to the rap of the heavy iron knocker. She recognized the man and nodded, "Come in, Senor. Everyone is in the dining room. You will eat with them?"

Donovan Gochais strode past her and on into the house, "Sure, Constantia. I can use a bite."

Wetmore raised his hand in greeting, "Well, well, the sailor home from the sea. Come on in. You remember BJ?"

"Sure do. Hello, ma'am. Hello, Amos ... Major."

"Hello yourself, Donny. How's everything with the family?"

Gochais flopped into one of the large chairs and said, "Tommy's surgery is scheduled for Tuesday. Everything's great."

The maid came in from the kitchen with a platter of sandwiches and asked, "What do you prefer to drink?"

Wetmore quickly replied, "*Cervesas* ... all around. That okay with you, BJ?"

BJ said to Constantia, "I'll have iced tea, please."

When she returned with the drinks, Constantia said, "Excuse me, Senores. If you are done with me here I will return later."

Wetmore answered, "Sure, thanks, Constantia."

Mead opened a bottle of Budweiser and slid the opener to Gochais. "We can eat and work. It's time we get ourselves on the same page. Time's short before you sail, Donny boy."

BJ asked, "Do you want me here for this, Amos?"

"You, bet. You're part of this now. And when we're done here you and I need to have a long talk."

Kilometer 4 Via San Roque
San Antonio Del Mar,
Baja California, Mexico

Herr George Nicolaus sat looking out at his view of the Pacific Ocean. His fingers drummed on the painted tile table, a mindless motion that saw him in deep thought. Glancing back at the shortwave radio, he raised his arm, and the sudden slap of his hand on the table brought all in the room to attention. "Where do we get these people? These imbeciles?" He growled at the man seated across from him.

"*Pero, Senor* Nicolaus But, Mr. Nicolaus)—"

Nicolaus cut him off, "*No Pero*! No buts, no buts!" Then he rose quickly to his feet and spun to face the small group of men, raising his voice, "*No mas peros. Actiones* (no more buts. Actions)!"

All heads looked down and teeth gritted. No one dared reply as he rapidly continued to berate the group of cowed men, "I cannot report failure anymore! Do you understand?"

There were slow nods, but no one raised up their gaze to face Nicolaus' anger.

"You do not know *Reichsmarschall* Goering. I do. If we fail him there is no place on this earth we can hide. *En todo Mundo ... no podemos ocultar* (In the whole world ... no place to hide)."

Nicolaus turned away toward the ocean vista beyond the window. *"Wir können nicht uns verstecken* (we cannot hide)."

He stood for a moment at the window, then turned slowly and returned to the table. He leaned over, resting on his closed fists and looking at each of the men. Calm now, he spoke slowly, "Alright, gentlemen. We need a plan. We also need some help. Have you heard of the *Sinarquistas?*"

A Clandestine Location
Southern California

The radio hissed to life, *"Jaeger, Jaeger,* come in, *Jaeger.* Over."

The man jerked up from his slumping nap and responded with a keying of the microphone, *"Jaeger* here. Over."

"The subject is on the move soon. Do you have instructions from our contact? Over."

"Nein, no. We have been waiting for him. Are you in contact?"

"No, I cannot reach him from here. You must go active. My time is up. Out." The line went dead.

The man slumped back into the chair, but the nap did not continue.

Air Defense Wing Headquarters
Los Angeles, California

The small convoy of Army trucks sat idling at the curb on South Flower Street, as material from the 1st Fighter Squadron operations was being loaded. As the soldiers had been living on the 8th floor of the building, much of the material is their personal belongings and equipment.

The lead and tail vehicles in the convoy were jeeps. Most of the dozen or so trucks were deuce-and-a-halfs, but near the middle of the line sat two three-quarter-ton ammo carriers being carefully loaded with newly constructed crates cryptically stenciled *R-Tac-OE-USAAC*.

The offices on the 5th floor sat empty, save for the remnants of trash and discarded items.

Captain Bonfoey walked through the space, the last man out. He reached down to retrieve a telephone sitting on the floor and found it still active. He dialed. "It's me. We're out of here. Taking route 60 to Riverside. It's about 70 miles to March Field. Keep an eye out."

 **CHAPTER 10**

OSS Safe House
Los Angeles, California

Donovan Gochais received his instructions and began to gather his gear and head for home. He is to tell his family that he has to report to his ship in San Francisco early for preparation for loading special war cargo. Clearly uneasy with the deception, he knows it's wartime and nobody will question his story.

Wetmore handed him a brown envelope stamped SECRET. "One more thing, Don ... here's the code words we'll be using if we have to send a message in the clear to your ship."

Gochais took the envelope, lifted the unsealed flap and drew out the single piece of paper. He read a moment then said, "Clever, Chief." He chuckled as he read down the list. "Are these your creations?"

```
Orion's Eye — Constellation
Gochais — Sailor
Cape San Juan — Ark
Mead — Boss
Officer Spy — Spook
Hauptmann — Arnold
```

Wetmore just smiled, "Don't be a smart ass."

Gochais slipped the paper back into the envelope and picked up his gear. "Okay, gentlemen, I'm on my way."

Amos Mead rose from the table and started toward the patio door. Moving his arm in a *come-on* gesture, he nodded in the direction of the backyard and said, "Hold up a minute, Donny. Take a walk with me."

Gochais set his things down and followed. They walked side by side to the back of the expanse of lawn where a stone bench flanked by stone columns delineated the edge of the landscape. Mead said, "Sit down for a minute."

He drew a cigarette and lit it with the Globe and Anchor Zippo, blowing the first draw of smoke out with a sigh. "How're you doing with all this, Don?"

Gochais sat on the stone bench, leaning forward with his elbows on his knees, his hands joined in front. He stared down at his highly polished shoes and answered, "Okay ... I guess."

Amos waited.

Gochais continued, "It's comin' at me fast, Amos. I'm just barely figurin' out what my part is ... I mean, I know I'll be lookin' out for stuff at sea ... but just what I'm not sure ... yet ... well, you know."

He never looked up from his shiny shoes.

"We've all got that problem, Donny. Not quite knowing. Sometimes it seems like we're chasing smoke." Mead exhaled a cloud of cigarette smoke and waved his hand through it, adding, "Like this."

"I guess I understand that part. But, dammit, Amos, I don't like all the lies I have to tell Elma. I don't like it at all."

"You're mostly just not telling everything, Don Guess you could see that as a lie. It'll be over soon enough. When you go to sea it'll be just the same as always for Elma. But like I asked … are you okay?"

Standing up, Gochais answered, "Yeah. Let's just get on with it!"

Mead carefully snuffed out his cigarette in the grass and field-stripped it. He scattered the tobacco and stuffed the tiny wad of paper in his pocket. They headed back to the house.

While Mead and Gochais talked in the yard, Wetmore explained BJ's role at the house to everyone and then left to go over to the Federal Building for a scheduled call from London on the encrypted telephone. He'd also promised BJ that he would check for any word on her missing husband and that he'd be back in time to get her back for her things and work on her list. He didn't want to interrupt Mead so he missed saying goodbye to Gochais.

Gochais picked up his gear and headed to the front door. As he departed he said, "See you later, Amos. Hey, thanks for your concern." The heavy oak door closed behind him.

Amos turned to see BJ standing in the kitchen door. She said, "My turn."

Mead and BJ walked out to the Bougainvillea draped patio. The air, warmer than in the thick walled house, smelled of the Jasmine that bordered the tiled space. "Strange thing, BJ, I've thought of you often since the war started."

Gazing up at the crimson flowers, she said, "You never wrote."

"You were married."

"Before that."

106

Quiet settled for a while. He pulled out one of the heavy chairs and she sat. He walked to the edge of the tiles.

"You're right. My work with the Bureau, well, I kind of detached myself from my old world for too long."

"Your folks kept me up on your career for a while. Then I didn't stay in touch with them as much. After the war started Phillip and I decided to get married. You know, before he shipped out and all."

Amos turned to face BJ. "You know I have to leave again pretty soon."

"Why am I not surprised, Amos?" She shifted toward him in the deep cushioned chair. "At least I can keep track of you from here."

Mead walked back to the table and pulled a chair close to BJ. He sat, took her hands in his and leaned slowly closer. "Maybe, when I get back—"

She leaned closer.

The raucous ring of the telephone Wetmore left sitting on the patio table crashed in on them. Mead reached over and picked up the receiver. With a sigh, he answered, "Clinton 58873 ... yes, speaking ... hello, Lieutenant .... missing? What the hell do you mean, missing?"

He stood abruptly and waved a hand in the air. "Holy shit, Lieutenant, how does a convoy go missing? Yes, yes, I'm sorry. Yes, I understand .... Okay, thanks for the call, Lieutenant."

Mead set the phone's receiver onto its cradle. He crossed his arms and looked down at the table. "What the hell do we do now?"

BJ looked beyond Mead to her quarters in the bungalows beyond, struggling with her thoughts.

Should I say anything about what I thought I heard? Maybe not now. Did I just imagine it?

Route 60
At the Riverside County Line
California

The faded red paint on the sign read EATS.

The condition of the ramshackle building beneath the sign didn't do much to promote an appetite. Nevertheless, there were cars in the dusty, windswept gravel parking lot—and three U.S. Army trucks.

Picking up his sandwich, the pimply faced soldier, a private first class, whined, "We're going to get our asses in a sling for this one, Sarge."

Technical Sergeant Driest chewed the oversize bite he'd removed from the greasy hamburger barely held together with both his hands, then set the dripping sandwich on his plate, took a swig from a Coca Cola bottle and answered, "Don't sweat it, boy. This Captain Bonfoey's all screwed up. He's got this convoy spread out halfway back to L.A. They ain't gonna miss us for a few minutes. Besides, I had to pee. No sense wasting a stop."

He took another bite.

The olive drab Jeep with the white star on its hood and a yellow rotating light on a pole jutting up from the rear bumper slid to a stop, almost disappearing in the cloud of desert dust. A red-faced Army captain vaulted from the seat and hit the ground in full stride toward the door under the sign marked EATS.

The door crashed open, its hinges barely surviving the assault.

The Army private first class jumped to rigid attention, knocking a full tray from the grasp of a beehive coifed waitress, its contents spewing over the truckers sitting in a booth. Someone muttered, "Oh shit."

Technical Sergeant Driest calmly took another bite. He set the remnants of grease shined bun on his plate, wiped a bit of mustard from his chin with the crumpled paper napkin, tossed a dollar bill on the counter, then rose and strode the four paces to the door—followed by a parade of utility clad soldiers and two food covered truckers.

He stepped out into the desert sun, flipped a half salute, and said, "Afternoon, Captain."

Eyes ablaze, hands on hips, all the officer can spit out is, "What in the holy hell!"

The three U.S. Army trucks spun their tires, carefully avoiding hitting the double-parked jeep, as they re-entered traffic on Route 60 headed south toward March Field.

 **CHAPTER 11**

USAT *Cape San Juan* - Pier Side
San Francisco, California
Two Weeks Later

Lieutenant (JG) Donovan Ignatius Gochais, USMS, stood at the bottom of the gangway, the steady sea breeze gusting around from the Golden Gate sending a chill through his shoulders.

He set his Valv-Pak down on the worn planks of the pier and looked up at the ship as if seeing her for the first time. Gochais noted the large hull number, 249, beginning to show the effect of salt water spray. *Doesn't take long to grow old in war.*

He looked out beyond the ship at the vista of the bay. Everywhere he saw ships of all shapes and sizes moving purposefully on the water. The ferry boats crisscrossed San Francisco Bay from Oakland, Marin and up the San Joaquin river, through Suisun Bay to Pittsburg, California. The plodding Liberty ships moved with purpose, singly and in forming convoys, some returning, he knew, from war. Others heavily loaded with decks nearly awash moved toward the Golden Gate and their fate outside the protection of the bay.

This is the war and he is about to rejoin it.

Gochais made his first voyage to the South Pacific on this ship that loomed above him just a few months earlier, then brand new and on her maiden voyage.

The USAT *Cape San Juan* is a C1-B type cargo ship converted to carry troops as well. Her design is *full scantling* with three deck levels of the same width below the main deck for the cargo and troops. At four-hundred-seventeen feet in length and sixty feet in width she can maintain a top speed about fourteen knots with her oil-fired steam turbines.

He looked around at the bustle of activity on the pier. Heavy rope net slings were swinging mountains of equipment aboard the ship in a dance of heavy cables and muscular booms. In between the ever present seagulls swooped and dove in their perpetual food fights. From tinned food to toilet paper, from shoes to shells and from cannons to coffins—it's all going to war.

These tons of war materials will soon be joined by over a thousand flesh and blood human beings—the warriors. And, as Gochais noted to himself, *at least one spy*. He hoisted the heavy bag at his feet and started his climb up the gangway, stopping mid-way for the customary salute to the red, white and blue standard flying from the stern.

Captain Walter Strong, Master of the USAT Cape San Juan sat regally at the head of the wardroom table looking over the assembled officers.

The Master is an old-school merchant seaman. A naval officer in WW I, he is nearing sixty years old and wanting to make it to retirement. He has the gruff air of an old sea captain, but he's known to mentor his young officers. Short, paunchy and bearded, he's agile and in good health.

Quietly assembled around the table, the officers waited for Captain Strong to speak. In his own good time he looked up and said, "Gentlemen, some of you have sailed with me before ... to the rest of you, welcome aboard. You will be advised of our final sailing time in due course. In meantime there is a lot of work to do in preparation for embarking the troops." He paused and looked around the table. "We will have over thirteen-hundred souls sailing with us to Australia. We're sailing alone, unescorted. However, we will have a Navy dirigible with us for the first three days. The Japs patrol close in and sinkings off the Farallons are all too common. I don't intend to become a statistic this close to home."

The men nodded and quietly processed the meaning of *alone* at sea, especially those few on their first voyage.

The captain continued, "I'll be meeting with each of you soon enough. Get your gear stowed and get familiar with what's going on around here. That's all."

Asking for no replies, Captain Strong rose and stepped out into the passageway, striding toward his quarters.

Gochais looked around as the group began to mill about as they greeted old friends and introduced themselves to the new faces. He knew Chief Mate Earl Manning and 2d Mate Bill Dorcey from his first voyage. The Army officers he'd meet soon enough.

During his briefing in the OSS house in Los Angeles, Wetmore had provided him with a list of officers and non-coms with whatever background information he had on them. The chief included the non-coms 'in case the translators in London had misread the *officer involved* stuff.' The list included the transport surgeons, Army Lieutenants Schurts and Davis, the transport commander, Major Barth, and the senior passenger aboard not attached to a unit, Major Floyd Shinn.

Gochais thought, *the three Army units coming aboard will have their own officers ... Bonfoey among them.* He knew that this is just the beginning. *Are these all suspects? One the spy? At this point, I guess that's the case. Now I know what the Lone Ranger feels like ... except I ain't got no Tonto.*

As he moved to join the activity a yeoman stepped into the space. "Lieutenant Gochais. The captain wishes to see you in his quarters."

Chief Mate Manning quipped, "In trouble already, Gochais?" He flashed a wide grin, driving his handle-bar moustache to a most impressive spread.

With a shrug and a grin of his own, Gochais followed the yeoman into the passageway, brushing by a naval officer arriving late. Gochais noted, *don't know that guy.*

The yeoman knocked on the captain's door.

"Enter."

"Lieutenant Gochais as you ordered, sir"

"Send him in."

The yeoman stepped back and held the door open for Gochais. Captain Strong leaned back in his desk chair. "Welcome back, Don. I hope you're ready to tell me what in the living hell this is all about."

Gochais remained standing at attention but looked down at the captain and replied, "Aye, aye, sir ... at least as much as I can. But first, sir, can you tell me what *you* know?"

The captain scowled. "I know that you've got some damn highly placed people fronting for you. Missing our coastwise sail up here could have put you in deep shit. But my orders are to just go with whatever you do. I'm not used to that, Mister, not used to that at all." He stared hard at Gochais, who didn't break eye contact.

Gochais paused before he spoke, "I understand, sir. Is that all you were told, Captain?"

Strong leaned forward, elbows on his desk, right hand slapping the grey linoleum top. "Damn it, son, I'm supposed to be the one asking the questions."

Gochais looked straight ahead at proper attention. "Sorry, sir. I meant no disrespect."

His voice a little softer, Captain Strong said, "I suppose you didn't, son. All I'm told is that you're under orders from some goddam high government agency." He looked down at his folded hands. "And that it's a war related assignment." He looked back up at Gochais, spreading his hands, palms up. "And now you're back with us."

"Yes, Captain, I'm back with you for this voyage." Gochais relaxed the stiff posture he had held since entering. "Captain, I think I need to take a chance here and share what this is all about."

"Good thinking, son. Take a seat. We're secure here." Captain Strong rose and stepped the three paces to his door, securing the latch. He sat down in the other chair that faced his desk. "What the hell is this all about?"

Gochais looked up at the pale grey overhead and took in a breath. "I have no authority to tell you, sir. But neither has anyone told me that I can't. So, I guess I'm making a command decision here." He paused, absently putting his hand over his mouth and sliding it down to stroke his chin. "I'm feeling a little alone here, sir ... and frankly I'd like you to be aware of my mission."

"Mission? You're on a mission? On my ship?"

"Aye, aye, sir. And this is it."

For the next few minutes Captain Strong listened, alternately sitting on the edge of his chair and rising to pace, head down, his hand rubbing the nape of his neck. Gochais explained his status with the OSS and his training on Catalina that had kept him from the last voyage. He related about the secret technology coming aboard. "It's known by its code name *Orion's Eye*. It's coming aboard as part of the equipment of the 1st Fighter Control Squadron."

Now showing a deeper interest in Gochais' mission, Captain Strong asked, "Okay, tell me why the OSS is interested in you and this Army stuff."

Gochais answered, "Well, sir … I've saved the best for last. There's a spy, a German spy, in the picture. And it is suspected that the spy is a U.S. military officer."

"A goddamn spy on my ship? I'm not liking this at all, Gochais. Who the hell is it?"

"That's my mission, Captain … to find out who it is … and to stop whatever he's got planned."

Captain Strong rose and moved behind his desk. "You said German. We're going to the Pacific. I thought we're fighting the Japs down there."

Gochais took an audible breath. "Guess I might as well tell you everything, Captain."

He spoke of the Fort Monmouth spying, the captured Germans—which Strong knew about from news reports and now understood their mission—the attack at the Los Angeles Center, and even the screwed up scare by a hungry Army convoy driver.

"So that's it, Captain. I don't know what's going to happen on this ship … if anything. I've just got to keep my eyes open and check everything out."

Strong shook his head. "Sounds like a damn Bogart movie plot. Okay, Don, what do you need from me?"

"Nothing really, Captain. Just be aware of my mission and back me up if it ever comes to that. I may come to you for information. Don't know where it'll go ... not yet."

Captain Strong stood up and moved away from his desk. "Okay. Keep me informed. I don't like surprises on my ship. Go get your quarters squared away and do what you need to do."

"Aye, sir," Gochais stood, "Thank you." He turned toward the door.

"One more thing, Don," the captain added. "Watch your back. I don't intend to have any casualties among my crew."

Gochais took the short step to the door. "Aye, aye, Captain."

He moved down the passageway to the wardroom where some of the officers still sat at the table. The chief mate said with a wave, "Hey, Gochais, come on over here ... somebody you need to meet."

A Navy lieutenant stood up and extended his hand to Gochais. "Hi, I'm Graham Harris ... the new communications officer."

Gochais shook the hand and replied, "Welcome aboard, Harris. Don Gochais, third mate."

"*Still* third mate, Donny?" The Chief mate jibed. "Captain let you off Scott-free, did he?"

Gochais grinned. "Free as a bird, Mr. Manning, free as a bird. Then he asked Manning about the regular communications officer, "Say, what happened to Smitty?"

"Oh, you haven't heard? Nasty car accident. He got run off the road. He's in pretty bad shape."

Gochais asked, "Wow, too bad. He's a good guy. Where is he?"

Manning replied, "Over at Oak Knoll Naval Hospital."

"Thanks, maybe I can get over there before we sail. I'm going down to stow my gear. Catch you all later."

Gochais nodded to Harris and Manning and started to his stateroom where a crewman had already stowed his bag. He started to open his door, then hesitated, shut it and turned toward the quarterdeck and the gangway to the pier below.

With the usual acknowledgements from the Officer of the Deck, he left the ship and made his way to the bank of phone booths at the entrance to the pier. Dropping a coin into the slot he waited for the operator to come on. He instructed, "Los Angeles, California, Clinton 58873," then adding his authorization and priority code. The call is answered in the familiar manner, but the voice more pleasant—and female.

"BJ? How's it going? This is Don ... yeah, Don Gochais. Is Wetmore or Mead available?"

Wetmore came on the line, "Hello, Don, what's up?"

"Chief, I'm a little new at this spook stuff, and maybe just a little too jumpy. But I want you to check something out for me. We've got a new commo officer. A guy named Harris, Graham Harris. Lieutenant (JG) Navy Reserve. He's a replacement for our regular guy."

"Replacement? That's not unusual is it?"

"Yeah, Chief, this time it is. The regular guy had a bad accident. Run off the road. He's alive, but he's in bad shape. They've got him over in Oak Knoll

Hospital. Name's Delbert Smith. Same rank. Don't know exactly what I'm asking you to find, but can you follow up, Chief?"

"You bet, Don. You never know. Everything good up there? Army boys there yet?"

"Yeah, Chief, everything's good. Army's not aboard yet. Say howdy to the major." He hung up the phone and stood for a minute, wondering if he had over-reacted. A rap on the glass door snapped him back to reality. "Sorry, sailor, phone's all yours."

Gochais stepped out into the chilling air and looked back toward the ship.

Steady as she goes, he thought.

OSS Safe House
Los Angles, California

Mead placed his carefully folded clothes, a mix of uniforms and civilian, in the Valv-Pak that lay open on his bed.

BJ stood leaning against the heavy oaken doorframe, trying to look more relaxed than she felt. "I always thought those military issue bags looked like a little life raft when they're opened up like that. What do you call them?"

Mead replied, "Valv-Pak. Don't know where that name came from." He casually continued his packing. "Does the job though."

They heard Wetmore before he appeared in the doorway. "Major, our sailor-boy sends his regards. He's got some people he wants me to check out. Don't know if the suspect list is growing or if he's just finding his first boogieman."

Mead looked up, thankful for the break in the unspoken tension. "Cut him some slack, Chief. What's he got?"

Wetmore related what Gochais had asked for, then added, "We seem to jump on new arrivals ... first Bonfoey, now this guy Harris."

While the two men talked, BJ moved over by the bed, carefully slipping a small envelope into the folds of Mead's packed clothes.

Mead said, "We go with what we've got, Chief. It's cat and mouse with these guys. All we know is they want our toy real bad." He folded the Valv-Pak over and secured the heavy zipper and leather straps. "Hey, Chief ... I'm adding one more thing to your check out list. Damn, I don't know why I didn't click on this one before. He's with the 1st Fighters and he worked with Orion's Eye at Monmouth. His name is Lieutenant Harry A. Gibbons. He's Air Corp."

Mead hefted his bag off the bed and turned toward the door. "Time to go."

The three walked out to the front door. Mead stopped, set down the bag and faced BJ. He placed his hands on her shoulders and said, "Take care of yourself."

She slipped forward and embraced him, her cheek pressed to his chest. He closed his arms around her. She whispered, "You take care, Amos."

He walked away toward the car where Wetmore had already loaded his bag. Climbing in the car, Mead thought, *Townsville, Australia, is a world away ... In more ways than one.*

Naval Amphibious Base Coronado
San Diego, California

The Pan Am Navy PB2Y maneuvered away from its ramp and taxied out into the bay.

Trying not to think of the long journey ahead of him, Mead leaned down to look out the porthole for a last glimpse of the mainland. The flight from Los Angeles to San Diego on the cramped C-47 had been only tolerable for him. He settled deep into his seat, hands folded in his lap, as the four engines of the giant flying boat roared up to take-off power, reminding him once more that he hated to fly.

What first is the slap of the sea on the bottom of the craft soon became jarring metallic whumps that caused Mead to squeeze his eyes shut and form his clenched fingers into a painful ball. He didn't feel the pain. *Just get this over with.*

After what seemed an eternity, less than a minute, the giant Navy transport broke loose from the sea and began its climb out over the Pacific.

First stop Pearl Harbor, Hawaii.

Major Amos Mead is finally going to war.

 **CHAPTER 12**

OSS Safe House
Los Angles, California

Chief Wetmore told BJ, "Well, he's off by now. Let's you and me get the Velazquezes in here and make everything official. Then I want you to go through this place and set things up the way you want to run the joint. We've got more Marines coming through from Catalina next week. It's your show now, BJ."

Her hands on her hips, assuming a proper fishwife stance, BJ quipped, "You're a little too overjoyed about that, Harmon. I may just write some rules for you while I'm at it."

Chief Harmon Wetmore feigned a cowering posture and laughed. "Whoops, shiver me timbers. There be trouble afoot aboard this 'ere vessel."

The quick meeting with Pedro and Constantia Velasquez produced no reaction, as they maintained their usual subservient, eyes down demeanor. Wetmore noticed a glance exchanged between BJ and Constantia that seemed a bit out of character. He shrugged it off as *girl stuff*.

Wetmore had work to do. He had his end of the project to hold up. Besides he wanted nothing to do with being an innkeeper.

As he headed out to the car, he said with a wave, "BJ, I'm headed over to the Federal Building for a late communication with London. Lock things up. I don't know how long I'll be."

A while later BJ felt the ebb of the adrenalin that had kept her ignoring the weariness she felt. She glimpsed Constantia finishing up in the kitchen. With a last glance around the room she became aware of the fading light and turned the switch on a large ceramic lamp that sat on a table near the patio door, its glow soothing but further reminding her of her weariness.

BJ walked outside, noting the soft air smelled of jasmine and the first star now visible above the soft pink of the late sunset, as she walked slowly on to her quarters.

She sat on the edge of her bed, her face in her hands gently massaging her forehead. It had been a confusing day for her. The swirl of feelings ... seeing Amos again, and then watching him leave. *The new possible searches for Phillip and the change in her circumstances ... yes, a confusing day.*

Federal Building
Los Angeles, California

Wetmore patiently waited out the fifteen minute process of connecting the SIGSALY encryption telephone in Los Angeles to the same in London.

"Hello Chandler, how's things in Limey-land?"

Morse replied, "You are the irreverent one, Mr. Wetmore. Things are peachy keen. How are things with you and the major?"

Chandler Morse headed up SIRA, the joint operation of American OSS Research and Development and British Strategic Intelligence known internally as *the enemy objectives unit*. Morse and Wetmore had teamed up to supply Mead with continuing information on the Nazi players. The high level support for the protection of the Orion's Eye project gave them access to the best intelligence sources and technologies available.

Wetmore continued, "The major's on his way to the South Pacific. He's getting ahead of the transport ship that's carrying our project. We've had a couple of scares with it here ... but it looks like it'll make the ship."

"Then it's with Gochais now, right?"

"Roger, that Chandler. Gochais' already feeling the new-boy pressure ... which is why I'm calling. I've got a couple of folks Gochais needs you to check out through your sources. You've already got Bonfoey. The new ones are Graham Harris, Navy JG, and Rhinehart Meuller, Navy Lieutenant. Oh, and Mead added an Army Lieutenant name of Harry Gibbons to the list."

"Send me what you've got Chief, I'll get on them. One more thing. A dossier on Heinrich Hauptmann went to OSS Headquarters in DC. We've discovered some interesting details that might shed a little light on his son Otto Hauptmann's motivation."

"Roger that, Chandler. By the way, Otto has dropped out of sight again. Nobody's seen him in a couple of weeks."

"Hope that's not bad news, Chief. Hard to protect yourself from something you can't see."

The SIGSALY call to London ended on that note, but Wetmore stayed in his seat. "Sergeant, can we connect this thing up to Washington, DC ... OSS headquarters?"

Kilometer 4 Via San Roque
San Antonio Del Mar
Baja California, Mexico

The radio connection to Berlin is a relayed system that served them well for the last year. The Mexican authorities had not searched it out. Even with American government pressure, Nicolaus and his group still had enough friends to keep up their work.

George Nicolaus, nervous about staying on the air too long, had a need to get some answers. He keyed the microphone, "Ja, we have good intelligence on its movements. Our people are close by, but it is nearly impossible to make a move. Over."

Releasing the talk-switch, he listened for the distant voice. The electrically scratchy reply, "You must take action. Time is short. Too much is at stake. Make every effort. Do you have a plan? Over."

Nicolaus pressed the talk switch again, shaking his head in frustration, "Yes, yes of course ... we have another option. But what of our contact in their military? We have not been told of his identity. And where is Otto Hauptmann? What is he up to? Over."

Static, humming, then, "*Wir wissen nicht.* (We do not know where he is). The American military officer is his contact. We are trying to get the information, but Himmler's people are not talking to us anymore. What is important, George, is that you continue your work … successfully. Goering is reaching the end of his patience, and that is not good … for any of us."

Deployment Staging Area
1st Fighter Control Squadron
March Field, California

Captain Edward Bonfoey sat erect behind the shaky olive-drab field desk, one of many that crowded the large oiled-canvas tent that served as the processing center for the 1st Fighters.

Technical Sergeant Driest stood at rigid attention in front of the desk.

Bonfoey hissed through clenched teeth, "Driest, you should be facing a Courts Martial. You're stunt is beyond belief!"

Driest spoke to the space above the captain's head as he stared straight ahead, "Yes, sir!"

"Mister, I've decided I want to see you in combat with the rest of us instead of sitting around in a nice safe stockade. Get your sweet ass back to work. We have a train to load and people to move."

Technical Sergeant Driest saluted, made a soldier-perfect about-face and strode away from the desk.

Bonfoey watched him go. *You don't realize, sergeant asshole, what a frigging scare you gave me.*

Camp Stoneman
Pittsburg, California

The Southern Pacific Troop Train steamed into the yard at Camp Stoneman near Pittsburg, California, the major U.S. Army embarkation point for the war in the Pacific.

The soldiers of the 1st Fighter Control Squadron rose stiffly from the wooden seats, gathered their personal gear and moved lock-step off the train and onto waiting busses.

Before them they saw a sea of over eight-hundred wooden barracks, glowing cream and khaki in the late afternoon sun that is home for the next two days as they received last minute medical checkups and completed their lists of required personal combat gear.

The third day dawned California sunny as the 1st Fighters marched from their temporary barracks to the piers that lined the Carquinez Straits—officially known as the San Francisco Port of Embarkation, but is actually 65 miles east of the fabled city.

Here the Sacramento and San Joaquin Rivers flow together to empty into the San Francisco Bay, an impressive sight for the majority of east coast and Midwest Army boys. Marching onto waiting ferries, the 1st Fighters sailed down river into the Bay marveling at the views of Alcatraz Island and the Golden Gate Bridge towers that loomed beyond—then on across to the San Francisco waterfront to board their transportation to the war, the USAT *Cape San Juan.*

Federal Building
Los Angeles, California

The cryptology clerk handed Wetmore the file. "Here Chief, we've finished decoding the stuff from DC."

The cover page had the diagonal red stripe of secret designation—and the word SAINT that Wetmore knew meant OSS counterespionage

126

message content. He opened the cover and began to read the first page

SECRET
(**SAINT** – Austria)

Subject: Hauptmann, Heinrich
(1)   Reference CASSIA, Austria

Heinrich Hauptmann died in Vienna after a prolonged illness, age 51.

Heinrich Hauptmann, born 5 August 1892 in Brunn am Gebirge, a village near Vienna, Austria.

He married Gretl Alt in Vienna, Austria in, 1914. Gretl Alt is Hungarian, born in Odenberg, Austro-Hungary in 1893. Son, Otto, born 1914 (date unk.)

Contacts report Heinrich abandoned his wife and son in 1915 and traveled to the United States. We found that he reappeared in Germany in 1938 and has been active in the Third Reich as an official in the Ausland Institute.

His son, Otto, regularly visited him in hospital until recently.

Investigation shows that he and his son have been in regular contact for at least 10 years.

There are also reports that another son
appeared periodically and that the three
shared strong sentiments about the
mistreatment of Germany and the promise of
the Nazi Party.
From his accent they suspect he's
American.

We have only hearsay and can find no
records in Austria on the other son.

Otto's mother, Gretl, has remarried and is
reported in Vienna.

Chief Wetmore scanned the page once more,
noting the key points. The second page looked just as
interesting as he turned it over and read.

SECRET

(2)   Reference FBI Nazi Surveillance
Records (1935-1940)

Heinrich Hauptmann immigrated to US in
late 1915 or early 1916. No record of US
citizenship. Subject active in the pro-
Nazi German-American Bund. A vocal
organizer and an official in the Ausland
Institute.

The Ausland Institute organized Germans
abroad into the Nationalsozialistiche
Deutshe Arbeiterpartei—the NSDAP.
Common name for NSDAP is Nazi Party.

```
At the Ausland Institute subject, Heinrich
Hauptmann, also tracked returnees to
Germany. Subject dropped out of sight
early in 1938. Reports from associates
interviewed here indicate he returned to
Germany.
Note to file: There is indication that
subject married and had children in the
US.

END of REPORT
(signed) Hyman, M.
OSS, Washington, DC
```

Wetmore sat back in his chair, crossed his arms and stared at the open file, his mind racing. Chandler Morse in London had come through for him with the Cassia investigation and Maurice Hyman in D.C. had pulled the FBI reports. *Not an easy task with FBI and OSS so unfriendly,* he thought.

So Otto's got a brother...

 **CHAPTER 13**

USAT *Cape San Juan* – Pier Side San Francisco, California

The Army's heavy equipment and cargo had arrived by train and been stowed low in the holds, equipment for the 1st Fighter Control Squadron—including Orion's Eye—stowed in #3 Hold.

Gochais watched as the crates, wrapped in the rope cargo nets, swung high over the deck then dropped from sight deep into the dark bowels of the ship. *Strange there's no special escort,* he thought. *Guess that makes sense. No need to draw extra attention.*

Gochais turned from the teak-capped rail and walked the few steps to the communications shack.

"Catching some ray's, Ted?"

The sailor sitting on the deck, his back against the steel bulkhead and his head tilted to catch the warm sun on his face replied without moving, "Yes sir, Mr. Gochais, last of the California sun."

Petty Officer Second Class (PO 2) Thaddeus (Ted) Makowski is one of the ship's two radio operators. The short, muscular, but with a beer-fed paunch,

Petty Officer is older than most of the sailors aboard. A *'tween-wars China Sailor*, he had little use for the ninety-day wonder' officers this war produced, but took a liking to Donovan Gochais during the first voyage.

Gochais asked, "Where's your little buddy?"

"You mean the corporal?"

A voice from inside the radio shack called out, "Somebody looking for me?" A head popped out of the hatch. "Sorry, sir, didn't know it was you."

Corporal Manny McIntire, US Army, is the number two radioman for this trip. Even though Makowski had told Gochais that, "he's an okay guy … for an Army grunt," Gochais had still added him to his list for background checks.

Gochais said, only partly tongue-in-cheek, "Just wanted to be sure you're ready for sea, Corporal. We'll be a long way from home and your radio's real important."

Corporal McIntire stepped out on deck. Young and slightly built, the ill fit of his uniform added to an already awkward appearance—not at all athletic, or soldierly. He wore a lifejacket, tied and fully rigged.

Gochais looked the soldier up and down, a theatrical scowl on his face. "What's with the lifejacket, Corporal? We're tied to the pier."

"With all due respect, sir, you handle water your way and I'll handle it mine." McIntire shrugged and leaned back against the radio shack, as far from the rail as you could get on this deck.

Gochais knew from Wetmore's reports that McIntire feared water. He also knew that the boy is an expert with his weapons and had scored well in all his Army training. McIntire had graduated from the radio school at Fort Monmouth, New Jersey. And the real surprise for Gochais, he had worked briefly on the final phase of the project *Code Name: Orion's Eye.*

The metallic clang of a steel hatch opening caught Gochais' attention. He looked past Corporal McIntire into the dark interior of the radio shack as a figure moved to the chair in front of the Radiomarine 4U radio console that filled the rear bulkhead of the small room.

The beam of light through the single porthole showed him who it was. Gochais stepped up next to McIntire in the doorway and said, "Good afternoon, Mr. Harris."

Lieutenant Graham Harris turned and gave a startled reply, "What? Oh, yes. Hello Mr. Gochais. Sorry, I'm kind of wrapped up in this thing. New to me, you know."

The twenty-seven-year old, dark blonde, blue eyed, Yale Law School graduate appeared awkward and ill at ease to Gochais.

"I understand that, Lieutenant Harris, we've got lots of new stuff aboard this trip."

No reaction from Harris as he turned back to the console.

Gochais, stepping back out toward the rail, asked, "Hey, Ted, did we get the HF unit installed?"

"You bet, Mr. Gochais. We got her all set up on the coastwise trip you missed. She's real sweet. It's got a range from 3 to 30 megacycles. The 4U in there is 435 to 500 kilocycles—we call that medium frequency."

Gochais chuckled. "Whoa, belay that, Petty Officer Makowski ... you're in the process of making me look real dumb." He glanced back into the radio shack. Harris was not in sight, but he knew that Harris' quarters adjoined the space. *Gonna be hard to keep an eye on him.* "Carry on you two. I've got a ship to load. There's a war on, you know."

"Aye, aye," from the sailor and "Roger," from the soldier, were the replies.

As Gochais walked forward toward the bridge he could see the Navy Armed Guard in the gun tub mounted out on the bow already tinkering with their 3" gun. He stepped into the wheelhouse as Chief Mate Earl Manning scanned eastward across the bay.

Manning spoke to the bridge crew on duty, "Looks like we're about to get our company."

Raising his own glasses, Gochais followed Manning's view and saw the ferry boats approaching, troops lining the rails.

Captain Strong stepped through the hatch from the weather bridge and said, "Mr. Gochais, take this and get down to the quarter deck. See that everything's in order to board those troops."

Gochais took the offered sheet of paper and saw the headings:

855th Engineer (Aviation) Battalion
    809 personnel

1st Fighter Control Squadron
    366 personnel

253d Ordinance Company (Aviation)
    163 personnel

The captain added, "By the way, Mr. Gochais, those engineers are colored troops."

Gochais responded, "Aye, aye, sir." *Sleuthing for a German spy will have to wait awhile.*

He stood near the OD on the quarterdeck and watched as the Army captain climbed the gangway.

Captain Edward M. Bonfoey, US Army Air Corp, stepped onto the quarterdeck and saluted the duty OD. "Cap'n Bonfoey, sir. CO, 1st Fighters. Where do you want us?"

Gochais stepped closer. "I've got 'em," he told the OD. "Welcome aboard, Captain. I'm Don Gochais, third mate. Your guys are in #3 Hold. Your gear's already aboard. Have your people board on the forward gangway."

Bonfoey followed Gochais' pointed finger. He glanced down at the bar on Gochais' collar. "Got it, Lieutenant. Say, these guys are hungry —"

Gochais cut in, "Quartermaster'll meet 'em on deck, Captain, and get all that worked out for you." He returned the unexpected salute, *The Army salutes everything*, he thought as he watched Bonfoey return to pier side and his troops. *So that's Bonfoey.*

Gochais heard the sound of clipped marching commands. Leaning over the rail he looked out toward the entrance to the opened main gate as the lead ranks of soldiers made a precise marching turn from the Embarcadero onto the pier. The dark faces told him that this is the 855th Engineers. Leaning on the rail he watched, thoughts running together, *Sharp looking troops. Never seen that many colored guys in one place. All those officers are white. This sure ain't Minnesota.*

Petty Officer Makowski stepped out of the shadows, jolting him back with his voice, "Mr. Gochais, there's a radio-telephone message for you. A Chief Wetmore. I can place the return call when you want."

"Thanks, Makowski. I'll go up with you now." *Wetmore, eh. Hope to hell he's got something I can use.*

134

He followed Makowski to the radio shack and watched him do his magic with knobs and dials. Makowski handed Gochais the headset. "He's all yours, Lieutenant. Remember to say 'over'."

"Thanks." He placed it to his ear and spoke into the microphone, "Chief. How's the home front? Over."

"Hello, Don. Home front's peachy. Got a couple of things for you. First, the major's on his way to Australia. He'll be setting up that end. Second, we've confirmed that Hauptmann has a brother. But we don't know yet if that's connected to our problem. Also, we don't know where Hauptmann is. Over."

At Wetmore's pause, Gochais keyed his mike, "Strange, Chief. If this guy Hauptmann is such a hotshot he should have hit us before this. We're gonna be out to sea soon enough ... and the stuff is safe aboard. Over."

"Roger, that, Don. All I know is that the major said to never count Hauptmann out. Hey, I checked out your people. Rhinehart Meuller's clean as a whistle. Nothing negative on Harris, either. At least not yet. He's a Yale lawyer boy. Record gets kind of fuzzy. We're trying to have a little deeper look. Your Corporal McIntire seems okay. He was at Monmouth, but you knew that. Keep an eye on Bonfoey. We just can't get a good track on him ... still trying. Over."

"Thanks, Chief ... I guess. We're loading the last of our troops ... a colored engineer outfit. Looks like probably tomorrow we shove off. Over."

"Okay, smooth sailing ... and keep your head down, boy ... I mean, sir. Over and Out."

Gochais slipped the headphones off and sat back at the console, mumbling, "Yeah, Chief, I'll keep my head down."

 **CHAPTER 14**

Pacific Ocean
German U-835 Underway
Same Time

Kapitän zur See Ernst Kalbruener watched from the conning tower as the last of the three whaleboats floated free from the U-835's sloshing deck.

The calm sea had only enough breeze to occasionally ripple the red and black *Kriegsmarine* ensign flying from the stern. The sun sparkled off the surface forcing the lookouts to shade their eyes and squint into the light as they scanned the horizon.

Time on the surface is necessary, but dangerous. The repeated practices that Otto Hauptmann had driven seemed to be producing a semblance of smooth performance from the whaleboat crews.

The rumble of the diesel engines found its way up to Kalbruener's ears as the boats dispersed to their assigned positions—an extended arc with the U-boat in the center. The power of the engines' sound is pleasant to him.

Hauptmann yelled up through cupped hands from his station at the rear of the conning tower, "That is better, *Herr Kapitän.*"

He turned back toward the deck officer. "Recover the boats, *Herr Leutnant.* That will be all for today."

Otto Hauptmann climbed the rungs toward the top of the tower. Stepping over the rail, he stood next to Kalbruener and watched the *Bootsmannmaats* maneuver their craft back to the U-835.

"*Herr Kapitän,* these crews have their *u-boot-päckchen* (leather U-boat battledress) on board, I presume?"

The *Kapitän* replied, "Ja, of course, Herr Hauptmann." Keeping his binoculars to his eyes as he watched the boats return he added, "You are going to tell me what this is about?"

"Soon enough, *Herr Kapitän,* soon enough."

USAT *Cape San Juan* – Pier Side
San Francisco, California

Donovan Gochais arrived on the quarterdeck just as Lt. Col. Harold Keefer, the commanding officer of the 855th Engineer (Aviation) Battalion, stepped off the gangway. "I've got eight-hundred hungry boys here looking for a bunk and a meal. Can somebody point me the way?"

Gochais, his hand extended, answered, "That'd be me, sir. Don Gochais, third mate. Welcome aboard. Your people are in #2 Hold forward. That's the gangway they use." Gochais pointed. "There's a quartermaster stationed at the hatch to direct your people below."

Lieutenant Colonel Keefer said, "We'll board my Headquarters Company first, Mr. Gochais."

"That's fine, Colonel. Follow me, sir ... we'll meet them at the head of the gangway."

Gochais motioned to Keefer to follow him and proceeded forward along the deck to the large canvas and wood superstructure installed above the #2 Hold. He walked to the head of the gangway and motioned down to the white officer waiting on the pier to proceed with boarding his colored troops.

Keefer said, "That's 1st Lieutenant Muchler in the lead. He's the XO of Headquarters Company. The colored man behind him is First Sergeant Rivers."

Pointing to the quartermaster and the head of the ladder that descended into the #2 Hold, Gochais called out, "This way, gentlemen."

The USAT *Cape San Juan*, originally built as a cargo ship, had been converted to carry troops by adding rows of three-high bunks in the upper levels of the ships holds. Quarters are so tight that a man can't roll over in his stretched canvas bunk without hitting the man above him. Shelters—deckhouses— are built over the hatch openings on the main deck to provide troop washrooms and a weather cover for the ladderways down into the ship.

As the men made their way into the ship they found a set of safety instructions on each bunk discussing use of rafts, lifeboats and life jackets. It took a while for the eight-hundred-nine troops of the 855th Engineer (Aviation) Battalion to make the climb and to find the cramped space that would be their home for the next couple of weeks.

Gochais stood and watched the parade of black men pass by him. Growing up in northern Minnesota and coming to the west coast as a young sailor he had not met many colored people.

A few of the soldiers made eye contact, some even smiled and nodded. One young technical sergeant even offered a simple hand-to-the-forehead salute. Gochais returned it, also casually, noting the man had lighter skin and finer features than most of the others. The stenciled name on his fatigues read JETER, A.

Gochais thought as he turned back toward the bridge, *I guess they're not all alike.*

A bosun's pipe shrilled out over the public address speakers followed by an announcement that blared throughout the ship, "Now hear this. Now hear this. Ship's officers and senior military officers report to the wardroom in twenty minutes."

Gochais started up to the wardroom. *A cup of coffee would taste good before another meeting.*

Seats at the wardroom table filled early and the assembled officers sat or leaned wherever they found space.

Captain Strong entered, a sheaf of paper in his hand. Someone announced, "Attention on deck!"

Captain Strong moved to his chair at the head of the table and said, "As you were, gentlemen. We're shoving off at first light tomorrow. As some of you know we're sailing alone. We've just been informed that a Navy dirigible will escort us for the first day only. This is our second voyage to Townsville and I anticipate no difficulties. However, there are rules of conduct we have been given should the enemy find us."

The captain handed a paper to the Navy lieutenant sitting nearest him. "Mr. Harris, please read this aloud."

Harris scanned the first few lines and began to read the document.

Instructions to Masters from the Secretary
of the Navy
Op-23L-JH (SC) S76-3 Serial 097923
    NAVY DEPARTMENT, WASHINGTON
    1 October, 1943

    From: The Secretary of the Navy
    To: Master USAT Cape San Juan

    SUBJECT: Instructions for Scuttling
    Merchant Ships.

    1. It is the policy of the United
       States Government that no U. S.
       Flag merchant ship be permitted to
       fall into the hands of the enemy.
    2. The ship shall be defended by her
       armament, by maneuver, and by
       every available means as long as
       possible. Then, in the judgment of
       the Master, capture is inevitable,
       he shall scuttle the ship.
       Provision should be made to open
       sea valves, and to flood holds and
       compartments adjacent to machinery
       spaces, start numerous fires and
       employ any additional measures
       available to insure certain
       scuttling of the vessel.
    3. In case the Master is relieved of
       command of his ship, he shall
       transfer this letter to his
       successor, and obtain a receipt
       for it.
                        /s/ FRANK KNOX

```
Received 13 October 1943
Port Director San Francisco, Calif.
Edward C. Kaminski, Port Master
```

A murmur spread through the room as Harris finished reading the message.

Captain Strong rose from his seat and retrieved the paper. "Pretty clear, gentlemen. I expect you to make any necessary preparations. Any leaves and passes are over at midnight. We answer bells at 0500 hours, feed the troops and cast off at 1000 hours. Good day, gentlemen."

With permission to go ashore from Second Mate Dorcey, Gochais headed for the telephone booth at the head of the pier. The line of sailors stood too long for his time frame so Gochais flashed his ID to the gate guard and walked out onto the Embarcadero looking for a public phone.

Across the street a dark green 1936 Hudson sedan sat parked, its distinctive vertical chrome grill reflecting the afternoon sun. Two men sat inside. They both wore fedoras that shadowed their faces from distinct view. Gochais thought they looked quite out of place on the waterfront. As he looked across the street the sedan's driver seemed to quickly avert his eyes. *My imagination's running away with me,* Gochais thought as he spotted what he looked for near the next pier gate. He walked on down the street toward the phone booth.

With the drop of a coin, a number given, and a priority authorization shared, Gochais heard the charming voice of BJ answer his call, "Clinton 58873."

"Hi, BJ. I need the chief ... Thanks."

The upbeat voice of Chief Wetmore came on the line, "Hello, Donny ... everything good up there? You get a sailing time?"

"You bet, Chief. We sail tomorrow mid-morning. Everything and everybody's on board. Guess it's going to be my show now for sure."

"Roger that, Don. I'll pass the word. Good luck and fair seas, sailor."

"Thanks, Chief. Say, Chief, can you do me a favor?

"Sure thing, Donny. What d'ya need?"

"On second thought, Chief, nothing. Never mind."

"Okay, Don. It's your call, just let me know. So long."

"So long, Chief." *I really wanted him to look after Elma and the boys ... but OSS calling might be too scary. I did leave her that envelope in case somethin' happened. Damn, I'm thinkin' too much.* He hung up the phone, slipping a finger into the coin return out of habit.

Gochais turned to walk back up the Embarcadero, but stopped suddenly.

Across the street and nearer to the pier gate he saw someone standing by the dark green Hudson. The man leaned into the driver's window, talking to the two fancy dressed guys inside. Gochais eased into the shadow of a doorway as the man turned away from the car and crossed the street toward the pier.

The man wore a uniform.

Army. An officer.

Gochais watched the Hudson pull away from the curb, coming toward him. Acting like he wasn't aware of anything amiss, Gochais lit a cigarette and started to walk back toward his ship. The driver looked straight at him as he drove by and Gochais turned to watch the dark green car turn up Sansome Street and speed out of sight. He quickened his pace toward the ship and got to the edge of the fence where he could see down the pier, in time to see the man, the Army officer, moving half way up the forward gangway.

It's Bonfoey!

Gochais took a last drag on the cigarette and dropped it to the pavement. As he crushed it out with a twist of his shoe he thought, *guess this really is my show now.* At a fast walk he returned to the ship, feeling no need to conceal himself. He climbed the forward gangway keeping his eyes on the deck ahead. Captain Bonfoey is nowhere in sight.

His mind swirled. His police training didn't have a chapter on spies. *Slow down, dummy. Think. Remember what you learned at Toyan. What the hell could he be planning? There's plenty of perimeter security for the ship. The crates are too big to put in his pocket ... stupid thought ... don't be stupid.*

Taking a deep breath and one last look around, Gochais moved along the main deck toward the #3 Hold. He put his hand on the leather holster clipped to his web belt. *Just checking.*

As he stepped out of the waning afternoon light into the shadows his eyes adjusted. Under the deck house rigged over the hatches he became aware of the soldiers. Some were sitting, leaning against the bulkheads with knees raised and writing last letters home. Others stood in small groups, having the smoke forbidden below decks.

His thoughts raced, *get your head out of your ass, Gochais ... be aware, look calm.*

Some of the soldiers stood as he approached. Gochais said, "As you were. You guys 1st Fighters?"

"Yes, sir," came a chorus of replies.

143

Gochais quipped, "Ready for a nice boat ride tomorrow?"

Followed by laughter, he moved on down the ladderway into the #3 Hold. The interplay with the soldiers had calmed him a bit. At the first deck level, crammed with the canvas bunks with a few soldiers on and about them, he began to feel the closeness of the space. He continued descending the steel ladders below the berthing and into the cargo hold. He slowed as palpable tension crept across his shoulders. He'd been down here before and knew exactly where the three crates are stowed – *Orion's Eye*.

The wire-caged safety lights cast little more than a glow on the narrow passageways between high stacks of crates and equipment. Shadows overruled the light. As he stepped onto the first catwalk he paused to listen, hearing nothing but the usual background groans and whirs of a ship. It's hard to be quiet because each step produces a metallic reaction from the stretched-steel grating that forms the ladders and walkways.

He crept forward. One step. Two. Listen. He heard more sounds as adrenalin sharpens his senses. *Which sounds are danger?* His eyes adjusted slowly to the dimness. He scanned side to side as he had been taught in OSS spook school. He remembered the instructor's words. *'Your eyes are more sensitive to darkness on the edges than in the middle. Stare straight ahead into darkness and you will be blind ... so scan, fool, scan.'*

Gochais moved his scan down to the next catwalk level, then out and left to where he knew the crated radar to be.

Nothing. Two more steps to the ladderway.

Damn, why am I so jumpy? What the hell could be down here? As he reached out with his foot for the first step Gochais froze.

A shadow passed over the grated decking below, quickly there and just as quickly gone. Something had passed between him and one of the dim lights.

Is it above me or below me? Or my imagination? Damn.

He peered up over his shoulder, shifting his feet and slowly rotating to get a better look around, his heart pounding in his ears.

Sounds blended together.

He reached down and released the flap on his holster, touching the butt of his 1911 Colt .45.

Only slightly reassured, he took his second step down the ladderway. Then another and another, feeling each step with his toe before putting weight on it. His eyes never left the spot, now nearly on the same level, where the shadow had flitted by.

Scan, dummy, don't stare!

Sweat beaded his forehead as he became aware of the stuffy sea-damp atmosphere in the space. First wiping his moist hand on his right thigh, Gochais slowly drew the Colt .45. He listened and scanned ahead. Reaching the catwalk he moved to his right toward the cargo he's watching over. Barely breathing he inched along the narrow aisle.

From above and to his left a raspy whispered order came, "Freeze! Set the piece on the deck ... slowly. Keep your hands where I can see them."

As a cold shiver enveloped him, Gochais said, "Okay, okay, easy ... I'm kneeling down ... Easy."

His training kicked in. *Calm. Assess. Slow moves, fast thinking. No heroics ... until you've got the upper hand.*

He heard the hissed whisper reply, "You move easy if you want to live."

Gochais rose slowly to his feet. He felt the man approach behind him. "Okay, okay."

The voice instructed, "Hands on your head. Turn around. Slow. Slow."

Gochais complied. They faced each other.

Captain Edward Bonfoey said, "So it's you ... I thought you were a little too interested in these crates."

Ignoring the comment, Gochais stared into Bonfoey's eyes and asked, "So how do you plan to get them out of here before tomorrow, Captain?"

"*Me* ... get them out of here? That's *your* game, Gochais."

"What the hell you talkin' about Bonfoey? We've been on to you for a long time." He motioned with his head, his hands still finger-laced atop it. "... and I saw your boys out there."

"We figured you'd pegged me, Gochais. That's why we decided to take you down before we sailed. Thanks for making it easy for me by coming down to check on your booty."

Gochais' strained reply, "Jesus H. Christ, man ... you're takin' *me* down? Who in hell are you, Bonfoey?"

The captain switched his pistol to his left hand and reached into his shirt pocket. "I'm your worst enemy, my kraut loving friend." He produced a leather folder that flipped open to reveal a glint of metal—a badge—and Federal ID. "Special Agent Edward Bonfoey, F.B.I. ... now, get your hands behind you! You are under arrest."

Gochais dropped his chin onto his chest, his fingers still entwined in his hair and chuckled out loud, "Man, this is too much. Look, I'm standin' still. Let me get my wallet ... in the hip pocket, right side. Get my ID."

The impatient reply, "I know you've got your sailor-boy papers. Hands behind you!"

Gochais, slowly shaking his head, dropped his hands and pressed them together behind him, palms out. Bonfoey snapped a handcuff on one wrist. "I see you know the position. Been busted before?"

The second cuff clicked into place. Gochais snapped, "Nope, but I've put a few of them on. Now, dammit, will you get my ID?"

Bonfoey grunted as he pushed Gochais forward until he leaned into the cargo stack. Placing a foot between Gochais' legs he fished the wallet from the pocket and flipped it open.

"Shit. I don't believe this." Bonfoey squinted to see the card with the blue band, the wings-spread eagle, with *Strategic Services – OSS* emblazoned at the top. Unmistakable. "You're frigging OSS?"

"I'm not Santy Claus! Now get these cuffs off me! You've got some goddam explaining to do, Captain ... or whatever the hell you are. Then I suspect we've got work to do ... together."

 **CHAPTER 15**

San Francisco, California
The Next Morning

The morning fog, typical for this time of year, rolling thick as cotton through the Golden Gate, followed the San Francisco harbor front as it clung low to the ground and water.

High on the bridge of USAT *Cape San Juan*, Gochais stood above the rolling fog in the clear air of a crisp fall morning. He watched the sun rising behind Mount Diablo in the east, casting its first rays to light the jutting towers of the great red bridge that spanned from Fort Point to the Marin headlands.

His favorite expression, he thought, *This sure ain't Minnesota.*

He noted the line of Liberty ships steaming past Alcatraz, the first of the ship convoy already disappearing into the fog bank.

Down on the main deck early-bird soldiers lined up for their morning meal, still learning the procedures for moving about the ship. Longshoremen on the pier prepared the rigging to hoist the gangways and disconnected shore power. Slowly, piece by piece, this fine ship came alive and took responsibility for herself—and the voyage ahead.

A phone call the night before to Wetmore set inquiries in motion and they'd come full circle. From what Mead told Gochais about the loveless relationship between senior FBI and OSS officials in Washington, he figured that there must have been a lot of shouting going on as they faced off about each unit's actions.

Gochais thought, *At least I've got a team mate now ... the Lone Ranger's found his Tonto.*

He laughed out loud, "Better not call him that."

The duty quartermaster said, "Pardon, sir?"

"Nothing, nothing, sailor ... just thinkin' out loud."

Headquarters CinCPAC
Pearl Harbor, Hawaii

The Pan Am Navy PB2Y maneuvered alongside the designated buoy and secured. The shuttle craft off-loaded the mail bags, secure document containers and passengers, including Major Amos Mead, USMC.

The first over-water leg of his journey proved uneventful—to his relief. Besides some rest, he had one stop to make in Hawaii. The Office of Naval Intelligence, Wetmore's old boss.

Rear Admiral Edward Layton, head of Admiral Nimitz's intelligence staff, said, "I appreciate you stopping in here, Major Mead." Adding with a chuckle, "How're you and Harmon getting along?"

"Chief Wetmore? Honestly, Admiral, he's my babysitter ... and that's a positive statement. I didn't know that he's your boy until just before I left L.A."

"Well, I don't know if he's anybody's 'boy,' Major, but I'm glad he's let you in on our needs. Frankly, all this infighting between agencies and commands over intelligence activities is pure ego-based bullshit. Now what's up with your project?"

"Agree about the infighting, sir, but it's way above my paygrade. The ship should be underway by now, Admiral, and to be honest, we don't know what the Germans have up their sleeve ... but it's damn hard to figure how they could steal this stuff off that ship."

"Like I told Wetmore, Major, stranger things have happened before. Have you found out any more about our military officer spy?"

"Nothing more, sir ... and it's got us on edge. Intercepts from German SS messages still lead us to believe he exists."

"Where do you go from here, Major?"

"Townsville, sir. Trying to get ahead of whatever's coming our way."

"Well, stay safe ... and keep me in the loop. I'll help you out anyway I can. But, frankly, Mead, this is all your show. One more thing. Listen to the chief and heed what he says. There's more to Wetmore than any of us know ... I speak from experience."

Mead rose and extended his hand to Admiral Layton. "Aye, aye, sir. And thank you, Admiral. Having back-up is appreciated. By your leave, Admiral. I've got a Pan Am flight to find."

The handshake, firm and genuine. "Have a safe flight, son. Remember, let me know if there's anything you need along the way."

Mead exited CinCPAC Headquarters and strode along the quay toward the Pan Am moorings. The giant Boeing 314-A with NC18604 on her vertical stabilizer is his flight. The Pacific Clipper rocked gently beside the loading dock, receiving the last of tons of mail and supplies headed for troops in the South Pacific. With a crew of ten she normally carried seventy-four passengers. This flight only twenty-four people are scheduled on board.

Mead joined the line, wishing he were someplace else, anyplace else but boarding another over-water adventure. As he reached the front he handed the Pan Am steward his papers and crossed the short gangway, then stepped into the lower deck of the two deck flying boat and looked for a seat.

Thirty minutes later the four Wright GR-2600 Cyclone engines roared to life. Their sixty-four hundred horsepower drove the nearly fifty tons of aircraft, treasure and flesh and blood people over the water and skyward toward the war.

The Clipper's range of thirty-six hundred-seventy-five miles is more than enough to make the island hopping route feasible.

With Japanese advances, their route went south from Hawaii to Penryhn Island, then on to Aitutaki, Tongatapu and finally Townsville, Australia. At 183 miles per hour they settled in for a long flight. Mead nestled into his seat, snugged the seat belt and found sleep to be the first order of business.

Federal Building
Los Angeles, California
Same Time

Wetmore initiated the SIGSALY voice encrypted call to Hawaii. The fifteen minute synchronization sequence seemed to him an eternity, but finally weaving through the layers of gatekeepers he had Admiral Layton on the line.

"Sorry for the interruption, Admiral, but you're the only place I knew Major Mead planned on stopping."

Layton replied loud and clear, "No problem, Harmon. But sorry ... you just missed him. The Pacific Clipper took off about twenty minutes ago."

"Thank you, sir. I've got some detailed reports on our German spy ... the Hauptmann guy ... from the OSS in London. I'll catch up to him in Townsville."

"Roger that, Harmon. You getting any closer?"

"Slowly, Admiral, bit by little bit. Nothing much changes from war to war, eh Admiral?"

"Sure seems that way. Keep me posted."

"Aye, aye, sir. Los Angeles. Out."

USAT Cape San Juan
San Francisco, California

The piercing steam-whistle signal announced the ship's departure. Getting underway, with the assist of harbor tugs, the four-hundred-seventeen foot long transport ship moved slowly away from the pier and out into the San Francisco Bay. The harbor pilot on the bridge watched every move as the ship angled out toward Alcatraz Island and into the proper lane toward the Golden Gate Bridge. Captain Strong and Chief Mate Manning observed the process that they had witnessed many times before.

Gochais wasn't scheduled for the watch until midnight. As the ship proceeded down the waterfront he stood at the port rail and watched the San Francisco skyline slide by. Finally full in the channel and turning toward the Golden Gate, Gochais walked forward to the bow and joined a group of soldiers who stood watching the pageant.

He recognized a few of the 1st Fighter Control Squadron, but most of the soldiers were colored troops from the 855th Engineers. The soldier nearest him wore a khaki windbreaker jacket and stood with his hands clasped behind his back.

As Gochais approached, the man turned, made eye contact and said, "Morning, sir."

Gochais answered, "Good morning ..." He glanced down at the name tape on the jacket. "Sergeant Jeter. Quite a view, eh?"

The sergeant replied, "Surely is, sir. Ain't nothin' like I've ever seen before."

Technical Sergeant Arthur L. Jeter, stood five feet nine inches tall and about one-hundred-forty pounds with a light brown complexion. A handsome and self-assured man, his face angular with an almost aquiline nose, Gochais thought, *He looks more Italian than colored.* "Where you from, Sarge?"

"Pennsylvania, sir ... Yeadon, Pennsylvania."

"Minnesota for me ... Duluth's my home town. California now, though."

Jeter waved toward the landscape. "We didn't get much time out here, but going through those mountains on the train sure be something for me. Ain't got no mountains like that in Pennsylvania, for sure."

Gochais nodded, "For sure."

The two men stood in silence as they slipped under the tall red spires of the Golden Gate Bridge, an awesome sight. But what lay ahead for them were private thoughts, private questions.

Captain Bonfoey walked up behind the group. "Hello, Mr. Gochais. Some view."

"Hey, Ed. Glad you came up. We need to talk." Gochais turned away from the bow. "Take care Sergeant Jeter."

"You bet, Sir."

Bonfoey and Gochais headed aft along the portside rail to find a quieter spot.

OSS Safe House
Los Angles, California

BJ walked into the kitchen of the large hacienda that served as a way station for OSS officers moving in and out of the Pacific war. She found who she looked for. "Constantia, may I have a word with you, please?"

"*Si, Señora. Con su servidor* ... pardon me, in English ... I am at your service, Señora."

BJ pulled out a chair at the work table and said, "No need for the formality, Constantia ... come, sit down."

Constantia sat, her expression unreadable.

Settling into the chair across from the maid, BJ began, "Chief Wetmore will return soon. Before he does though, you and I need to get a few things straight."

"Straight, Señora?"

BJ leaned forward, her forearms on the table, speaking in a stern, but not scolding, tone. "Don't play dumb with me, Constantia. Wetmore and even Mead may see you as the little immigrant lady. I see more than that. You are very alert and understand much more than you admit to."

Constantia looked straight into BJ's eyes, her lips, slightly pursed. She showed restrained tension, but didn't respond.

154

BJ held the eye contact for a moment then broke it and looked down at her folded hands. She began to speak softly, "Constantia, we need to work together. We don't need the tension. So, tell me about yourself. Where is home, originally?"

Constantia's face relaxed only slightly. "Uruguay, Señora. My father is Argentine."

"When did you come up here?"

"My husband and I moved here in 1938."

"And Pedro, he's Uruguayan?"

"Argentinean."

BJ rose and walked to the sink, leaning over to look out the window, her back to Constantia. "By the way, where is Pedro? I haven't seen him today."

"He has not felt well, Señora ... he is in our house."

"Does he need a doctor or medicine?"

"No, no, Señora. I can take care of him. It is not serious I am sure. Will there be anything else? I have some work to do." She stood and waited for a reply.

"Yes, okay. That will be all."

BJ watched Constantia as she bowed her head slightly then turned and walked into the dining room and on out into the patio toward her quarters.

She played that cool. Didn't lie about her nationality. BJ thought, *the Chief's information is good. But does it mean anything?*

Then she remembered what she thought she heard on her first day in her quarters.

 **CHAPTER 16**

Pacific Ocean
German *U-835* Underway

The German submarine U-835 had been running on the surface for two days. This part of the Pacific had few Allied patrols, but the lookouts were doubled just in case. They had sailed east on a course that Otto Hauptmann had given to *Kapitän* Kalbruener.

The *Kapitän* stood on the conning tower bridge, scanning the horizon with his Leica binoculars. Hauptmann stood next to him, enjoying the fresh air and sunlight. Not used to the confined space of the submarine with its stale humid air and the stench of unwashed men, he had no intention of ever becoming used to it.

"What is our position, *Herr Kapitän*?"

Kalbruener replied, "The last star sight had us at 42 South Latitude, 110 W Longitude. Are you ready to quit the games and talk to me?"

"These are dangerous games, my friend. We must move the pieces carefully if we are to survive."

"So what is the next move?"

"I believe we have one more day on the surface ... then we will be in dangerous ... more dangerous waters, *Herr Kapitän*. I suggest you have our position updated, and then we will submerge and proceed. Call me when you have completed the task. I will give you the next move. For now, I need some sleep." Hauptmann turned and descended the ladder into the submarine.

Kapitän Kalbruener tensed, but held his temper. *Someday I will even the score with that SS bastard.* His order to the talker, "Navigator to the bridge!"

USAT *Cape San Juan*
Underway, Abeam Fort Point
San Francisco Bay

The long, high swells that rushed through the narrows of the Golden Gate had the bow of the ship climbing and plunging with spritzing wafts of sea spray wetting the forward decks. While nothing unusual for the sailors, most of the soldiers sought shelter nearer their quarters.

On the lee weather deck just below the stack Bonfoey and Gochais watched the headlands and then the sands of Ocean Beach pass slowly by.

Leaning with his forearms on the teak capped iron rail, Gochais said, "I guess all we can do is watch and wait."

"Have you got anything in particular to watch in mind?"

"Well, shit, I've already lost my best suspect!"

"That'd be me, eh?

Gochais rambled through a chain of out-loud thoughts, "That'd be you ... nothing suspicious with the others. Except maybe Harris replacing Smitty ...

157

bad car crash … probably nothing but coincidence … Can't figure what any bad guy could do now anyway. They gonna hide those crates under a bunk?"

Bonfoey chuckled. After a moment of quiet as the two men gazed at the sea, he said, "Say, Don, you got family?"

"Yeah, two boys. Back in L.A. … how 'bout you?"

"Me, too. Wife's name is Sarah and my boy's Ned. They're back in Quincy, Illinois. You from California?"

"Nope, Minnesota. My Dad died on my thirteenth birthday. Kinda tough for my Mom with four kids. I went in the Navy when I could and ended up on the USS *West Virginia* in San Pedro. That's where I met Elma … that's my wife. Got out when they moved the Battlewagons to Pearl. Lucky, eh. Lot of my friends bought it on December 7. Anyway, I joined the LAPD and became a cop." Gochais zipped up his khaki windbreaker. "It's getting cold out here. How 'bout some coffee … and, hey, you be my guest in the wardroom for dinner tonight."

"Coffee, okay … but I'm thinking I'm going to be a little green around the gills for dinner."

"Okay, soldier, your call."

They climbed the ladder toward the wardroom, gripping the rail tightly as the ship rolled and pitched on the incoming tide. They began to hear the bark of sea lions and the smell of sea churned kelp as the ship plowed toward the Farallons, twenty-seven miles from San Francisco—beyond that, the open sea.

As they reached the hatch Gochais heard the drone of an engine on the wind. They both looked up to see the Navy LTA (lighter than air) blimp with ZP32 blazoned on her rotund side. The escort from Moffet field slipped into place over the ship. Gochais said, "That's good to see … at least for a day or two."

158

OSS Safe House
Los Angles, California

Wetmore had already poured himself a Chivas Regal over ice when BJ walked in from the patio. She wore a flowered house dress and platform shoes that gave the demure blonde a businesslike impression without losing any of her allure. "How is your day, Mr. Wetmore?"

Raising his glass in a toasting gesture, he said, "My day is perfect now. Oh, I tried to catch up to Amos but he's off in a big silver bird again. And how is your day, Miss BJ?"

She peered toward the kitchen, assuring that they were alone, and said, "Interesting, Chief. Your information on Constantia ... she confirmed it all. No lies."

"So maybe she's just what we see ... the maid."

"I'm sorry, Chief, but my intuition tells me different. I see it in her eyes. I'm sorry."

"Intuition is good ... nothing to be sorry about."

He tipped the glass high for the last sip. "One more of these is in order for this old sailor so far from the sea."

"One more thing, Chief. She told me that Pedro is sick in bed. But later I saw him come in from behind the bungalows ... looking healthy to me."

"Sneaking out was he?" Harmon Wetmore poured the last of the whiskey.

"Look, Chief, I don't know. But I've got a couple of things I want to check out." BJ went to the bar and retrieved another bottle of Chivas. "Lady needs a short one." She added with a sigh, "When's the next group from Toyan Bay arriving?"

159

"End of the week. Think there's four this time. Be here about three days. One's going into Mexico. That's different."

"I'll have Constantia make things up. I don't want to tip her that I'm suspicious ... suspicious about something ... and I'm going to find out what."

"Sounds like you're on a mission, BJ. Maybe we ought to sign you up."

"Okay, Chief ... have your little chuckle. But you guys'll find out that I'm not just another pretty face. Cheers."

**Federal Building
Los Angeles, California
Two Days Later**

Wetmore sat in the large room that housed the fifty-ton encrypted telephone system SIGSALY. The signals sergeant from the 805th Signal Service Company working to initiate Wetmore's call to Townsville, Australia.

Balancing precariously on the back legs of his metal chair, Wetmore said, "So McArthur gets his own phone, eh Sarge?"

"Pretty much, Chief. That one's carried on an Ocean Lighter called OL31. Moves around down there for him."

"The 805th service all of them?"

"Roger that. Wherever one of these big boys go ... we go with 'em. Okay, Chief, your calls synching up."

Wetmore donned the headset, heard the connection and the answer, and asked for Major Amos Mead. Earlier, Wetmore had radioed his need to speak with Mead, and Mead sent a radio message to arrange the time for the call.

160

From Australia, Mead quipped, "Hello, Chief, how're they hangin'? Whoops, maybe that's not protocol for this fancy phone."

"You're loud and clear, Major. And in exceptionally good spirits. What's up?"

"What's up is I got here in one piece ... and dry. What have you got for me?"

"We got some good stuff on Hauptmann from London and DC. Confirmed that he has a brother, and we're pretty sure he's here in the States. Actually he's a half-brother ... American Momma. Also, Heinrich ... papa ... is dead. Died in Vienna."

"Have you found, Otto?

"No, Major. He's dropped out of sight. There's been some activity and radio traffic ... mostly from Mexico ... so it could be him. But he's invisible."

"Or he could be on his way down here? Damn, like chasing smoke. What about our other suspects, Chief?"

"We have one less suspect, sir. Are you sittin' down? Bonfoey turned out to be a Special Agent for the FBI. He's workin' directly for Hoover ... same mission we've got. Do you believe that shit?"

"Yes I do, Chief. The FBI and OSS don't mix by directive of the super egos at their heads. Seems Roosevelt loves it this way for some twisted reason. Whoops, think I broke protocol again. Where's Bonfoey?"

"He's at sea with Donny on the *Cape San Juan*. Donny told me they're teaming up. So much for Roosevelt."

"Roger that, Chief. Donny's got to be feeling good about this."

"He is now, Major. But they came damn close to killing each other to get there. Listen, Major, there are a couple of others we're checking out. But one is giving us fits. There's a Navy Reserve lieutenant name of Harris on board the ship. This guy's a last minute replacement for their regular communications officer. He's clean as far as we can trace ... but that isn't very far. Trail goes real cold. That always makes me suspicious."

"So what the hell can I do about it, Chief?"

"We know he graduated Yale Law School, like you did. It's a long shot, sir, but we thought maybe you could give us some names of your frat brothers for us to find somebody who had eyeballs on him in school. Might let us go back further."

The call ended after a few more minutes.

Wetmore had a short list of 'Yalies', and he had Mead's itinerary in the islands.

Mead had assurances that BJ is doing well—and that Wetmore is impressed with how sharp the lady is. Mead had only laughed in reply.

Wetmore shifted in his chair as the call terminated. "Sarge, I need to talk with E Street, OSS, Maurice Hyman."

"Go get us some coffee, Chief. It'll take me another fifteen minutes to synch it up."

"How do you take it, Sarge?"

"Original recipe, Chief ... just beans and water."

"Smart ass," said Wetmore as he headed out of the air conditioned palace that housed his new favorite tool.

The call completed, Chief Wetmore headed for home, feeling good about the chances for getting some real clues out of this exercise. Maurice Hyman had become Wetmore's regular contact in Washington, D.C., and with Chandler Morris in

London, the three, with their contacts and networks, formed an effective intelligence team. Hyman took the list of Yale grads and began to search his sources— including Norman Holmes Pearson, the former Yale University professor that headed OSS X-2 in London—Mead's old outfit.

OSS Safe House
Los Angles, California

Wetmore pulled into the driveway and saw BJ standing near the garage in the rear. Curious, he continued toward her. As he stepped out of the car, he said, "Why the greeting committee?"

Glancing toward the main house, BJ answered, "Come with me," and began toward her quarters.

Wetmore shrugged his shoulders, looked over toward the main house, not knowing why, and followed. BJ unlocked the heavy oak door and entered her rooms, leaving it open for Wetmore to follow.

Leaving the door ajar, Wetmore said, "What's this all about, BJ?"

"Close that," BJ ordered as she peered through her curtains toward the house. "Constantia and Pedro are in the main house fixing dinner for our guests. I've got a plan and I need to talk it through with you. In fact, you've got to make most of it happen."

Wetmore furrowed his brow with guarded curiosity. "A plan, BJ? What sort of plan?"

She turned to face him, fixing a stern gaze that withered any thought he had of not taking her seriously. "I think I've got a way to trip up the people who've been trying to steal your stuff ... that radar stuff."

He crossed his arms and held her gaze and said, "You do know, BJ, that the stuff you speak of has already left the country?"

"Of course I do. And that's part of my plan."

BJ strode the three paces to the sofa and plopped herself down. She patted the space next to her as an invitation—or an order—to Wetmore to join her. On the heavy oaken coffee table sat an official looking document.

Her order to the chief, "Read."

Wetmore reached the bottom of the page. "I'll be damned! I see where you're going ... damned clever. But, what set you in this direction?"

BJ reached into the large patch pocket of her dress and retrieved a folded sheet of paper. Before she opened it she tapped Wetmore on the knee, catching his attention. Then put a finger up to her lips, moved it to point at her ear and wave it in a circle to indicate 'can't talk, somebody listening ... room wired?'

Wetmore nodded. She unfolded the paper and handed it to him. He read, then looked up at her with a quizzical look. She nodded yes.

He said, "We'll do it. I've got some calls to make."

"Thank you, Chief."

She placed her fingertips on his knee and smiled. "Let's go in to dinner."

4th Interceptor Command
March Field, California

Major General Manfield R. Nielsen, III, shifted the cigar in his mouth and picked up his telephone. "Yes? Put him through ... Chief, how are you? ... Good.

What've you heard from the major? Goddam it, son, nobody's talking to me!"

Wetmore answered, "Major Mead is fine, General. He's snooping around down in Townsville. We're tracking a few leads, but nothing red-hot. The reason for my call, sir, is that we've hatched a plan that I need your help pulling off. I think you'll like it!"

"Tell me about it, Chief... Damn sakes, it's about time I'm given an assignment in this thing!"

Wetmore relayed the details, leaving out only that the author is a petite young blond from Vermont. *Can't give it all away*, he'd thought.

"I like it, Chief. I like it a lot. Count me in. What can I do?"

"Great, General, here's what we do ..."

General Nielsen took notes.

 **CHAPTER 17**

Headquarters, Luftwaffe High Command
Berlin, Germany

Oberst (Colonel) Wilhelm Kohlbach prepared the message to be sent to George Nicolaus in Mexico. The message read:

> *Reichsmarschall* Goering has approved
> your plans to capture Auge Orions.
> The *Reichsmarschall* sends his
> congratulations on your progress.
> We remind you that your success is
> imperative.
> You will not, repeat, will not
> communicate with the SS - SD or any
> other Himmler operative on this matter.
> (signed) *Oberst* Kohlbach, Wilhelm

Kohlbach gave the message to the cryptographer. "Send this immediately. Use the Lorenz Cipher."

Kilometer 4 Via San Roque
San Antonio del Mar
Baja California, Mexico

Herr George Nicolaus had cast his lot with Goering over Himmler as the two struggled for supremacy and survival in 1943.

The message in his hand gave him much needed recognition and the opportunity to be on the winning side. This operation required more than his small team of infiltrators and Nicolaus had a plan. He prepared to fly in the *company* airplane south into the desert of Mexico's Baja peninsula to *Baia Magdelena*.

Even though Mexico officially joined the Allies in 1942, commercial activities by companies based in Axis countries are generally ignored. Herr George Nicolaus is an *importer/exporter* of various products. As such he arranged to bring a five passenger aircraft, an MS-500 Criquet, into Mexico from France with little difficulty—and of course a reasonable bribe.

The Criquet, actually an Fi-256 Fieseler Storch, is a mainstay observation and courier aircraft of the Luftwaffe.

Nicolaus's destination, the village of San Carlos on *Baia Magdelena*, is home base for the *Sinarquists*.

The right-wing *Sinarquistas* are an influential Catholic cultural organization with close affiliations to the Spanish Falange, the Nazi-styled political party that emerged from Spain's civil war. The radical *Sinarquistas* see the United States as driven by Jews and Communists and had a membership in Mexico of over half a million. Nicolaus is especially interested in working with the trained para-militaries in the movement—the Gold Shirts.

U.S. Intelligence keeps a close watch on the group at *Baia Magdelena*. There is concern that the Japanese will capitalize on the *Sinarquistas'* militancy and attempt to establish a base there. It is far enough removed from effective Mexican naval control for the concern to be real. The OSS is watching both at *Baia Magdelana* and at *San Antonio del Mar.*

As the MS-500 Criquet completed its takeoff roll and climbed onto a southerly course, a radio call went out on a discrete ground-based frequency, "Subject airborne. Flight following. Expect ETA plus four. Out."

Four hours later, the lightly loaded aircraft, Nicolaus the only passenger, touched down on the desert strip scraped out by the *Sinarquistas* near their compound. Two men dressed in Khaki uniforms and high front billed caps with the Mexican Eagle emblem on the front approached the plane as it rolled to a stop. The older of the two spoke, "*Buenas tardes, Senor Nicolaus. Bienvenido a San Carlos.*"

Nicolaus replied in flawless Spanish, "*Gracias, mi amigo. Tienes lo que yo necesito?*"

"Si, Senor. We have what you requested. The men can be on the border in two days *a su servicio.* Do you have the money?"

Nicolaus laughed aloud. "Of course, my friend. Are these men of yours going to be worth this fortune you demand of me?"

"On the soul of my sainted dead mother, Senor, these men are the finest thieves in all Mexico."

Everyone laughed.

Nicolaus said, "*Sie sind der Chef-Dieb!*"

He reached back into the plane and retrieved a satchel. He translated his remark to English, "And the chief thief shall have his booty." As he handed the satchel to the Gold Shirt officer, he said, "Get me in out of this sun and find your best tequila for me. It is no match for *Schnapps*, but I am growing to accept it."

Again, everyone laughed and headed into the desert shack that served as the airport terminal.

"Señor Nicolaus, what would you have us do?"

"You will be going to California, *Norte* California, my friend. My people have discovered a way for us to be very successful in our mission. You will help us."

"You have paid for our services. Tell me what we are to do."

Their planning session went long into the afternoon, fueled by growing optimism—and Tequila.

OSS Safe House
Los Angles, California

BJ sat leaning on the table, elbows supporting her clenched hands, as she waited for Wetmore to finish his call. He hung up the phone and turned to her with a wry smile. "It's all set."

BJ blurted out around her hands, showing white at the knuckles, "Tell me what's happening! Talk to me, Chief!"

Wetmore laughed and leaned back in a relaxed slump. "You've stirred up quite a hornets' nest, Miss BJ. General Nielsen gave us people from the 35th Fighter Control Squadron … the last piece of the puzzle. Maurice Hyman in DC got the U.S. Marshals to play. He cut through a lot of bureaucratic crap to make that happen. BJ, my fine feathered friend, we are ready to go."

BJ sat back in her chair and looked down as she moved her clenched hands to her lap. Almost in a whisper, she said, "Damn it, Chief. I hope I'm right."

"Oh, you're right, BJ. I'm betting on it. Sure, we're taking a bit of a chance. But what you found gives good cause to act. Hey, the worst thing that can happen is nothin' happens. No down side, I say."

"You're the expert, Chief." BJ stood and moved to pour a cup of coffee. "Refill?"

"No, thanks. I've got to get over to the office and tie up the loose ends. We're still looking for something on the Yale investigation, too."

BJ sipped the hot coffee. As she glanced up over the rim of the heavy Navy mug she saw Constantia coming across the lawn toward the house. "Good timing, Chief. Here comes our player."

Pacific Ocean – At Sea
German *U-835* Underway

Otto Hauptmann never got used to the claustrophobic feeling. The humid, rancid air felt like a mask pressing on his nostrils, closing his throat. He had no intention of getting used to it, only allowing it to pass like other unpleasant times in his life.

It had been three days of running submerged, surfacing only to take navigation sights at night. The grudging concession of *Kapitän* Kalbruener to use the *schnorkel* allowed them to progress this way.

Hauptmann called a meeting of the senior officers in the wardroom galley. Cramped together, sweating in clothes not changed in days, they waited.

Kalbruener broke the tense silence with a cynical tone, "Well, *Herr SS Oberst* Hauptmann, are you ready to bless us with a glimpse of your mission?"

Hauptmann looked up slowly, a steely stare fixed on the *Kapitän*, his words paced, "I will overlook your insolences, *Herr Kapitän*. But I do not condone

170

them." He passed a coffee mug to the officer across from him and gestured toward the grimy pot that sluiced dark liquid with every movement of the U-Boat. The mug back in front of him, he cupped it with two hands, raised it to his lips and blew on its steamy surface. "I can understand your feelings, *Herr Kapitän*. I am an intruder on your boat." He stared into the murky fluid in front of him. "But our mission supersedes our feelings. We will call a truce for now. I want to hear no more of anyone's attitude … only calls to action."

All the officers looked down or stared in any direction but Hauptmann's, except Kalbruener who never broke his stare into the side of Hauptmann's head.

Hauptmann continued. "I have a destination for you." He looked up and turned his head, returning the *Kapitän*'s glare. "22°15' South Latitude. 176°18' West Longitude." Holding his stare, he pronounced every syllable distinctly and slowly.

The U-boat's navigation officer wrote down the coordinates and quickly referenced the tattered chart affixed with yellowing tape to the bulkhead. "Ata Island, *Herr Kapitän*." Kalbruener asked, "And what is the importance of this island?" He crossed his arms and leaned back against the clammy steel.

"From this island we pounce, *Herr Kapitän*. This I will show you when we get there." Hauptmann rose and pushed around the officers to the curtain that covered the passageway entrance. He slipped the curtain aside, then hesitated and turned back to the group. "There is another location you must mark as well." He looked hard at the navigation officer. "18°52' South Latitude. 159°46' West Longitude. That is Aitutaki Island. Last year the Americans built a runway on this island. It is a regular route for American and New Zealand aircraft. If we are spotted by their patrol bombers you know the consequences all too well."

He turned his gaze to Kalbruener. "But that's your job, isn't it *Herr Kapitän.* To keep us out of danger."

Smiling, Hauptmann moved through the curtain.

Through his clenched teeth, Kalbruener hissed, "*Verdammt sein Esel* (damn his rotten ass)."

OSS Headquarters
Washington, DC

Maurice Hyman looked across his desk at the two men seated before him, each wearing the distinct VISITOR badge that allowed the select few to get this far into the E Street Complex. He asked, "Are you making any progress?"

The taller of the two men whose breast pocket displayed the U.S. Marshal badge near the clipped on visitor pass spoke first, "Yes, sir. It's slow going, but we're onto something that I think will get you what you're looking for."

The actions the men reported on were not the usual duties of U.S. Marshals. But when General Donovan, OSS, asked for help from Attorney General Tom Clark, the quick response put them on the case. Defined as war-espionage, it fit their job description well.

Hyman thought as he listened, *There's always 'a way' to get things done in Washington,*

The shorter Marshal said, "We got hold of all the student rosters and fraternity stuff at Yale. By the

172

way, Mr. Pearson greasing the skids for us really made things happen quicker."

Hyman leaned back in his leather chair, lit his first Lucky Strike of the day, and reflected, "Always nice to have friends in the right place."

The short marshal continued, "Yes, sir, it is. We found a guy who remembered Harris. In fact he chummed around with him for a while. The guy said he never talked about family much, but thinks he mentioned that he lived in upstate New York."

The taller man interjected, "He thinks Canton County ... in the Belleayre Mountain area. He said they talked about skiing in the Catskills."

Hyman asked, "Does that give you enough to go on?"

The taller one answered, "Think so, Mr. Hyman. We had some business to finish up here in DC, but we took the time to run names in the region."

The shorter man tag-teamed with his partner, obviously pleased with their work, "We ran the name 'Harris' and found twelve in Canton County. They're scattered. Some in a place called Big Indian, some in Margaretville and some in Fleishmann." He looked over at his partner. "We'll head up there tomorrow and start knocking on doors."

Hyman rose from his desk chair and reached over to snuff the remains of his cigarette. "Well done, gentlemen. Let's lay this one to rest. Harris is either a problem ... or you guys get a nice week in the Catskills." Hyman walked around the desk and shook hands with the departing men. "Hell of a way to fight a war, eh?"

The U.S. marshals laughed and moved out into the outer office. Hyman closed his door. *Yes, one hell of a way to fight a war.*

CHAPTER 18

**Van Nuys Airport,
Van Nuys, California
Four Days Later**

Misshaped shadows flowed along the wall of the old aircraft hangar-turned-warehouse that backed up to Sophia Avenue. The last of the five intruders squeezed through the opening cut in the chain-link fence then spread out, moving in a low crouch with practiced stealth toward the building.

The only guards roved the nearby flight line in a jeep but would not be back on this part of the airfield for another hour.

They had planned well.

The leader approached the door on the side of the building, tried the latch and found it locked. Motioning to the man carrying a crowbar, he pointed to the latch and whispered, "*Silencio* (Quiet)."

With only a little effort the door flew inward and the leader ordered, "*Entrada, rapido* (Enter, quickly)!"

The five moved in a line and disappeared into the black opening. In a little time the group became accustom to the darkened interior of the building, and in a moment they were moving through the aisles of stacked crates, searching for the one marked R-Tac-OE-USAAC—Orion's Eye.

The leader said in a loud whisper, "*Esta aqui* (It's here) ... I found it. Bring the tool. We will check what is in the crate ... then we move it."

The others gathered around as the top of the 3' by 2' by 4' crate popped up under the lever. He shined a small shielded light into the crate. Satisfied, he said, "All is in order. *Vamanos* ... we go now."

A sudden brilliant light flooded the space, blinding the intruders.

A voice from the shadows ordered, "Freeze. Stand where you are! *Plantear sus manos*! Hands in the air. Pronto!"

The crowbar clanged on the cement floor, its owner bolting back up the aisle, nearly colliding with the uniformed policeman standing his ground in a three-point stance, his weapon held in both hands and pointed straight at the fleeing Mexican.

The policeman shouted, "*Detener, mi amigo*! (Stop, my friend) ... or you're history."

The man slid to a stop and dropped to his knees, hands on his head. The policeman looked beyond him to see other intruders in similar positions, handcuffs being applied.

The man in the tweed jacket, a shiny U.S. Marshal badge clipped over his breast pocket, said, "Good job, everyone. Anybody hurt?"

"Good here," came a reply.

Others answered, "Me, too."

The marshal gave a quiet order to the few who were not working with the prisoners, "Fan out and be sure there's nobody else. Shouldn't be, but let's not take a chance."

At that instant they heard the outer door slam open followed by a muffled command, "Halt. Drop the gun!"

POP—POP—POP, the sound of a small caliber handgun echoed back into the darkened building.

The marshal ordered, "Hold your positions! Secure these prisoners!"

He carefully made his way toward the door, maneuvering with practiced skill.

BOOM—BOOM—BOOM, the sound and the attendant flashes of a shotgun assaulted his eyes and ears.

A shout came from outside, "They're down. All clear out here!"

The marshal answered, "We're secure in here. I'm coming out!"

Three masked men lay on the rough concrete apron of the old hangar, a uniformed police officer shining his flashlight on the trio. One moving in pain, the other two lay still, as blood pooled darkly around them. A police medic already moved toward the wounded intruder.

The marshal called back into the building, "Bring them out. We're finished here."

At the same time, some thirty miles away in downtown Los Angeles in the basement of the Los Angeles Air Defense Wing Headquarters at Eighth and South Flower Streets, a similar scene played out—but with no gunfire. The Los Angeles Police Officers and United States Marshals had pulled off the sting operation and arrested four additional members of George Nicolaus' hired thieves.

Soldiers from the 35th Fighter Control Squadron, provided by General Nielsen, had set up the bait—a lightly guarded radar control room featuring Orion's Eye—or so the thieves thought.

A fifth man is arrested in the basement—a Uruguayan named Pedro Velasquez.

Preliminary interrogation found that Velasquez is not a staunch Nazi militant, just a weak but willing pawn in his wife's dangerous game of picking sides in a world struggle. He quickly gave information that led officers to a real estate office only a half mile from the Federal Building. Here the officers found a radio station and evidence that the lone occupant of the office, a German-American named Adolph Müeller, is *Jaeger*—the mole contact for the Nazi spy network led by Nicolaus from Mexico.

OSS Safe House
Los Angles, California

Chief Wetmore placed the phone in its cradle and turned to face the group in the dining room of the Spanish style pseudo-hacienda. A smile slowly grew across his face as he raised his arm and pumped his fist in a gesture of victory. "YES! That's the last of the bastards! YES!"

BJ said, "Not quite, Chief," as she pointed to the three people walking toward the house from the quarters in the rear of the hacienda. "One more coming."

Constantia Velasquez, head bowed and hands secured behind her, walked onto the patio between two U.S. marshals.

General David P. Barrows, Coordinator of Intelligence and Information for the OSS on the West Coast, turned to Chief Harmon Wetmore and Mrs.

Betty Jean Williamson, and said, "Well done, you two. Well done."

Extending his hand to Wetmore he added, "You called in a lot of chits to pull these resources together, Chief. Someday you've got to tell me what your base of considerable influence is."

Wetmore grasped his hand firmly and smiled. "Someday, yes sir, someday." Turning to the Marshals and their prisoner, he flipped a thumb toward the door and said, "She goes with the rest ... to the Federal Courthouse for arraignment."

With a firm hand on each of her elbows, Constantia is steered toward the large oaken front door being held open by a wryly smiling BJ.

Constantia stopped suddenly in the doorway, startling her escorts. She hissed at BJ, "*Perra* ... Bitch!"

Two large muscular U.S. marshals lifted Constantia Velasquez a few inches above the polished tile walk and moved toward the waiting car.

Standing up from where he'd been sitting and observing the events, Major General Manfield R. Nielsen, III, USAAC, walked over to Wetmore and extended his beefy hand. "Let me add my well done, Chief. Looks like you've made a clean sweep of it."

"Thanks, General. But it's not quite a clean sweep yet. We've still not found Otto Hauptmann ... or that military officer spy."

Nielsen answered, "Damnation. That's a fact!" Turning to the others, General Nielsen said, "General Barrows, sir, may I invite you and your aides to dinner? It's awkward, sir, but I must ask that we use your car and driver. I flew up from March Field and am at a loss for transportation at the moment."

General Barrows threw back his head in a genuine laugh and slapped a hand on Nielsen's shoulder. "That you can, my friend! Dinner's on you ... and then we'll get your flyboy shiny-hiny back to the airport ... and back to work!"

Barrows turned to BJ and the Chief. "Pardon my 'French' folks. I've known this old fart for too many years to give him any respect."

BJ closed the great door behind the laughing generals and two rather bewildered looking aides. "What now, Chief? Are Donny ... and Amos... going to be alright?"

Kilometer 4 Via San Roque
San Antonio del Mar,
Baja California, Mexico

Herr George Nicolaus stood with his fingers laced above his graying head and watched the Mexican Federales and American FBI and OSS officers search his beachfront home. There is nothing he can say—nothing he *will* say—to these people. Obviously the operation had gone terribly wrong. He wondered about Hauptmann. *What is he doing ... and where? Is Hauptmann going to find the secret of Orion's Eye? And worse, is he going to bring it to Himmler?*

Herr George Nicolaus, spy for the Third Reich, decided that he will have nothing to say. *At least in a Mexican prison I am alive,* he thought as they led him to the waiting car. *Going home to Germany I am a dead man.* There had been no time to send a radio message to Berlin, the raid swift and a complete surprise. *Better Goering finds out from someone else.*

The door closed on Herr Nicolaus.

The car sped away casting a pall of dust that glowed red in the setting Mexican sun.

USAT *Cape San Juan*
The Equator

Technical Sergeant Arthur Jeter stood at the rail looking over the ship's stern at the sea churning behind the ship. He enjoyed this break from the dank, crowded quarters he shared with the other colored troops from the 855th Engineers. Growing up in Pennsylvania is a far cry from what he saw from this vantage point high above the tropical waters.

At night, Jeter marveled at the light show of phosphorous phantoms that boiled up like light bulbs in the wake of the ship. During the day he watched flying fish skip from wave top to wave top in a ballet of escape from the predators below. The days passed all too slowly.

The routine is always the same—calisthenics in the morning, chow lines, salt water showers, one canteen of water a day—and a cold Coke. *Amazing,* he thought, *just how good an ice cold Coca Cola can be. Back home you take it for granted, but out here, hey, it's a special thing.* Every afternoon Arthur Jeter found a shady spot on deck and nursed that Coke as long as he could.

He always rose early in the morning to be one of the first in the chow line, having learned early on that the food at least looked better at the beginning of the line than at the end, and also noting the mess hall cleaner and the floor not so slippery. The best part, though, is after the meal when he has his quiet time at the rail.

Jeter heard, "Morning, Sarge."

He turned to see who had greeted him, then stood up straight and saluted.

Captain Edward Bonfoey said, "As you were, Sergeant. Nice up here this time of day, isn't it."

Jeter turned back to the rail, "That it is, Cap'n, that it is."

Leaning on the rail next to the sergeant, Bonfoey asked, "You ready for all the festivities this afternoon?"

"Don't rightly know what's going on, sir."

Bonfoey said, "Well, I guess crossing the Equator your first time is quite a big deal to the sailor-boys."

"So, we gotta play too … is that it, Cap'n?"

"Yup, that's it. My first time too … so I'm going to be learning same as you."

A familiar voice interrupted Bonfoey, "Good morning, gentlemen! He turned to see Gochais arriving for their morning meeting.

"Morning, Don. Oh, this is Sergeant," he glanced down at the name tape on the uniform, "Jeter."

Gochais nodded. "I think we've talked before. How are things, Sarge?"

The soldier answered, "Fine, sir. Be better on dry land, but fine for now."

"Good enough, Sarge. Come on, Ed, we got work to do." As the two officers walked back along the ship, Sergeant Jeter leaned back on the rail and stared out at the sea. He liked the quiet time in the morning.

Later that afternoon the grand seafaring tradition of Neptune Day broke the monotony of the voyage. All personnel who had never before crossed the Equator were assembled on deck and told in no uncertain terms that they were *Polliwogs*—and they must be initiated into King Neptune's realm to earn the exalted title of *Shellback*. From there things went downhill fast.

From the upper deck came a parade of wildly costumed creatures—King Neptune and his Royal Court descended to the deck forming two lines that obviously would become a gauntlet of abuse for the Polliwogs. Besides King Neptune, the Royal Court included Queen Minerva (the ugliest and hairiest chief on the ship), the Royal Chamberlain, the Royal Barber, the Royal Fish Bearers, and the Royal Guards—various crew members who looked a little too gleeful for the comfort of the men. From the bridge Captain Strong served as Master of Ceremonies.

As the soldiers, officers, and a few sailors, pressed forward, the Polliwog officers were singled out for special treatment. They were covered with a thick liquid substance, content unknown, but dead, rotten fish products a major part if one's nose spoke true.

Then came the hosing off of all the men on deck with salt water fire hoses, and finally, the selective kissing the Royal Fish followed by a dubbing as *Shellbacks* by the Royal Chamberlain. Some officers fared a little worse as the new Shellback soldiers were allowed to shave a furrow down the middle of their heads.

Donovan Gochais enjoyed the festivities from high on the bridge. He'd been there before, just a few months ago. Edward Bonfoey stood by his side. Gochais had pressed him into *extra duty* on the bridge, sparing him a dunking and a possible fancy haircut.

Gochais turned toward the radio shack and caught a glimpse of Lieutenant Harris stepping through the open hatch. *Guess he bugged out of being initiated ... Strange guy.*

 **CHAPTER 19**

**Belleayre Mountain Resort Area
Canton County, New York**

"More coffee, gentlemen?" The teenage waitress asked. "You guys visiting?"

The taller man chuckled. "You could say that. How about you, miss? You from around here?"

"All my life. Right here in Big Indian. But I'm leaving soon as I get enough money together." She snapped her gum with authority as she topped off his coffee, then turned to the shorter man and raised the coffee pot. "How about you, sir?"

Placing his hand on his cup, the shorter man answered, "No, thanks ... Say, miss, where's a nice place to get a room around here?"

"Catskill Inn's nice. Just down the block. Should be rooms this time of year."

The taller man said, "You've been right nice, young lady." He laid a bill on the meal check. "You just keep the change ... Help you move on sooner."

"Gee, thanks, mister."

They all laughed.

"Oh, one more thing. Do you know anybody name of Harris around here?"

"Harris? There's some down on River Road. An old couple. He used to drive the school bus."

"Thanks, miss. Good luck to you."

The two U.S. marshals rose from the chrome dinette table, picked up their overcoats and hats and walked toward the door. The tiny bell on a spring chimed their departure.

The day long drive from DC and a hot meal had them both ready for some sleep. They saw the Catskill Inn just beyond their parked the car. The taller man said, "We'll start door knocking in the morning."

The fall colors were waning, but still spectacular enough to provide a pleasant diversion between stops.

Harris family after Harris family, from Big Indian to Margaretville had produced many cups of coffee and more than a few blueberry muffins, but no Graham in the family tree.

As they passed the sign announcing, YOU ARE LEAVING MARGARETVILLE, the tall man quipped, "Friendly folks up here."

The short man looked out at the passing woods, and answered, "Sure are. Must be blueberry season. Beats pounding pavement in DC"

A carefully carved and freshly painted slab of wood confirmed the next stop: WELCOME TO FLEISHMANN.

Checking their list and map the two marshals pulled up to a neat rustic cottage that had seen many seasons but spoke of loving care. They walked up to the gate and saw a man in a plaid shirt and worn straw hat pruning spent flowers from a bush.

He turned. "Can I help you fellas?"

"Are you Mr. Harris?"

"I am."

"U.S. marshals. May we come in and talk with you?" I.D.'s shown and handshakes shared all around produced an invitation into the parlor—and a cup of coffee. But this time, no muffins.

In response to the opening question, the man said, "Yeah, we got a Graham in the family." He ran his fingers through tousled graying hair. "But I ain't laid eyes on him since he be a mere babe. He's my little sister's boy. Family had a fallin' out … you know how that is. She married a fellow t'was new to these parts. Nobody liked him much, least not in the family. They moved away. Downstate. She visited one day, brought the little guy with her. Just stayed a few days. Haven't seen her since. Still a lot of hard feelin's, especially among the women folk … you know how that is."

The taller marshal asked, "Have you heard from her at all?"

"Been a lotta years. Got a Christmas Card. Funny thing … y'know how you toss things like that in a drawer? Well I found the doggone thing in this here drawer just the other day."

The man stood and walked over to a sideboard laden with rows of family pictures and a tall cut glass vase cradling a plastic rose. He pulled open a drawer. "Yup, here 'tis. Guess I kept it 'cause I been wonderin' what had become of her … my sister."

He handed the envelope to the taller marshal, who looked at the return address, then handed it to the shorter man.

They exchanged glances.

The return address, precisely written in a fine female hand read, *Mr. and Mrs. Heinrich Hauptmann.*

Federal Building
Los Angeles, California

Wetmore sat staring at the familiar massive face of the fifty ton monster dubbed SIGSALY. He'd asked the signals sergeant where the name came from and learned that it's 'just made up.' The forty racks of electronic equipment spread out on both sides of their seats as the sergeant tried to explain how *pulse code modulation* worked. Wetmore could only nod and be thankful that all he had to do is talk into the machine that hid his voice from the enemy.

The call to Australia synched up on the two turntables—which Wetmore didn't understand either—and Amos Mead came on the line. "What have you got for me, Harmon? Sounds urgent."

"Good news and bad, Major."

"How about the bad first, Chief. Save the rest for dessert."

"Okay. Bad news is we still haven't found Otto Hauptmann ... or our military officer spy."

"So, no change there, Chief. So gimme the good news?"

"Good news is we've cleaned up the rest of the Nazi gang that's been lookin' to steal our prize ... the Herman Goering side of the family it seems. And you've got your old childhood sweetheart to thank for it."

"What the devil does that mean, Chief?"

"It means, Major sir, that BJ uncovered things and hatched a plan to lure 'em in for the kill. The short version is she heard things coming from the Velasquez quarters, investigated and found a small radio transmitter. She didn't let on to Constantia what she found ... or suspected."

186

Mead asked, "And she reports this stuff to you?"

"More than that, Major. She went operational on me. She comes to me with an official looking message all typed out and tells me we need to let it be lying around on the table with other work for Constantia to see. BJ figured if she's a bad guy something would happen … if not, well, no foul."

"You're telling me that BJ's playing spy catcher? Is that a good thing?"

"Didn't think so at first, Major, but it sure as shootin' turned out to be. See, what she wrote in this phony message said that Orion's Eye being on the *Cape San Juan* is just a ruse to get the Nazi's off the trail. And that the radar stuff is really set up in the basement of 8th and South Flower … and still being used. Then she adds that another Orion's Eye unit is in a warehouse at Van Nuys Airport waiting to be flown to the South Pacific."

Mead said, "I can see how that would get their juices flowing … but I'm still not sure about BJ's getting involved."

"That's what I thought at first … so I dove in and talked with our senior players. General Barrows got on board and General Nielsen's happy as a pig-in-shit to play. Hyman said we should use the U.S. Marshals … not the FBI … and he got that arranged with Attorney General Clark. Said Clark loves to tweak J. Edgar's nose from time to time."

"Good God, Harmon, did you call in President Roosevelt?"

"Naw, that'd be showin' off, Major. Anyway we set it all up and Constantia bit on it. BJ heard the radio transmission. It went to another station called *Jaeger* … from there we didn't know. Thought we might have

Hauptmann on the other end ... least wise we hoped so."

"So the sting went down. You already told me no Hauptmann ... so who'd you net?"

"Mostly we snagged a bunch of Mexican Nazi sympathizers. They call themselves *Sinarquistas*, or something like that. But here's the best part. We nabbed Pedro Velasquez in the Flower Street hit ... and he led us to the Real Estate guy that rented us the house! Don't that beat all? This guy squealed like a stuck hog. Turns out he's *Jaeger* ... and his boss is Herr George Nicolaus. The OSS and the Mexican Federal police swept him up. Oh, yeah, we also let the FBI play with us in Mexico ... and got a lot of good Intel from his Mexican *palacio*. He's locked up in a Mexican jail for the duration. Says he's not interested in going back to the Fatherland 'cause Goering will be really pissed at him ... and that's usually fatal."

"I'd say, Mr. Wetmore, that you, and BJ had a good day's work. Anything else of your exploits to report?"

"That's it, Major. I'll be back when there's more."

"Thanks, Harmon. And, uh, give BJ a hug for me." As Wetmore stood to leave the radio room a clerk waved him down. "Hey, Chief, while you were chatting on the Big Sag you got a clear call from a guy name of Hyman ... in DC. Says he's sent you a report on the Harris investigation. Give me a minute and I'll get it for you."

Wetmore answered, "Thanks, I'll wait."

A few minutes later he took the folder marked SECRET, a red stripe running diagonally across the manila cover, opened it and flipped back to the last page thinking, *what's the bottom line?* "Holy shit!"

Pacific Ocean
22°15' South Latitude-176°18' West Longitude
German Submarine *U-835*

Only the sail—the superstructure of the German U-Boat—rose above the calm sea.

The waning moon laid a silver line across the blue black water and stars crowded the sky, the Southern Cross preeminent among them. Tonight they were not needed for navigation as the destination of *U-835* loomed into sight, rising as a dark mass above the sea.

Lookouts were posted.

Kalbruener and Hauptmann stood on the bridge. Kalbruener spoke first, "These shallow waters worry me, Herr Hauptmann. You can see the waves break on the atoll between us and the island. What is in your plan for hiding my boat?"

"The whaleboats will be hidden by the island, *Herr Kapitän*. Your U-boat will be there," Hauptmann pointed to the south, "in the deep water by day ... periscope depth at night."

"What of the island? Are there people there?"

"My last information is that the fisherman, I think about seven or eight, left the island when the Japanese began pushing this way. We shall come up and launch the small boat for a reconnaissance around the island. Have the boat party look for lights and check out any piers and such for recent use— with your permission, of course *Herr Kapitän*."

"Good idea, Hauptmann. I do not intend to be sent to my grave in these waters. We are too close to American airfields to be reported by some native eager for a reward."

After the *Kapitän* called the orders below to fully surface his submarine and launch the small boat, Hauptmann said, "I suggest, *Kapitän*, that we also launch the whaleboats and crews. We can hold them here until the shore party returns. That will save time. We must be submerged before dawn."

"I would have been submerged before dawn ... even if you were still on my bridge, Herr Hauptmann."

Kapitän Kalbruener passed the order below.

U.S. Ship: *Ocean Lighter OL-31*
Townsville, Australia

Mead sat at the familiar encrypted telephone system built into the ship.

It had been only an hour since the last call and had he not stopped in the ship's wardroom for coffee he would have missed this new one.

He doodled around the few notes he took as he listened to Chief Wetmore from Los Angeles. "So that's it, Major. They told me that she seemed relieved when the marshals identified themselves, like she knew the government would catch up to her someday. She said it never was a good marriage. Broke up her family. After Hauptmann got into all the trouble over his activism with the *Ausland Institute* ... the Nazi Party ... in the '30's she'd had enough. So Hauptmann took off back to Germany. She stayed here, but never went back home. She just took her maiden name back and raised their son by herself."

"Interesting, Chief. What about the boy? Is he our Lieutenant Graham?"

"We think he is. The boy took his mother's name ... Harris ... when he went to college. She said he took a trip to Germany after his senior year in high school.

190

Heinrich had sent the money. In college, and after she thinks, he made more trips. She didn't know how many."

"So he's back with his father. That fits your report on Heinrich ... the visits of the American son —"

Interrupting Mead, Wetmore added, "Yes, sir. But it gets deeper. Mrs. Harris said after her son graduated from Yale Law he came home and proceeded to erase every record of his name as Hauptmann ... all the way back to kindergarten. Even his church. He knew the legal ways to do it. She didn't mind. In fact it pleased her."

"Okay, Chief. So far nothing illegal."

"Last nail in the coffin, Major. A month before Pearl Harbor Graham joined the Naval Reserve as an officer. I've sent you a picture of him. Don't know how you'll get it out to Gochais to see if he's our boy, though."

"It all fits, Chief. I think we've found our military officer spy?"

"Sure as God made little green apples, Major ... our boy is on the *Cape San Juan*. Even so, for the life of me I can't figure out what the hell he can do to get Orion's Eye. I mean, he could destroy it or something like that ... but that doesn't get it for the Krauts."

"Haven't got an answer for you, Chief. But he sure as the devil isn't on a pleasure cruise. Thanks for your good work, partner. I'm going over to Suva and see if I can get a ride out to the ship."

As the machine disconnected, Mead thought, *Long shot ... but there's not much else to accomplish sitting here. The action is at sea.*

 # CHAPTER 20

USAT *Cape San Juan*
Underway – At Sea Pacific Ocean
South of Aitutaki Island
Late Afternoon

The ceremony with King Neptune had been a welcome break in the daily routine, at least for many of the soldiers aboard. For most, though, any sight of land, especially land they may put their feet on, would be the most welcomed and cheered event.

For the few 'blue-water' sailors—like Gochais—being at sea is where the magic is. Gochais had almost convinced Bonfoey—Almost.

The sea that moved along the ship at 14 knots gleamed cobalt blue, now and then blended with inky green. The two men stood side by side looking down from the teak railed bridge. The passing sea produced a near hypnotic trance on both.

Bonfoey said, "Times like this it's hard to believe we're going to war."

"I never tire of it, Ed ... being at sea. Something about it—" Gochais didn't finish his thought, just gestured with a sweep of his arm. The slow rolls of the ship tugged on their sense of balance. For people new to the sea, like Edward Bonfoey, trying to counter the feeling produced a palpable sap of energy by days end. But, once it's accepted as part of his reality it no longer has that effect. Bonfoey's almost there.

Gochais chuckled. "We'll be on this course until late tomorrow, then it's back toward the northwest and up to Townsville. By the time you get your sea legs you'll be diggin' fox holes."

Bonfoey shrugged his shoulders. "Doesn't look like anything's going to happen here. Might as well get on with the war."

Gochais heard his name called and turned to see Ted Makowski coming around from the radio shack. "Mr. Gochais ... been looking for you. You said to keep an eye out for any message that had those words ... you know, ark or sailor.'"

"Sure did, Petty Officer, what've you got?"

Makowski handed a piece of paper to Gochais and said, "Here, sir. Sounded like it came out of Suva ... but there weren't no call signs or nothing."

"Okay, Ted. Thanks."

Gochais unfolded the message form and read:

```
Message to:
Sailor guarding constellation. Stop
Spook definitely on ark. Stop.
Arnold not in sight. Stop.
Have ID on spook. Stop.
Will get out to you when possible. Stop.
(signed) Boss
```

Gochais looked at Makowski. "Anybody else see this, Ted?"

"No sir. Just me."

"We'll keep it that way, Petty Officer Makowski. No logs or anything. Understand?"

"Aye, aye, sir. That's no problem. Wasn't sent to us anyway. Just out there in the air for anybody to pick up."

"Good work, Ted. Keep an eye out for any more. Is Corporal McIntire in on looking for the words?"

"Aye, sir, he is. I'll tell him mum's the word." Makowski turned and headed back to the radio shack.

Bonfoey asked, "What's that all about, Don?"

"Love letter from home, Ed." Gochais looked around, then quietly added, "They've identified our spy and confirmed he's on board. But they can't tell me who it is yet ... 'cause we don't have a goddam code word for the name."

Bonfoey slowly shook his head. "Well shit ... that's nice to know."

German *U-835*
Ata Island

Leutnant Hans Schultz climbed the steep ladder up the side of the sail and joined Kalbruener and Hauptmann on the conning tower bridge. He saluted and reported, "We find no signs of recent activity on the island, *Herr Kapitän.*"

Hauptmann answered first, "Good work, *Leutnant.* Have your men secure the boats to the deck. You and the Chief *Bootsmannmaat* (bosuns mate) from each whaleboat join us in the wardroom at once."

Leutnant Schultz looked first at *Kapitän* Kalbruener, who gave a small nod of his head, and then back at Hauptmann. "Yes, sir." He turned and leaned out over the rail, cupped his hands to his mouth and gave the order, "*Chef Bootsmannmaats. Sicherung der Bootes und Ein Treffen mit mir in der Offiziersmesse. Schnell* (Chief Bosunsmates. Secure the boats and meet with me in the wardroom. Quickly)!

Hauptmann said, "Very good, *Leutnant.* Now let us go below."

The wardroom, crowded, damp and hot, smelled of the many long days at sea. Sweat beaded on every face that watched Otto Hauptmann enter from the passageway followed by the *Kapitän.*

Hauptmann began, "Gentlemen, it is time. Within three days an American ship will pass by this island. She carries over a thousand American *soldaten* (soldiers) and their equipment. We do not want a fight with the soldiers. What we want is in the hold of the ship. They carry a new tactical radar that the *Führer* wants very badly. So badly that we have been sent to get it for him."

An officer asked, "Sir, excuse me, but a radar unit is heavy and large. How can we—?"

Hauptmann interrupted, "Not this one. The Americans have put the power of our best units into less than one square meter. In fact, they have put *more* power than we have into this small package." Looking around at their faces, he continued, "Gentlemen, you have not been home for a long time. The Americans and British are exacting a terrible toll on Germany. They are bombing our homes by day and by night. They have long range fighter escorts for the bombers. The Luftwaffe is losing many good men. Our radar cannot give them the support they need to attack first and hardest."

Every man in the cramped space stared intently at Hauptmann as he continued to speak in measured tones, "The cargo on the ship does exactly what we need. It can guide our Messerschmitt 109 to the tail of an American P-51 Mustang in the dark of night so quickly that the American pilot would know only a moment of terror as the tail is shot away from his airplane. The Americans know this radar by a code name: *Auge Orions*. The star constellation Orion has always been known as the hunter. The *hunter's eye* is a poetic, but accurate, name for this device. Gentlemen, with your success in two days it will be the *eye of our hunters.*"

Otto Hauptmann looked at the chronometer on the bulkhead and turned to *Kapitän* Kalbruener. "*Herr Kapitän*, we have three hours before dawn. We must provision and launch the whaleboats in two hours. Each boat will have food and water for two days, also full fuel and at least three rounds of ammunition for the heavy gun. Be sure the high intensity lights are in perfect order. The crews will dress in their *u-boot-päckchen* battledress. I will go in *Leutnant* Schultz's boat and we will tow the launch with us. Any questions?"

No one spoke.

"One more thing. I will need the suitcase radio with me, *Herr Kapitän*. We captured it from an American OSS agent in France and it has the frequencies we need."

Kalbruener shrugged in resignation.

Hauptmann continued, "When we are on the island I will brief the boarding party and instruct you all on the final assault. You are dismissed to prepare your boats. We cast off in one hour and fifty five minutes."

He stepped aside as the officers and bosun mates trailed out of the space. After it had cleared, the submarine *Kapitän* said, "What of my boat, Herr Hauptmann?"

"You will stay at periscope depth and watch. We will signal from the shore. When we begin our attack you will watch. When the American ship stops you will surface and light your sail for five minutes. I want them to see the fine insignia on your side."

"The ship will be at full speed and the night is moonless. How do you plan to chase—"

"If all goes well, *Herr Kapitän*, we will know of the ship's approach before we see her ... or she sees us."

"So you have secret radar for that trick also?"

"No secret radar ... but I do have someone on the ship who will be sending a signal.

 **CHAPTER 21**

Suva City
Viti Levu
Fiji Islands, South Pacific

As the Army C-47 aircraft circled to land on Viti Levu, Mead marveled at the beauty of the island.

With clearances received from traffic control the military transport lined up on final approach and descended smoothly to the threshold of the blacktopped runway. Touching down at the Allied Air Base brought him back to reality. The palm trees and blue sky were just a backdrop for machines and men of war.

Mead grabbed his kit-bag and walked over to the Operations building. He asked the duty sergeant, "Where can I catch a ride to Suva Harbor?"

"Check outside, Major. You can thumb with somebody headed into town ... or you can get brave and grab one of those motorbike jitneys."

Mead said with a wave, "Thank you kindly."

He stepped outside and looked around. *Hell, when in Rome ...* He opted for a jitney.

Suva City is the capitol of the Fiji Islands. Located on the easterly, rainy side of the main island of Viti Levu, it has been a Major commerce and shipping center of the South Pacific since the 1880's. Now it is a Major shipping center for the trappings of war.

Although more than a little rough, Mead enjoyed the open air ride into the city. They rode down Victoria Parade, dodging jeeps and pedestrians, to Albert Park. He marveled at the impressive weathered stone buildings of the Parliament and its soaring stone clock tower. *Looks downright civilized,* he thought—just as a pothole jarred him back to hanging on for his life. The next turn took him past Thurston Gardens and the impressive white-washed colonial buildings of the Fijian President's residence.

The jitney slowed and the driver pointed toward the gate. Just beyond, Mead saw a changing of the guard ceremony in progress with sulu-clad soldiers drilling as sharply as any unit he'd seen before.

Pomp and circumstance—even in war.

Another turn took them down Cumming Street, a narrow pillar-lined street of shops and what appeared to be taverns. *Where there's GI's there's taverns,* he thought as the jitney's brakes began to complain of a too fast stop behind a queue of vehicles entering the guarded gate to Suva Harbor. When their turn at the guard gate came, the jitney driver showed his ID and the guard saluted Mead as he checked his military card.

Mead returned the formality and asked, "Which way to the Pan Am docks, Sergeant?"

"Your driver knows where it is, Major. It's not far."

With a neck-stiffening jerk, a pop-pop noise and a puff of blue smoke, the jitney proceeded into the base—its driver nodding assent that he knew just where to go. Mead hung on tight.

Inside the combined Pan Am and US Navy Operations building a fan kept the air moving over a hubbub of activity. Pilots got weather briefings, clerks shuffled manifests, and passengers lounged in a variety of rest-seeking positions wherever they could find room. The only breath of air wafted through the louvered glass windows that faced the ramps leading down into the harbor.

Mead could see two of the great flying boats at their moorings, a four engine Consolidated PB2Y Coronado like the one that had brought him to Townsville, and a twin engine Martin Mariner. They each wore the large white star in a dark blue circle field—and, of course, the Stars and Stripes.

He thought, *Hard to believe those things can fly.*

He waited his turn behind some Pan Am pilots to see the Operations Officer on duty. Mead offered his ID card—this time using his OSS identification. "I need to see your commanding officer, Lieutenant."

"Yes, sir. I'll call him."

The officer took the card. He dialed while he scanned the card with its blue band, the wings-spread eagle and *Strategic Services – OSS* emblazoned at the top.

He spoke, then hung up the phone and pointed to his right. "Up those stairs, sir. Third door on your left." With one last look, he handed Mead his card.

Mead rapped once on the door jamb and stepped into the office. A Navy commander stood behind his desk and extended his hand. "What can we do for the OSS today, Major?"

"I need one of your airplanes, Commander. Preferably one that can land on water."

USAT *Cape San Juan*
Underway – At Sea
Southwest of Aitutaki Island

"May I join you gentlemen?"

Gochais felt a brief jolt up his spine at the sound. Still leaning on the rail he turned his head toward the approaching officer and recognized Lieutenant Graham Harris, USNR. "Sure, Harris. You know Captain Bonfoey?"

"Haven't had the pleasure." He offered his hand and said, "I'm Graham Harris, Captain."

Bonfoey said, "Make it Ed," shook the offered hand and turned back to the rail.

Gochais used the polite banter as a cover to slip the folded piece of paper received a moment before from Petty Officer Makowski into his pocket.

Harris asked, "First deployment, Ed?"

Bonfoey replied, "Yup ... the outfit's been training up. This is our first time out."

"Which is your outfit?"

"I'm CO of the 1st Fighter Control Squadron."

Harris nodded. "I saw that designator. What do you guys do exactly?"

Gochais listened to the exchange, wondering why the sudden buddy-buddy stuff from Harris. *This guy knows about the 1st Fighters. But he doesn't seem to know about me or Bonfoey ... or does he?*

Answering Harris, Bonfoey said, "We use radar to vector fighters in on the bad guys. These kids can run a P-40 up a Zero's ass before he knows we're in the neighborhood."

He purposely exaggerated the image.

Harris said, "Wow, hadn't heard that stuff before!"

Bonfoey responded, "Well, you're gonna hear about it pretty soon ... and so are the Japs,"

Harris nodded and leaned on the rail. For a moment no one spoke as they looked out at the passing sea. Then Harris asked quietly, "They got that stuff in Europe yet?"

The answer hung, delayed for a long moment until Bonfoey said, "That's way above my pay grade, Lieutenant." Glancing at Gochais, Bonfoey signaled the end of conversation.

Gochais caught the meaning and said, "Gotta be dinner time somewhere."

The three officers headed for the wardroom. Bonfoey and Gochais exchanged a knowing glance, but all they knew is that they didn't know anything.

Later that night, Bonfoey found sleep avoiding him. The officers' quarters are not palatial, though certainly not the cramped canvas stacks of the enlisted soldiers. But tonight it wasn't the quarters that stole his sleep, as his mind refused to let go of the puzzling possibilities waiting in the near future. *What the hell am I doing here*, echoed in his head. *I've got a job to do ... but there's really nothing to do. Bad guy on the ship ... maybe, maybe not.*

He rolled over looking for a cool spot on the damp pillow, not to be found. *What the hell am I doing here?*

After a moment he rolled out of his bunk, sliding quietly to the deck, and slipped into his fatigue trousers, half way lacing on his boots.

In the dim red glow of the after-dark lighting he shuffled toward the ladderway that led down into the #3 Hold beneath their quarters. Not sure why, he felt like going down to where Orion's Eye lay stored and see that all is well. *At least it's something to do until I can find some sleep.*

Step by careful step he descended into the cavernous hold. The widely spaced mesh-covered red lanterns barely touched each other's glow. Shadows ruled the night. The heart of the ship throbbed with an incessant rhythm. Sometimes he couldn't hear it so much as sense its power coursing through every muscle fiber. It enveloped Bonfoey as he reached the level where the three crates awaited. His mind isn't focused and that's a relief as it helped to rid him of the racing thoughts.

A sound.

Cough.

He froze, instantly alert, listening, he crept forward.

Cough.

To the left—close. Seems to come from the small space between the stacks of crates—near Orion's Eye.

Adrenalin flooded his veins. Every sound, every whiff of breath in the salty moist air, became acute.

Cough.

At the opening in the wall of crates he peered around the corner, exposing as little of his head as possible. He saw a leg, bent at the knee.

Cough.

The leg straightened, the other appeared crossing the first at the ankle. Bonfoey slowly reached down to his right hip.

Nothing. Damn.

He had not strapped on his weapon.

Back away? confront? His thoughts challenged him for only an instant. *No more thinking. Now!* He swung around the corner kicking the extended feet, "Freeze!"

A high-pitched voice bounded from the dark recess of the other end of the small space. "Shit ...

What? What ... what's the matter? .... What'a you want?"

The feet recoiled but did not move to stand.

Bonfoey hissed his command, "Put your hands out toward me. Stand up real slow and move this way. Real slow, mister."

"Yuh ... yuh ... yes, sir."

The face of a confused and frightened Corporal Manny McIntire materialized in the red glow. Bonfoey said, "What the hell are you doing down here, Corporal?"

He saw how McIntire looked him up and down—*looking for my weapon?* Then saw the look on McIntire's face harden. Bonfoey tensed and mentally prepared for—*for what?* He didn't know what.

McIntire spoke, but his face remained a blank, "Sleep better down here, sir. Doesn't roll so much this deep in the ship. Not like up in the radio shack."

Bonfoey stayed on guard. "Why right here? This spot?"

McIntire looked around then back to fix his eyes on Bonfoey. "Oh, you mean by Orion's Eye?" He patted the nearest crate stenciled with *R-Tac-OE-USAAC*. "He's an old friend, sir. I worked on him at Monmouth."

A faint smile crossed his lips as he turned and looked at the crate. Bonfoey eased back away and checked his balance, still not sure if there might be anything more. He said to McIntire's back, "We'd better head back topside, soldier."

McIntire turned very slowly to face Bonfoey. He looked down and tied the strings on his life vest, one at a time. "Okay, sir." He fixed his blank stare into the half-light and gently pushed past Bonfoey, moving for the ladderway.

Bonfoey stood fast, his heart still swishing in his ears. *What the hell is that all about?*

Sicherheitsdienst (SD) Headquarters
Berlin, Germany

Heinrich Himmler sat behind his ornate oversized desk, perched on the edge of the high-backed leather chair as he read the report.

Artur Nebe, Chief of the German Intelligence Service (SD), sat across from him, his hands clenched in his lap, staring at Himmler's face, searching for a reaction. It came slowly as Himmler began to smile, and then to laugh out loud. The laugh turned to almost giggles as Himmler sat back into the chair and removed his round spectacles, rubbing his eyes.

Nebe sat back and allowed himself to smile.

Between chuckles Himmler blurted out, "So the little *hurensohn* (son of a bitch) Nicolaus screwed himself! And he will take that *fett schweine* (fat pig) Goering down with him."

Nebe's own smile turned to a nervous laugh. But Himmler cut him off with a sudden silent stare. "Before you get too gay, Herr Nebe, tell me where Otto Hauptmann is!"

Nebe cowered, "I, I, we, that is—"

"If he ... and that means *you* ... fail in this mission," Himmler stood, leaning on clenched fists. "I promise that it will be your last failure."

Nebe leaped to his feet and stood at stiff attention. "*Ja mein Reichsführer, I verstehen.* I understand completely. The last we heard he is at sea on the U-boat that you authorized through Admiral Dönitz. He seems to have a plan, *mein Reichsführer.*"

"It will be a *winning* plan, Herr Nebe, you will see to it."

"*Ya, mein Reichsführer.*"

With a stiff-arm salute, "*Heil Hitler,*" Nebe turned and strode from the office.

OSS Safe House
Los Angeles, California

Wetmore sat at the table nursing a Chivas over ice while the new maid cleared the last of the dinner dishes. The three other men, Marines all, sipped coffee. Wetmore asked, "Nobody up for a sip of this nectar?"

Two nods and one reply, "Not tonight, Chief. We've got an O'dark thirty wake up ... as you well know. Catalina beckons."

"Oh, that's right ... school boys you are." Wetmore chuckled and looked across the large oak table at BJ who sat shaking her head slowly and smiling back at him.

Tonight she looked especially fetching with her blond hair curled and swept back on one side ala Veronica Lake. All the OSS guys, Marines or not, who came through here enjoyed the view—but no one dared get out of line.

Grizzled old and wise Chief Harmon Wetmore, USN, saw to that.

BJ heard the loud *thunk, thunk* of the heavy iron door knocker. No one else seemed to, so she rose and walked toward the door, all eyes following her every move. She opened the door a crack, and then wide.

On the broad stone step a pretty young woman, barely 5' tall stood looking straight at BJ.

Wearing a flowered dress and a cardigan sweater, she held the hand of a small toe-headed boy, maybe two years old, by her side. The young woman looked into BJ's eyes then slowly looked down without a word. BJ saw a look on her face that reflected either sadness or seeing a ghost.

BJ asked, "May I help you?"

Then she looked beyond the woman to the green Chevrolet coupe parked at the curb. An older man sat at the wheel, looking intently at the house.

Slowly looking up at BJ the woman answered, "May I please speak to Donny Gochais?"

 **CHAPTER 22**

Suva City
Viti Levu,
Fiji Islands, South Pacific

The Navy commander looked incredulously at the sheet of paper that Mead handed him as he asked for the aircraft, the signature at the bottom not to be denied, *... all assistance ... anything requested.* He mumbled, "Looks like you've got the key to the candy store, Major."

"Too bad I don't like sweets, Commander. Do I get one of those, sir?" Mead pointed out the louvered window at the flying boats.

The commander turned his chair to look out the window. "Afraid not, Major. The Coronado is headed to Sydney on a priority run for MacArthur. She'll be pushing off any second now. And the Mariner is red tagged for repairs."

Mead crossed his arms, sat back in his chair and started to speak, but the commander spoke first, "Honestly, Major, I hate to divert any of the ships coming through here with troops headed over to New Guinea. You can understand that, I'm sure. But

208

there's a Mariner due in the day after tomorrow that will be unloading cargo completely. I can divert it to your use. Will that work?"

Damn, I don't know how much time I have. "It'll have to work."

The commander looked up at the large chronometer on the bookcase behind Mead and said, "Okay then, Major, we'll get you a room in the pilots' quarters. But for now ... the sun must be over the yardarm somewhere. Let's walk over to the Marlin Bar and find a cool one of something."

Mead stood and picked up his khaki fore-and-aft cover with the silver oak leaf, and resigned himself to the delay. "After you, Commander."

The Marlin Bar could have been on any island in the Pacific. The rattan chairs squeaked with every shift of attention—like up to the blowfish lamps, the carved tiki posts that held up a rattan mat ceiling, or the almost pretty, but definitely female, *wahines* balancing trays of cold beer and avoiding the occasional gropes.

"So Major, just how far out to sea do you wish to fly our Mariner?"

"How far I don't know for sure, Commander. I need to find a ship that's en route to Townsville. Best I can calculate she'd be no more than four-hundred miles out from here by day after tomorrow."

"And just what are you going to do with this ship when you find her?"

Mead took a double swig of his beer. "Frankly, Commander ... I don't have a clue."

OSS Safe House
Los Angeles, California

For a moment BJ stared, mesmerized by the woman's intense gaze. "He's not here, Mrs. ..." she glanced down at the baby boy.

The lady spoke up, "... Gochais. Elma Gochais."

BJ stepped back and pointed the way into the living room. "Come in, please, Elma."

Wetmore walked into the room with a quizzical look on his face. He said, "Can we help you?"

BJ cut in, "This is Elma Gochais, Chief. Donny's wife ... and is this little Tommy?"

Elma corrected her, "No, ma'am, this is Bobby."

BJ tried to keep it on track, "I'm sorry, Tommy's in the hospital, right? How's he doing?"

Elma Gochais pleaded, "How do you know all this? And where is my husband?"

BJ turned to Wetmore for help. The chief said, "Sit down, please, Mrs. Gochais."

BJ reached down toward Bobby. "May I?"

Sitting on the edge of the leather sofa, Elma looked up and nodded assent. Wetmore took the chair across from Elma Gochais and asked, "How do you know about this house ... and why do you think your husband might be here, Mrs. Gochais?"

"Donny gave me an envelope before he left. He said to open it only if something happened to him. I didn't like that kind of talk, but we tell each other everything and I respected his request." She sat with her hands clasped in her lap, looking carefully at her fingers. "Yesterday Mrs. Dorcey ... her husband is an officer with Donny ... came over to visit. She asked me why Donny had missed the two week coastal sailing of his ship."

Wetmore put his head down and rubbed the stubble on his chin. "Uh, oh. I see the problem."

Elma Gochais replied through clenched teeth, "Well then maybe you can tell *me* what the problem is!" She glanced over at BJ, then back down at her hands regaining her composure. "I was frantic. I didn't know where to turn. I remembered the envelope ... and I opened it. Inside, well ... this address. My father drove me here. He's waiting outside. You seem to know Donny and a lot about me and my boys." Her tension rising again, she asked, "So what is going on here?"

Wetmore responded calmly, "Would you like to invite your father in, ma'am? This may take a minute."

A half hour later Elma Gochais and her family left the Wilshire Avenue house with a mixture of relief and fear of what may be happening in the Pacific. She also had the second OSS payment of $500 in her purse—a blessing that would have to last until Lieutenant Donovan I. Gochais returned home.

USAT *Cape San Juan*
At Sea - Well South of the Cook Islands
Next Day

Gochais listened to Bonfoey's account of the night's encounter in the #3 Hold with growing frustration. "Corporal McIntire? That's bizarre. What's your gut feeling, Ed? Could he be the military spy? Is it possible they're mistaken about the officer bit?"

Bonfoey answered, "Gut feeling? I flat don't know. He scared the shit outa me for a minute though. Weird ... like he had to get a story together real quick."

"We'll just have to keep an eye on him, Ed."

"Sure, keep an eye on him ... like we're keeping an eye on Harris and the gunnery officer with the kraut name ... yeah, and Rhinehart Meuller ... and every other swinging dick on this boat."

Bonfoey leaned on the rail clenching and unclenching his fists.

Gochais chided, "Frustrated, little brother? Look, Meuller's okay, best we can tell. Harris and McIntire ... lotta weird stuff for sure, but nothin' solid. Everybody else? Who in hell knows."

Ed Bonfoey, noticeably more relaxed, said, "Okay. So it's wait and watch."

"Mr. Gochais." Petty Officer Ted Makowski walked up to the two officers. "Sorry to interrupt, sir. May I have a word with you?" He looked straight at Gochais, ignoring Bonfoey.

Gochais glanced at Bonfoey, then back at Makowski and said, "Speak freely, Makowski." Nodding his head toward Bonfoey, he added, "It's okay."

"Aye, Sir. You asked me to let you know if anything strange happened with the radio."

"I did ... and?"

"Well, sir, I tried fiddling with the new HF unit ... you know, listening to see if anybody might be transmitting on it and stuff like that, and I heard something on 30 Megacycles ... that's the high end ... dit da, da da da, dit dit dit da da."

Gochais asked, "And that is?"

Bonfoey spoke up, "That says A – O – 3."

"That's it, sir, A-O-3. That's two days ago. I listened, expecting more, but that's all, A-O-3. I didn't think anything of it ... until yesterday I heard dit da ..."

"Okay, A-O again?"

"Yes, sir. A-O ... and then dit dit, da da da. 2. So this time it's A-O-2."

Gochais asked, "What the hell do you—?"

Makowski interrupted, "There's more, Mr. Gochais. After that second one I started scanning regular. Just a few minutes ago here it comes again."

Bonfoey asked, "A-O?"

"Yes sir, and then, dit, da da da da — 1 ... A-O-1."

Gochais probed, "That's a count-down of some sort. Any identification ... where it came from?"

"Negative, sir. But it's plenty strong. I'd say close by. But there ain't *nothin'* close by."

Federal Building
Los Angeles, California

Wetmore sat down at the SIGSALY console to take Chandler Morse's call from London. He asked, "Hello, my friend, how are things in jolly old England?"

"Fine as can be, Mr. Wetmore. I'm calling to tell you that things have gone dead quiet with our friends on *Prinz Albrecht-Straße* . Himmler hasn't shown up for a couple of days ... at least not with *Auges Orion* in the script. Analysts at Bletchley Park seem to think it's either because they've got what they want ... or they've given up on it."

"Could be a third option, Chandler. Could be they're executing a capture plan as we speak. Keepin' it operationally hush hush."

"Good point, Harmon. That would put Gochais and Mead out front for sure. What do you hear from them?"

"Nothing from Gochais ... ship's on radio silence. Mead's in Suva looking for a ride out to the ship to finish up the Harris question."

TOM GAUTHIER

"Understand. Well, that's all I've got, Harmon. We're kind of missing jolly old *Auge's Orion* around here. Give me a shout if anything pops up out your way. Cheerio for now."

"Yeah, cheerio, Chandler, tally ho and tata."

Chief Wetmore cut the connection with a chuckle. *Gotta meet that guy sometime. Buy him a beer ... a cold one.*

USAT *Cape San Juan*
Underway – At Sea
Southwest of Tongatabu Island

Captain Strong stood looking at a chart of the South Pacific on his stateroom wall.

Donovan Gochais sat in front of the captain's desk.

"So let me get this straight, Mr. Gochais. The CO of that Army unit is an FBI Special Agent. You have a couple of suspects for your spy ... but no solid proof, so you can't act on it. You can't figure out how they could steal the radar equipment anyway. You've heard a couple strange radio transmissions. Is that about it?"

He turned from the chart to face Gochais, who answered, "That's about it, sir. Not much of a report ... but I said I'd keep you in the loop."

"That you did. Guess I should be thankful that there *isn't* any more to report."

Strong took a seat behind his desk.

Gochais continued, "You could look at it that way, sir. Frankly, it frustrates me ... and gets me a little worried. We know that something is going to pop. Just can't get a clue on where or how."

"Okay, Gochais. By dawn tomorrow we'll be about 300 miles east of Fiji and we should start getting some air cover."

"Understood, Captain. I'm on the morning watch." Gochais stood and walked over to the chart. He ran his finger along the track that Captain Strong had marked in pencil. "What's that speck there, Captain?"

Captain Strong peered past Gochais at the chart he knew so well. "Oh, that's Ata Island. Nobody on it last I heard, maybe a few fisherman. Why? You looking for a desert island to get marooned on?"

"No sir, just curious. Guess I slept through that one last time we were along this way. Good night, sir."

"Good night, Mr. Gochais. Sleep well."

Suva City
Viti Levu
Fiji Islands, South Pacific

Mead watched as the dark gray form of the looming aircraft, a Pan Am Martin Mariner, roared through the amber and pink clouds, banked steeply and lined up for its final approach to landing on Suva Bay. The large twin engine flying boat touched down in a spray of translucent green water that shimmered in the setting sun. It bounced once and then settled firmly into the Bay.

The Port Captain said, "She'll be off-loading and refueling. After some crew rest she'll be all yours before first light. By the way, your pilot's name is Bill Moss ... one of the best."

"Thank you, Commander. You've been a great host."

Tomorrow we'll know something. I hope.

 **CHAPTER 23**

USAT *Cape San Juan*
Underway – At Sea
Just East of Ata Island
11 November, 1943
0300 hours Local Time

Third Mate Lieutenant Donovan Gochais had the con. The binoculars around his neck of little use as the night is without a moon and the Southern Cross is obscured by gathering clouds. The barometer dropped like a rock, promising rough seas by morning.

Second Mate Bill Dorcey, Officer of the Deck, stood on the starboard side of the wheelhouse. Noting the date, Dorcey quipped, "Armistice Day. 11/11 ... the end of the war to end all wars. Ha! Somebody miscalculated!"

Captain Strong stood on the port side of the binnacle stand. He had just asked for some coffee to be brought up for the watch. He started to answer Dorcey, "You got that ri —"

A sudden blinding light filled the wheelhouse.

It went out just as suddenly, leaving everyone with green spots dancing in front of their eyes.

Rubbing his eyes, trying to regain some vision into the darkness, Captain Strong yelled, "What the hell is that?"

FLASH

The beam of light returned.

Then another beam, equally as intensely bright, and a third, all from different directions swept across the forward and aft gun tubs.

Gochais new this would literally blind everyone on watch.

Dorcey groped his way to the alarm switch and sounded general quarters—one long and one short blast of the claxon.

All over the ship sleep groggy men rolled out of bunks and rushed to their assigned stations. The claxon fell silent. And as suddenly, the brilliant light flooding the wheelhouse went black.

Gochais stepped out on the weather bridge to try and get his bearings.

From far below on the surface of the black sea a voice on a bullhorn rose, "Ahoy, Captain Strong."

Gochais turned back into the wheelhouse. "Captain, out here. Did you hear that?"

Stumbling to the opening, Strong answered, "Hear what?"

The voice came up again, "Captain Strong. You must stop your ship. We mean you no harm, but you are covered by four torpedoes aimed at the heart of your vessel. You have more than a thousand men on board. Do not sacrifice them. Stop your ship."

The brilliant light once again flooded the wheelhouse. Strong yelled, this time with a note of fear in his voice, "Jesus, what's happening? How the hell does he know my name ... my ship?"

The augmented voice rose again, its tone more intense, "Ahoy, Captain Strong. If you are on the bridge, listen carefully. Hold your fire. Do not endanger your men. A radio will be brought to you shortly. You must speak with me. Stop the *Cape San Juan* immediately!"

Confusion showed, not panic but confusion because there is nothing in the book to deal with what is going on. *The lights are coming from four different directions. They said four torpedoes are aimed at us. A bluff?* Captain Strong spoke to the officers on the bridge, "Best to just listen. Nobody's been hurt yet."

A figure appeared in the hatchway, silhouetted by the bright lights, and said, "Captain, this is for you, sir."

Corporal McIntire handed the Captain a hand-held radio the likes of which he had never seen before. The radio came alive with, "Captain Strong. Are you there? Push the red button to talk to me."

Strong complied, eyeing the corporal for a moment. He took and spoke into the black bake-a-lite box in his hand, "Who the hell are you?"

"You will know soon enough, *Kapitän*. I will introduce myself when I come aboard."

Strong responded as he tried to peer through the lights, "Come aboard, my ass!"

"Captain Strong. This is my last warning. Stop your ship or we fire and you will have killed a thousand and more good men." The voice on the radio spelled ultimatum.

Captain Strong looked around the wheelhouse, the hand with the radio dropped to his side.

Every man looked back at him, happy they did not have to make the decision, and anxious for him to make it soon.

Scanning the space, he said, "I don't have a choice. I don't have a God forsaken choice!"

Gochais spoke, "Captain, if he does have the torpedoes we lose. If he's bluffing, we get him when he boards."

Captain Strong looked at Gochais with a stern glare. He picked up the interphone, "Stop all engines. Stop all engines." He returned the small radio to his lips, "You've got your wish. What's next?"

"Well done, Captain Strong. You've made a wise choice. Look over your stern, sir."

The glaring lights went out. The men looked back over the stern of the Cape San Juan in time to see a light appear near the surface of the sea. It glowed against what soon took shape as the sail of a submarine.

The man's not bluffing.

As their eyes adjusted to the change in light they made out the ensign with the red field, black cross—and the swastika.

Gochais yelled out, "That's *Kriegsmarine*! The frigging *German* Navy!"

Dorcey asked the question on everybody's mind, "What're the Germans doing here?"

Gochais answered, "I think I know, gentlemen … I think we are about to meet Herr Otto Hauptmann!" He turned to Captain Strong. "This is it, Captain … My mission." Gochais looked out for what he could see.

With a tone of resignation, Strong said, "I'll be damned." The radio in his hand crackled, the voice in clear, unaccented English, "Captain. Please deploy a

Jacobs ladder over the port side … and tell your men to stand easy."

"Mr. Dorcey. See to it."

"Aye, aye, sir."

Gochais turned to Captain Strong, "Sir, please excuse me from the bridge. I need to make some preparations for our guests."

"Get to it! But, God damn it, Gochais, don't get anybody hurt … or my ship sunk."

Strong then reached for the public address microphone. "Now hear this. This is the captain. All hands, including all Armed Guard personnel, stand easy. Do not, repeat, do not fire any weapons until further order."

Gochais slipped out the starboard side of the wheelhouse as Captain Strong saw the first of the leather-clad armed German sailors climb over the port rail and take up defensive positions. The last man over the rail wore the black uniform of the Nazi SS, a Knight's Cross, First Class around his neck.

The engines of the *Cape San Juan* had stopped as ordered and all hands on deck watched the scene unfold.

The ship grew virtually silent.

The SS officer looked up toward the bridge, raised his arm and shouted, "Good morning, Captain Strong! May I join you on your bridge?"

The bright lights stayed trained on the gun tubs, but lowered below the level of the wheelhouse so the people on the bridge could see the German SS officer make his way aloft.

Two *Kriegsmarine* Naval Infantrymen carrying MP-40's, stocks unfolded and ready for action at his side.

Of all the ship's officers and men on the bridge, only Corporal McIntire knew that the thirty-two rounds of 9x19 mm Parabellum ammunition carried by each MP-40 could slaughter everyone in sight.

The others knew simply that they were badly out-gunned. Everyone stood in place.

The SS Officer entered the wheelhouse. He stopped and swept his hand over his black uniform blouse, pulling it down for best fit. Looking at Captain Strong he saluted—not the Nazi straight arm salute, but the hand to the cap bill, palm down salute of a military officer.

"Good morning, *Herr Kapitän*. My name is SS *Oberst* Otto Hauptmann. Thank you for remaining calm. We do not want to damage your ship or injure the men aboard."

Staring straight at him, arms crossed in a defiant stance, Strong asked, "And what the hell do you want, Mr. Hauptmann?"

"There are three crates in your #3 Hold, *Herr Kapitän*, that we will be removing to lighten your ship's load. If you do not resist we will delay you for only a few more moments. However, sir, if you do resist, the boats surrounding you will sink your ship immediately."

Hauptmann stepped to the public address system control, picked up the microphone, and handed it to Captain Strong. "Announce to the ship that we are to be unmolested and that no one will move from where they are right now."

Captain Strong did not move.

Hauptmann thrust the microphone forward again. "Captain, you are very brave. But soon you and many others will be very dead. So do as I say!"

This time Strong took it in his hand, held it a moment then keyed the button. "Now here this. This is the captain. Everyone stay in place. Be vigilant, but do not, repeat, do not interfere with the people moving around the ship. Stay calm. Armed Guard stand down. That is all." He replaced the microphone on its clip and turned to Hauptmann. "What now?"

Hauptmann replied, a taunting grin on his face, "Well done, Herr Captain! Now we will need an escort to show us where the crates are located." He looked out of the wheelhouse toward the radio shack. "And I believe our escort is about to join us."

Captain Strong and the others looked toward the doorway in disbelief as a naval officer stepped onto the bridge.

Hauptmann smiled wide and said, *"Hallo, mein kleiner Bruder. Sie auf der Suche gut* (Hello, my little brother. You are looking well)!

They embraced, and Lieutenant Graham Harris answered, "Hello to you, my brother."

Around the ship each of the sentinels on duty at bulkhead doors and hatch entrances is joined by a *Kriegsmarine* Infantryman.

The captain's announcement effectively turned any confrontation into a stare-down by the opposing forces. The ship's sentries are not armed, their duty primarily for fire watch and blackout safety—not for repulsing boarders. Throughout the ship, faint red battle lanterns cast an eerie glow on these odd-couple pairs.

Gochais made it to the officers' quarters above the #3 hatch and roused Captain Bonfoey before the announcements started. He saw the first of the *Kriegsmarine* Naval Infantrymen come over the rail in the light reflected from the brilliant beam that had moved below the level of the bridge.

"Ed, we've got company on deck ... Germans. I think we know what they're after. Let's head below and stay out of sight so we can figure our next move."

Bonfoey responded, still groggy from sleep, "Lead the way, Don. Where'd the frigging German Navy come from?"

He strapped on his sidearm.

"Wherever, Ed ... They're here." Gochais started down the darkened ladderway into the #3 Hold. Bonfoey followed.

On the bridge the officers and men stared in disbelief at the fraternal reunion they were witnessing.

Corporal McIntire, his anger exploding, stepped toward Harris and screamed out, "You're a slime-sucking traitor!"

The nearest German swung the barrel of his MP-40, catching McIntire on the side of his head. He spun around and dropped to his knees, holding his head. Blood oozed between his fingers as he sank further to the cold steel deck.

Hauptmann said to his escort, "*Einfache, Soldat* (easy, soldier). This skinny one is no danger to us."

Dorcey hissed, "Bastards!"

He held his place.

Hauptmann spoke sternly, "Everyone settle down. No more violence!" He turned to Harris and quietly said, "*Kommen, Graham, zeigen den Weg.* (Come, Graham, show the way.)"

"I will show the way, brother, but please ... English. It has been awhile."

Two more *Kriegsmarine* Infantrymen stepped up onto the deck outside the wheelhouse and

Hauptmann ordered, "*Beobachten. Niemand verlässt das Zimmer.* (Watch them carefully. No one leaves the room)."

"*Sehr gut, Oberst Hauptmann.*" (Very good, Colonel Hauptmann). Gun barrels are lowered and dark eyes glare in the harsh shadows of the beams of light as Otto Hauptmann and Graham Harris left the bridge of the *Cape San Juan.*

Deep in the #3 Hold, Bonfoey and Gochais took concealed positions near the three wooden crates marked with large letters: *R-Tac-OE-USAAC* (Radar-Tactical-Orion's Eye-U.S. Army Air Corps).

His Army issue Model 1911 Colt .45 sidearm in his hand, Bonfoey whispered across the top of the crates to where Gochais crouched, "If this is what they're after we're going to have a lot of company real soon."

Gochais whispered back, "Roger that. Only way they get them out of here is muscling up the ladders … and that'll take a few folks." He racked a round into the chamber of his own Colt .45 and lowered the hammer to half-cock, then added, "Those krauts that came over the rail had MP-40's. These peashooters ain't enough."

Bonfoey responded, "Discretion is the better part of valor, they tell me. We pick our fight when we can win it. Sit tight, Donny. First we watch."

Bonfoey flattened himself against the crate. He'd seen the beam of a battle lantern before he heard the first footsteps on the grated ladder.

Here we go.

Gochais saw it too. Away from the main aisle and flattened against the top of the cargo crates, he and Bonfoey could not directly see the men who approaching their Orion's Eye prize.

One of the intruders spoke, "Here ... These three crates."

Gochais lifted his head slightly, straining for a look, thinking, *that's not a German!*

A second voice ordered, "*Das sind die Boxen. Vorsicht* (These are the boxes. Be very careful with them)!"

Six large *Kriegsmarine* Infantrymen slung their MP-40 *Maschinenpistoles* on their backs and began to remove the three crates. Gochais watched the three pairs of muscular Germans begin to carry the heavy crates up the ladderway. Staying in the deep shadows he raised himself up to look, then quickly dropped down again when he heard the voice with a heavy German accent. "Let us go. They are at the top."

Looking up again, Gochais saw the crates disappear over the combing above, and heard the other men moving below and away from his position. He began to inch himself toward the aisle—out of the dark shadows. He couldn't see Bonfoey, but assumed he would have his back. He brought his pistol to bear and thought, *now or never!*

Gochais dropped to the steel grating deck behind the two men and shouted, "Freeze! Stay where you are!"

The pair stopped, still gripping the hand rails that snaked to the base of the ladder. One turned and faced Gochais, and for an instant Gochais hesitated in confusion, then said, "Harris? Are you okay? Step over here ... I've got this one covered."

Holding his 1911 Colt in both hands, leaning in, aiming directly at the German officer's back, he motioned Harris to move his way. He shouted at the officer, "Hands on your head!"

As he moved toward the figure in the black uniform he heard Bonfoey sliding over the crates to his left. He didn't see Harris step to the side and slowly draw his sidearm. "Sorry, Gochais. *You* drop your weapon. NOW!"

In the dim light Gochais looked into the barrel of the .45 caliber Colt and slowly dropped his hand to his side. He knelt to set his pistol on the deck and heard Harris say, "Otto, we'll take him up with us."

Gochais blurted out, "Otto? Otto Hauptmann?"

Harris smiled. "Yes, Mr. Gochais. Meet my brother."

Hauptmann ignored the banter and said, "You have done well, my brother, very well indeed. A few more minutes and the mission will be accomplished. You will be well rewarded ... and father will be proud."

At the same instant Bonfoey appeared atop the crates and shouted, "You all freeze!"

Suddenly a voice boomed down from far above them, "*Die Boxen sind auf dem Deck, Herr Hauptmann* (The boxes are on deck)"

A battle lantern glared, lighting the deck—and Gochais.

Hauptmann whirled to face Gochais and yelled, "*Töten* (Kill him)!"

The Lugar in his hand spit flame, but the shot went wild, ricocheting off steel girders.

Gochais dropped and grabbed his already cocked pistol.

A burst from the German MP-40 held by the *Kriegsmarine* at the top of the hatch slammed into the crate next to Gochais' head, spraying splinters in his face.

He squeezed off a .45 round where his target had been and heard it twang off metal—not flesh.

226

Bonfoey got off one shot before he dove back into the dark shadows. His foot slipped over the edge of the stack of crates and he spun toward the dark deck. Landing hard, his head slammed into the grating. But his shot had hit home. Hauptmann groaned and fell forward onto the ladder grasping his arm.

Harris moved toward him. "Otto!"

Another burst of fire from the deadly German *Maschinenpistole* above lit the space with sound and fury.

As a sailor on the Battleship USS *West Virginia* before the war, Gochais had been a champion boxer. Never in his life had he felt a punch as hard as the one that spun him around and crushed him into the cold steel mesh of the deck. At first it wasn't pain, just a crushing blow—then it *was* pain, a burning, pulsing pain. His ears rang and he smelled the cordite from the spent rounds. His senses were acute—then began to fade.

Through narrowing, darkening vision he watched the Nazi SS officer and the U.S. Navy lieutenant climb the ladder. *Discretion is the better part of valor,* played over in his mind as blackness enveloped his still body. He never knew that Bonfoey had shaken off the stunning fall and made it painfully to his bleeding side.

Out on deck the wind rose as Otto Hauptmann appeared gripping his hand over a blood soaked sleeve, Harris supporting him as they moved to the rail. They watched the first crate being lowered into the waiting German whaleboat bobbing in the dark water below the Jacob's ladder, and the second being moved into position.

WHAM—BOOM

A massive explosion wracked the ship.

An intense flash of flaming light came over the gunwale on the starboard quarter, eclipsing the flood lights that were playing on the ship. The flames reached as high as the bridge and higher, spreading thirty feet wide and glowing reddish white and yellow against the black sky. Men closest to it had bare skin seared.

Everywhere on the ship men were thrown down from where they stood or laid. Immediately behind the flames a plume of choking black smoke boiled over the ship like a specter, reflecting all the lights and flames in a devils brew. In an instant a huge sheet of seawater cascaded over the flying bridge and sent seamen flailing for something to hold onto before they were swept into the black waters below. The ship shook, then shuttered violently, rose up out of the sea, then settled back with a fifteen degree list to starboard.

She began to settle by the bow.

Below decks the soldiers were thrown from their bunks and chaos reigned in the darkness. The chaos lasted only a moment as the relentless drilling kicked in and men donned life vests, moved to aid the injured and found their way up the ladders to the main deck. As they emerged on the main deck the soldiers paid little heed to the German *Kriegsmarine* Infantrymen, who were themselves seeking safety, their weapons hanging loosely by the sling, the men looking to their officers for direction that wasn't coming. One jumped over the rail in panic falling toward the waiting German tender. He hit the boat's gunwale and rolled into the sea, sinking from sight.

No one noticed.

Down in the #2 Hold, the colored troops of the 855th Engineers took the brunt of the torpedo explosion. The deck below their feet buckled up like a swelling dome and seawater poured in through the gaping hole below the waterline. Overhead, the beams of the makeshift deck structure fell in, trapping many and killing a few.

Screams came from deep in the sloshing darkness.

Men were trapped.

Men were dying.

On the bridge Captain Strong reeled and smashed hard into the binnacle cabinet. He regained his balance and lunged toward the open doorway. The Germans did not stop him, as they moved along with him and the others toward the deck below. Strong reached the top if the ladder and stopped, his head clearing. He grabbed Dorcey by the arm as the others flailed their way past them, and ordered, "Find out where we were hit. Get me a damage report,"

Dorcey, starting down again, answered, "Aye, sir."

Captain Strong went back into the wheelhouse. As he called down to the engine room he noticed Corporal McIntire still dazed and seated against the binnacle holding his head.

Strong spoke into the intercom, "Engine room. Are you flooding?"

Chief Engineer Ted Hall responded, "Negative, Captain. We're dry. Engine fires are out, but I've got the emergency diesel plant running. You can have lights when you want them."

Strong answered, "Okay, we'll take the lights!" He reached up to the alarm controls and activated the abandon ship alarm. The squawker alarm sounded seven short and one long blast—then repeated it.

When the squawker sounds all hands are to abandon ship—even the Navy gun crews.

The blinding lights from the German boats still played on the ship adding to the confusion.

In the radio shack, Petty Officer Makowski sent out the SOS:

```
Ship torpedoed. Sinking fast. 22°01′
South Latitude - 178°13′ West Longitude.
```

He couldn't find Harris, the communications officer, so he followed his training and destroyed the radios and sensitive documents kept in the space.

Deep below decks in the darkened #3 Hold, Captain Bonfoey struggled to get through the labyrinth of crates dislodged and scattered in the explosion. He couldn't believe that the chaos of crates had not crushed him and Gochais. Ears still ringing from the concussion he pulled Gochais' dead weight to the bottom of the ladder. He didn't know if Gochais was alive or dead—but he wasn't going to leave him.

The hold was still dry but he can hear the growing roar of flooding from the #2 Hold just beyond the bulkhead. The ships lights came on and the pool of light above provided him a target for escape.

Not expecting and not getting an answer, Bonfoey asked his friend, "What the hell happened, Don? I think the bastards sunk us anyway!"

He hoisted Gochais onto his shoulder and began the climb.

 **CHAPTER 24**

Suva City
Vita Levi
Fiji Islands, South Pacific
0345 local time

Bill Moss climbed back into pilot's left seat of the Martin Mariner, wondering who the Marine officer standing alone on the dock is, when his radiophone brought Commander Mare's voice to his ears and the news of the sinking troopship.

In a matter of seconds Makowski's distress signal had flashed from ship to ship and base to base across the South Pacific. But it looked hopeless, as the location fix Makowski sent is a good three hundred miles from the nearest shore station, and the closest ship is hours away.

A minute later the big, blond, soft-spoken pilot, William Moss, Jr., climbed from the cockpit and down to the pier. A civilian pilot assigned to the Navy, his boyish face belied the half-million miles of flight in his log. He called his crew together and gave them the news—the troopship USAT *Cape San Juan* has been torpedoed and is sinking.

Marine Major Amos Mead heard him, too.

Moss looked around at their faces and said, "I'm not ordering anyone to go. The weather's foul and getting worse. We'll be lucky if we can find the ship. Even if we do find it, the Navy tells me the seas are running twelve to fifteen feet out there ... and I've never set one of these tubs down in that kind of water. If we do get down in one piece, remember we still have to get back in the air. I've already asked permission to go. If any of you —"

The entire crew stepped forward.

Amos Mead among them.

USAT *Cape San Juan*
Dead in the Water
11 November, 1943
0350 Local Time

The waves rose steadily in the approaching squalls, the rolling sea adding to the precarious footing aboard the stricken troopship.

Captain Strong reached the main deck in time to see Hauptmann leaning on the rail, wounded, Harris at his side.

Strong shouted, "Where do you think you're going, you slimy kraut bastard!"

Hauptmann turned toward him, looking around with a nervous twitch in his eye. "Now, now, Captain. Such name calling. We will leave you to take care of your men."

Strong screamed, "You said you would do this ship no harm. Why did you torpedo my ship?"

Hauptmann responded, "We did not do this, Captain." He grimaced in pain as he moved his wounded arm, trying in vain to appear calm, a proper stoic SS Officer. He glanced at the two crates still on deck. "Under the circumstances, Herr Captain, we will leave these with you."

Captain Strong stepped toward Hauptmann, but a leather-clad German infantryman stepped between them, machine gun at the ready. The other German *Kriegsmarine* Infantrymen moved toward the rail sweeping their gaze around nervously, expecting some kind of assault from the Americans. But the crew of the *Cape San Juan* ignored them while they proceeded to release lifeboats and rafts over the side.

Hauptmann said, "Please, no more violence, *Kapitän*. There has been enough already. Save your men. We are—"

WHOOM

A thunderous roar and flash of fire cut off Otto Hauptman and froze everyone in place.

Simple reflex had men ducking and throwing arms up to their faces.

Almost immediately a blistering hot shock wave rolled over them.

Graham Harris, standing at the rail with his back to the American officers, faced the explosion and only his grip on the rail kept him on his feet as he shouted, "My God, my God, my God, NO!"

Hauptmann spun around in time to see his submarine, *U-835*, rise up out of the sea in a mushroom of oily fire.

He watched in unbelieving horror as she broke in two and settled back into the inferno of burning oil, the men on her bridge, including *Kapitän* Kalbruener, flung like rag dolls into the churning caldron. In too fast a time the sea closed over the *U-835* sucking her crew to a watery grave—far from Germany.

Coming as a prayer, Otto Hauptmann said, "*Mein Gott, was ist passiert* (My God, what happened)?"

For a moment he stared in disbelief, trying to make sense of the carnage that spun surreally in front of his eyes. Regaining his schooled composure, he leaned over the rail and yelled down to the tender still tied below the Jacobs ladder that lay at nearly twenty degrees angle with the hull, *"Radio Walboote zu kommen, die in* (Radio the whaleboats to come in)!"

The stunned sailors did not even look up. He had to yell again, "Radio the whaleboats to come in!" Hauptmann turned to Strong. "I have called in my whaleboats. We will see to our own rescue. It seems we shall be castaways together, *Herr Kapitän.*"

The two men stared at each other while all around them trained seamen went about the business of reaching safety somewhere away from the stricken vessels. In a moment they each turned to give orders as needed. But they stayed at this spot, one not willing to leave the sight of the other.

Harris kept his back to Strong, keeping his death grip on the rail and staring at the spreading oil slick that fouled what could be his final route of escape.

Suva City
Vita Levi
Fiji Islands, South Pacific

To save every spare ounce of weight for survivors, Moss left his three junior officers ashore. They joined the summarily stranded passengers and helped to lug the last of the heavy cargo onto the pier while the crew quickly converted the transport aircraft into a rescue ship. All possible running gear is stripped from the cabin and replaced with inflatable rafts, life jackets, rolls of manila line, blankets, medical kits and containers of hot soup.

Mead began to board the plane behind Captain Moss, but Moss said, "Sorry, no more passengers, Major."

"Captain, I'll save you reading all of my credentials and orders, but I'm going with you. The *Cape San Juan* is my destination. I've got friends aboard. I'll work with the rescue."

Bill Moss saw the look in Mead's eyes. "Get strapped in, Major. It's going to be a rough morning."

Three minutes later the overloaded Martin Mariner strained into the air, lifted her dripping nose into the leaden sky and headed into the unknown, as Moss thought, *This aircraft has a wingspan of one-hundred-eighteen feet, a length of eighty feet and stands twenty-eight feet high — nearly three stories above her floats. She can carry over twelve tons of people and cargo, and she will need every bit of that capability on this mission.*

The first hundred miles provided a nightmare of lightning flashes, blinding rain and turbulent winds that tossed the flying boat like a leaf. Every man aboard strapped himself to the braces and worked feverishly to prepare the rescue gear.

Amos Mead, out of his element, helped where he could. After a particularly violent lurch he looked out at the storm and thought, *I don't like to fly, I really do not like to fly.*

USAT Cape San Juan
Dead in the Water
11 November, 1943
0445 Local Time

Despite the chaos and fear, brave and selfless acts took place all over the ship.

Technical Sergeant Arthur Jeter woke to a dark world of chaos. Ignoring the collapsed timbers and broken stairs he donned his life jacket and made it up out of the #2 Hold and onto the pitching deck. Groggy from sleep and the confusion around him, he heard the abandon ship signal and could see many of his friends going over the side of the ship.

He also heard the screams from below.

First Sergeant Shelton moved past him toward the hold. "Give us a hand, Jeter."

He didn't hesitate.

Joining Sheldon and Sergeant Rivers, Jeter headed back down into the darkness, the first man they found pinned under a beam. With new found effort they got him out and passed him up on deck. Others were helped as they were found. All the while they heard the sloshing of the incoming sea and the crunch of floating timbers in motion.

For a moment no more human sounds came from below. Then Jeter heard a moaning call from deep in the #2 Hold that moments before had been his home. He started to climb down toward the sound.

Captain Bass joined the sergeants, saw Jeter and yelled, "Hold on, Sergeant! It's too damn dangerous to go deeper. You'll be crushed."

They heard the panicked cry again, this time interrupted, then again. From further down the ladder Jeter saw the man being sucked under the water and yelled up, "Sorry, Cap'n, he needs me ... I'm goin' down."

There were no more orders. The sergeants secured a rope around Jeter and he climbed down. The ladder to the lower #2 hold had collapsed, and the deck plate warped up six or seven feet with the highest point just to starboard of center. Hanging from the collapsed ladder's last rung, Jeter could barely touch the high point of the warped deck. He dropped the last few inches. Now he saw the man clearly—a man he knew named Hayden.

As he went deeper into the water, Jeter saw that every time the ship rolled water poured over Hayden's head and he emerged screaming and praying for help. Jeter felt his way through floating wood and stuff he couldn't identify that had blown loose from the ship to finally reach Hayden, water up to his chest and flowing over his head in every roll.

Jeter prayed, "Lord give me strength."

In utter panic, Hayden would not let go of the timber he'd been hanging on to. Jeter got a rope around his leg and together with the others managed to pull him free and up onto the deck.

Through the tangled debris, Jeter called up, "You can get me outta here, Cap'n."

Following the rope tied to his waist that the others kept taut, he made it up on deck in time to see them pull a tarp over Hayden's dead face.

Jeter left the ship with the other soldiers from the 855th. He didn't look back. They would have to survive in the sea on their own.

Bonfoey, carrying Gochais, made it up to the main deck from #3 Hold with great difficulty. He arrived ready for a fight, but found the Germans abandoning ship with everyone else, weapons discarded. He laid Gochais down next to a row of other casualties, where Army Lieutenant Schurts, the unit surgeon, had already begun to sort out the dead from the badly mangled wounded.

Pain and frustration wracking him, Bonfoey thought, *that's all I can do for you now, buddy.* He called out, "Doc, Gochais' bad hurt!"

When he saw Schurts move toward him, Bonfoey stood, looked around and saw Captain Strong. Then he spotted Otto Hauptmann and Graham Harris at the rail.

Bonfoey rushed toward them, shouting, "Hold it right there Otto ... and you too, you slimy traitor!" He had his 1911 Colt trained on the pair who slowly turned to face his wrath, backing up along the rail. Bonfoey shouted over the rising wind to Strong, "Captain, these two are my prisoners ... they killed Gochais and I want them alive. For now!"

Captain Strong reached for his own weapon, "Killed Gochais —?"

A shot rang out from high on the bridge and a black spurting hole appeared in the side of Graham Harris's head above his ear. A spray of gore painted his opposite shoulder crimson and gray and blood and brains washed over Hauptmann.

In a dying reflex gesture Harris wrapped his arms around Hauptmann's neck and fell heavily against him. Off balance, Hauptmann clawed the air as the two disappeared soundlessly over the rail and into the dark sea.

The German tender, just ten feet behind the splash of the two bodies, cast off and moved away without seeming to notice.

Bonfoey and Strong looked up to the bridge. Corporal McIntire, his face bloodied, smiled down at them over the sight of his smoking Colt, shouting over the wind, "Did I get him, Cap'n? I'm a little dizzy and my aim might be off."

Strong said, "Your aim's just fine, Corporal."

A loud and jolting thud hit the side of the Cape San Juan and everyone snapped back to the reality of war. Another torpedo.

238

Japanese Imperial Navy Submarine I-21
Underway—Submerged
11 November, 1943. 0450 Local Time

Executive Officer Tanaka peered through the periscope and reported, "The last torpedo did not explode, Commander!"

Commander Inada, veteran of the Pearl Harbor operation and two successful deployments off the west coast of California, did not change his expression, but continued to smile and answered, "It is strange that they were not underway ... and carried so much light. But we can be satisfied with this night's work!"

Inada turned to face the sailors and officers in the Conn, raising his voice over the sounds of his submarine, "Sinking an American submarine and her supply ship will bring great honor to the *I-21*. You can be proud of your accomplishment."

He shook the hands of the officers and waved to the crewmen in the cramped space. As he turned and started to leave, he ordered, "Mr. Tanaka, I could not identify those other strange lights. There must be ships that I cannot see. Take us down to one-hundred meters and leave this area before they begin an attack."

Commander Inada, Imperial Japanese Navy, smiled broadly to himself. *A very good night's work for the I-21. A very good night, indeed.*

USAT Cape San Juan
Dead in the water
Listing badly and down by the bow

Pre-dawn light seeped through the storm clouds when survivors in the water felt a strong vibration— just before the loud thud slammed against the hull of the mortally wounded Cape San Juan.

The torpedo a dud.

No one wanted to think about the carnage another explosion would have caused.

Captain Strong looked around and saw that the deck officers were getting the job done. All the large lifeboats were away successfully, except the #4 motor launch that he could see had been swamped by too many troops trying to get aboard. He could also see that the large German whaleboats gathered rafts of floating men, securing their lines to the gunnels. Seeing it as a strangely calming site, he thought, *Brotherhood of the sea.*

Strong finally turned to Bonfoey, noticing his blood-stained fatigue jacket. "Where's Don?"

"I got him up as far as the #3 Hold cover, Captain." Bonfoey started in that direction, Captain Strong followed. Gochais' body could not to be found. A smear of blood on deck marked the spot, but it merged with other smears that tracked out to wherever men worked to save themselves and their shipmates.

"No more to be done here, Bonfoey, Captain Strong said, "You'd better see to your men."

Captain Edward Bonfoey took to the rafts with the last group of 1st Fighters.

It would be a long, cold, perilous time for them, with the outcome unknown.

 **CHAPTER 25**

Suva City
Aboard the Pan Am Martin Mariner
Approaching 22°01' S. Latitude – 178°13' W.
Longitude

The co-pilot wrestled with the controls while Moss studied the diagrams showing how two other Pan American captains, John Hamilton and Red Williamson, had worked their giant flying boats in and out of emergency landings on seas nearly as stormy as what he now faced. Satisfied he understood, he then rehearsed the crew in the procedure they were to follow once they hit the stormy water.

The process took Mead's mind off his fears—at least for the moment.

The Martin Mariner bucked and pitched to within ten miles of the sinking *Cape San Juan* before she broke out of the last rain squall.

Captain Moss yelled to his second officer who had struggled with the complex navigation to get them to this point, "There she is, dead ahead. Good job, Roblin!"

Mead peered through the streaks on the window at the scene below. The USAT *Cape San Juan* lay far over on her side, deep down by the head, rolling helplessly in the high-breaking seas. He peered well behind the ship at what seemed to be dots. He realized that the dots he saw strung out beyond sight, downwind of the stricken ship, are men—Gochais and Bonfoey among them.

The pitch of the engines changed and the wind-stream took on a banshee scream as the great airplane nosed over and dove to the level of the ship's smokestacks. They saw only a handful of survivors near her fantail, no one in the water near the ship, wind and currents having carried them away.

Moss pulled the aircraft up to about two hundred feet and swung around the ship for a second look. Then he and the flight deck crew saw what Mead had seen about five miles away—a long dark patch of water filled with floating specks.

Climbing through three hundred feet they saw that what had appeared to be wreckage was in reality hundreds of men bobbing in a great oblong oil slick three miles long. Patches of men clung to overloaded life rafts. One, almost awash, pitching and rolling, is framed by a solid ring of heads and arms being held above water by the men who crowded the inside of the raft.

As Moss made a final pass to set up for a landing clear of the bobbing heads, he spied a separate oil slick and debris under a mile away to the east from *Cape San Juan*. He had only a moment to wonder what it might be before a sharp gust of wind whipped the plane from side to side and brought him back to the mission at hand.

The seas were running so high that brown oil-coated spray from breaking waves streaked the Mariner's windshield. Through one clear patch, Moss

242

kept his bearing on one lifeboat which he saw most clearly as it rose to the crest of the racing swells.

Mead and the others in back braced as Moss inched toward the surface. Holding his rudder against the vicious cross wind, he felt for the top of a swell that would hold his keel to the sea. Mead exchanged nervous glances with the others just as the keel struck the top of a wave with a terrific crash and the plane careened back into the air. He felt sure that her 80 mph landing speed had increased to 800.

Moss nosed her over again, and again she is thrown back skyward by the angry sea. Seven times he tried. Each time the men aboard knew, *it had to be the last ... no flying ship could stand this beating.* But on the eighth try the keel of the Mariner caught a wave at just the right second and the pilot held the shuddering ship doggedly to the water.

Mead's eyes were tightly shut, every muscle in his body tensed for impact when suddenly the engines went quiet. The only sound he heard is the sharp, almost explosive booms of the waves slapping the thin metal hull. They were down in one piece.

Mead and the man next to him threw open the cargo hatch and went to work. As they had rehearsed, they threw over an inflated life raft and ran it out to the end of a one hundred foot rope. *Like a weighted bait on a fishing line*, Mead thought.

The pilot maneuvered the airship to drag the line through patches of men. The tension on the line gave them something solid to cling to, and often with their last remaining strength, the survivors were able to throw an arm or leg over the line and slide down it to the raft at the end. When five or six had been caught they slackened the rope and Mead and the others hauled their catch through the open hatch.

It took almost superhuman strength for the rescuers to haul a man up the final three feet to the hatch in the thrashing swells.

The troops had abandoned ship in such a hurry that many were still wearing packs, ammunition belts, helmets and other heavy equipment.

Mead is assigned the task, as each man is dragged aboard, of cutting off their gear and throwing it back overboard. He wrapped each man in blankets and helped drag him forward toward the galley, where the airship's steward took over and poured hot soup and a shot of bourbon down each salt-parched oil-clotted throat.

While the crew of the Martin Mariner worked, Navy orders hummed over the Pacific. Ships steamed toward the scene.

After nearly two hours on the churning oil-slick sea Moss spotted two dark dots above the horizon. Binoculars and blinker lights identified the dots as patrol bombers of the Royal New Zealand Air Force. The rescue work went on. But a few minutes later one of the bombers fired two red flares in the direction of the Mariner—a signal of approaching danger.

Moss thought, *Maybe a Jap submarine.*

At the same time another black rain-squall bore down on them from the south. Time to finish up. Moss shouted back to the crew, "That's it, guys. We've got to get back in the air while we still can!"

The final three survivors were dragged hastily aboard and the cargo hatch shut. The crew couldn't bring themselves to look out at the men they'd left in the sea. A hasty count put the number of men rescued at 48—more than twice the normal capacity of the flying boat.

Mead tended to the last of the survivors. He saw that the last man dragged into the plane did not have on any pack or ammunition belt. The man's uniform appeared black. He thought, *But then all of the men are oil soaked, some are Negroes, hard to tell the difference.*

Then he saw it.

Tucked into the top of the semiconscious man's shirt—a ribbon.

Mead tugged it free and stared at what fell into his palm—the Iron Cross First Class of a German SS Officer. He ripped the buttons from the front of the man's coat and thrust his hand into the breast pocket, retrieving a bloodied, black leather wallet. He didn't need to open it. As Mead wiped his palm across the front of the wallet gold embossed letters appeared.

SS Oberst Otto Hauptmann.

Mead replaced the wallet in the pocket. He ripped open the rest of the jacket front, found the holster and removed the Luger and stuck in his own belt. Nearby rescuers stared.

Before Mead could speak orders came down from Moss on the flight deck, "Toss any floatable gear overboard to those men and get everyone arranged for best weight distribution."

The orders followed, the crew quickly took flight stations. Mead stayed with Hauptmann.

Captain Moss eased the Mariner slowly in and out of the valleys formed between wave crests. He sought a rolling wave that would give him and the hopelessly overweight airplane enough surface for a takeoff run. Finally, one appeared and the ship spun around and the throttles jammed full forward.

In the next fifty seconds, Mead and his mates lived fifty years.

The surging engines blanketed them in a deafening roar. Crossing waves slashed at the hull with explosive blows. Walls of oily water closed over them as the ship raced forward.

The violence rose.

With engines in full throat the ship gave a final convulsive shutter that shook fittings from the bulkheads and peaked fear in half a hundred souls. She seemed to stop dead in her tracks—but an instant later reached fifty feet above the water.

The wave had split in two beneath her, literally throwing the Mariner into the air before she'd reached flying speed. With no lift from her wings she hurtled back to the teeming surface, violently struck another crest and got thrown again into the air—still too slow to fly. The next crash nearly laid her on her side, her starboard wingtip stabbing at the water—and catastrophe.

Mead lay across Hauptmann holding them both tight to the bunk where he'd placed him. *I do not like to fly*, raced through Mead's mind.

Moss's actions are above and beyond normal skill as he righted the great plane, aimed at the next wave and caught its crest in a way that catapulted her a hundred feet over the next two swells. Her engines dug into the sultry air and with a final seam-straining effort she's airborne.

It wasn't only the 48 survivors who had some quiet words for God during the next few moments. But, once aloft the airmen were in their element and there is still much work to do.

The Pan Am Martin Mariner with her precious cargo banked toward Suva and home. Within the hour radio messages from the Navy informed Moss and the others that the destroyer USS *McCalla* (DD

488), the destroyer escort USS *Dempsey* (DE 26), the Liberty Ship SS *Edwin T. Meredith* and others had reached the USAT *Cape San Juan* and were rescuing the remainder of the survivors.

One message in particular Moss received caused conversation on the flight deck for the rest of the flight—*what the hell are German sailors and marines doing in the Cape San Juan's lifeboats?*

Rescues at Sea
22°01' South Latitude – 178°13' West Longitude

Throughout the long day, rescue ships steamed back and forth along the extended line of victims of the Imperial Japanese Submarine *I-21's* torpedoes.

Winds and currents had strung out the oil soaked survivors over eight miles from the *Cape San Juan*. Some in boats, others clinging to whatever they could find, the men tried to help each other as best they could. It would be a long night and another day before all are found. Some would give up and slip under the sea—others fought valiantly against the marauding sharks—and lost.

Feats of personal heroism were repeated countless times as mariners on the various ships risked their lives to dive into the shark infested waters to rescue men who had spent their last ounce of strength getting through the night in the oily maelstrom.

The final count is 1,359 men rescued of the 1,429 who had set sail from San Francisco. The 28 Germans rescued added to the score.

Seventy men lost their lives in the stormy sea. Only eleven bodies were immediately identified.

The last to leave the stricken *Cape San Juan* were the Navy Armed Guards, their commanding officer, Lieutenant Rhinehart Meuller, USN, Chief Mate Manning, Second Mate Darcey and Captain Strong. They were picked up by the last motor launch sent over by the SS *Edwin T. Meredith* before nightfall ended the rescue operation.

On 16 November 1943, *Meredith* steamed into Noumea, New Caledonia and delivered 359 survivors of the USAT *Cape San Juan* to Advance Navy Base 131 for care and debriefing. The other rescue ships headed for Suva Bay, Fiji.

CHAPTER 26

Suva Bay
Vita Levi
Fiji Islands, South Pacific

USS *Dempsey* and USS *McCalla* sailed into Suva Bay, Vita Levi, Fiji Islands, with 845 oil soaked survivors and two unidentified bodies. Two Navy minesweepers brought in the rest.

As the bedraggled survivors walk or are carried down the gangways onto the pier at Suva Bay, some into waiting ambulances, Mead searched their faces, getting smiles and nods in return—even an occasional salute rendered. He recognized no one.

As the last gig tied up to the pier, Mead stood at the head of the short gangway. A name tape on the jacket of the last officer ashore caught his eye— Bonfoey— and he said, "Captain Bonfoey ... you don't know me, but—"

Edward M. Bonfoey interrupted Mead and extended his hand, "Oh, I think I do, Major. You're Mead. Gochais told me all about you."

"That's me, Captain. Where's Donny?"

Bonfoey looked down at the crumbling concrete pier. "He didn't make it, sir ... he didn't make it."

Mead blurted out, "Shit, man! What happened?"

"Shot by the Germans. They had us pinned down in the hold. Gochais had the drop on Hauptmann and Harris ... but Hauptmann's men came back in. They were above us. Donny didn't have a prayer. They didn't see me."

Adrenalin taking over, Bonfoey spoke rapidly, "He gets hit pretty bad. I couldn't tell if he's dead or alive. I got him up on deck, but—"

"Did you bring him back?"

"Negative, sir. I went after Hauptmann and Harris. McIntire killed Harris. Lost 'em both over the side. Went back to the hold, but Donny's body isn't there. Other bodies are on deck ... but not his. Don't know whether he got loaded onto ..." Bonfoey sagged, everything catching up to him.

Mead took his arm and led him up the pier. "Okay, Captain, let's get you out of here. By the way, Hauptmann is in custody. We got him. He's wounded but he'll make it."

"He's here?" Bonfoey said with a last burst of strength. "I want the son of a bitch!"

"Later, Captain, later." Mead helped Bonfoey into a bus taking the soldiers for debriefing and any treatment they needed. Mead watched it drive away, and then turned to the naval officer who processed the men in. "Are these all the survivors ... and bodies, Lieutenant?"

"No, Major, *Meredith* landed more survivors over at Noumea."

Mead found a flight leaving for Noumea, New Caledonia in about three hours, his credentials got him a seat. He used the time until takeoff to go to the 18th and 142nd General hospitals on Suva—*just in case.*

Noumea, New Caledonia
Same Day

For Major Amos Mead, the C-47 hop to Noumea, New Caledonia, was stressful. Not the flight itself, but his anxiety for the unknown—possibly tragic—fate of Gochais. His fear had replaced the adrenalin of the rescue flight, and he noticed a tremor in his hands not there before.

His thoughts raced, *Come on. There's always a chance. Info's not complete ...*

The plane landed at the old French airport outside Noumea. Mead hopped a ride in a jeep to Army Hospital #31 where he'd been told that the injured had been taken. The scene that greeted him as he stepped into the hospital seemed at first glance as pure chaos, so he stayed to the side of the entry hall to get his bearings.

What first seemed like chaos turned into an efficient system as he watched the medics care for the oil soaked survivors, many having eyes flushed and wrapped, badly irritated and burned by the caustic oil. He heard no words of pity or complaint.

Mead approached the desk manned by a harried sergeant. "I'm looking for someone from the ship. Any chance—"

"Sorry, Major, no way right now. We've still got marines coming in from the Bougainville landing ... plus the troop ship. Just hang in there, sir. They'll have things sorted out pretty quick."

"I understand, Sergeant." Mead wasn't going to pull rank or credentials this time. *If Donny's alive I'll see him ... if not,* he thought as he stepped slowly to the side of the small crowded entryway. Shuffling out of the mainstream of activity, he backed up to a door that led to a ward not involved in the survivor processing.

Mead idly looked through the glass, letting his eyes wander down the row of bandaged battle casualties. He glanced down at the bed just inside the door. Its occupant swathed in bandages and traction cords from both legs that said he'd had a really bad day at the office. Without quite knowing why, Mead pushed open the door and stepped in.

A nurse in starched white uniform with Army major's leaves on the collar turned to him. "Can I help you, Major?"

"Uh, no, thank you."

Mead's eyes never left the boy in the bed.

The nurse asked in a pleasant, almost hopeful voice, "Do you know him, sir?"

Mead spoke softly, not knowing whether the patient could hear him, "No, uh, no, I don't. Who is he?" He didn't know why he'd asked.

The nurse spoke matter-of-factly, professionally, glancing at the chart in her hands, "We're trying to pin that down, Major. He just got here this morning. Pretty banged up. All we know is he's a pilot, that he flew in the fight over Guadalcanal, and that he crashed in the mountains on Santa Isabel Island. No way of knowing how he got that far north."

"How'd you get that much information?" Mead glanced at the patient. "He doesn't look able to talk much."

"An Australian Coast Watcher, guy named Clemens, found him stumbling around in the jungle. He didn't have any ID and wasn't very coherent. Seems he'd been captured by the Japs. When we pushed their fleet north their evacuation caused a lot of confusion and he escaped. Anyway, Clemens hid him out, patched him up best he could ... the poor kid's all chewed up with bug bites. He's got malaria. He hasn't been able to talk to us yet."

Mead asked, "How'd he get here?"

The nurse kept up her rapid-fire report, "Clemens got a PT boat to come in and pick him up as soon as he could. He hasn't been really coherent since we got him. All told, we figure he's been out over four months."

The talking seemed to ease a pent-up tension in her. Mead could feel this happening and held his questions to the obvious, letting her talk it out.

She continued, "There were a lot of pilots down in that time. Too many. We think ... we hope ... this guy's malaria's the falciparum strain. At least then that won't be what kills him. We're giving him Quinine."

Mead let it be quiet for a second, then asked, "No name?"

"No name," she answered. "Flight suit's gone before Clemens found him—"

Mead interrupted, "My God, it can't be." He stared at the tattoo partly visible through the gauze wrapping the arm of the pilot.

The nurse asked, "What can't be, Major?"

"No, sorry, I didn't mean ... Major," he looked down at her name tag, "Major O'Hare, I've got something here ..." Amos Mead hesitated. He put his hand to his forehead, eyes covered. He struggled with his thoughts, and his next words. Then he retrieved his wallet from his uniform blouse pocket and drew out a photograph. He handed the photo to the nurse and said, "Major, check your records for Lieutenant

(JG) Phillip J. Williamson, USNR. Either from *Lexington* or *Enterprise*."

"My God, Major, you sound certain."

"I think I am, Major O'Hare ... but I hope I'm not. Look at the back of the picture."

"What's that?"

"Never mind. Just check it out." He looked down at the wounded warrior and touched the tattoo on his arm. "Hang in there, sailor ... we might just get you home."

He'd found the photo of the young Navy pilot, with the drawing of a heart and the initials BJ on the back, in an envelope slipped into his bag. He turned and walked out into the crowded entry hallway, glad for the confusion. It matched his own.

A voice called out, "Amos. Son of a bitch ... Amos Mead!"

He wheeled toward the voice with a chill of anticipation.

"Amos Mead in the Marines. Boy, what a small world!"

Mead saw the U.S. Army Surgeon, standing in the doorway, his legs spread and arms outstretched, palms out—looking every bit as if he is greeting an old friend. Which he is.

Mead stared hard, then, as the two embraced with hard back slaps, stammered out, "Cosma? Mario Cosma? What the holy hell .... a doc? A Major? Son of a bitch ... it's good to see you, man."

Major Cosma said, "Guilty on all counts!" He stepped back to look Mead up and down. "You look fit and fine ... what're you doing in my hospital?"

"Looking for a friend, Mario. A guy from the *Cape San Juan*."

"One of these kids?" The doctor gestured back over his shoulder.

"I guess. He's an officer. Shot up pretty bad in the face-off with the Germans. Actually, I don't know if he made it or not."

"Shit, that's tough, Amos. What's his name?"

"Gochais. Don Gochais. He's Maritime Service. A JG."

"'Go-chay,'" Doctor Cosma pronounced it carefully. "I don't think so, Amos. As far as we know there's no officers in this lot. Come to think of it, we heard that some of the badly wounded were transferred directly to the AHS *Tasman*. She's an Aussie hospital ship the *Meredith* rendezvoused with. Could be where your boy is."

Old friend Mario Cosma had the look that says, *that's all I've got. Sure wish I had more. Good luck.*

Mead said, "Thanks, Mario. Damn, it's good to see you."

The doctor reached out and shook his hand. "Hope you find him, Amos. Good to see you too. Just wish it could be somewhere else." He nodded back toward the ward.

Mead started to leave. He stopped. "Oh, Mario, remember back in our former life a girl named Betty Jean Brown?"

"Damn right I do, Amos. You two were pretty sweet on each other as I recall."

"Yeah, at one point I guess. I think you've got her husband in there." Mead pointed to the ward he'd just emerged from. "Name's Williamson. Your nurse … O'Hare … is confirming. If it is him, BJ needs to be told."

Cosma began to say, "They'll get to next of kin—"

Mead interrupted, "Takes too long, Mario. I'll check back with you and O'Hare. If we're right I can get word to her quick."

"Okay, pal, I'm curious. Where is she and how do you get to her faster?"

Mead raised his OSS I.D. card for the doctor to see. "She works with us in LA."

Amos Mead got in contact with Suva.

The commander running the harbor checked and found the AHS *Tasmin* is headed into Brisbane.

Mead got the next C-47 for Suva—then a PBY-2 for Brisbane. A long shot. But he had time on his hands. And hope.

During his stopover in Suva, Mead had a chance to get word that two of the Orion's Eye units had been dumped over the side by the last people off the ship— and that one unit had been picked up from a German whaleboat that rescued American sailors. It was flown down to Brisbane where the 1st Fighters who were not in a hospital were being gathered at Camp Ascot. Mead inquired about 1st Fighters officers—and Bonfoey—and found him headed for Camp Ascot also.

Brisbane, Australia
Two Days Later

As the large flying boat made its final approach to landing on Brisbane Harbor, Mead could see the red cross of the hospital ship tied up to the pier. An hour later he had his information. The ship's officers had no identification on any of the *Cape San Juan* survivors, but the Americans they picked up from the SS *Meredith* had been transferred to the U.S. Navy

Hospital. The Germans had been taken to the POW facility at the 112th General Military Hospital.

Mead hailed a taxi and asked the driver as he slid into the left side front seat, "Do you know the Navy Hospital at Camp Hill?"

"You bet, mate. She's north of old Cleveland Road on Kennington." The driver raised the flag on the dashboard and gravel spun from the quick started wheels. "I'll 'ave you thay in a jiff, mate."

Mead smiled. *Where do I get a translator for English in Australia?*

He bounded up the wooden steps under the ADMINISTRATION sign at the less than a year-old hospital. He waited his turn in line, then asked, "Do you have ID's on the people who just came in from the hospital ship—guys from the *Cape San Juan* sinking?"

"Not here yet, Major. But I'll send you over to ER where they came in. Should be something there," the Navy clerk offered and pointed, "It's three buildings down."

Mead turned and walked fast in the direction. The ER stood empty save for an orderly mopping up and a Navy Nurse. Mead took his last shot. "Ma'am, I'm looking for an officer, wounded, that just came off that hospital ship. Name's Gochais." He spelled it carefully.

She didn't look down at her list as she said, "Okay, Major. He's in surgery. He woke up just enough to tell me his name and asked for ... let's see ... another French name ... oh, yeah—Bonfoey. Then it was nighty-night again and into surgery." Then, seeing the look on Mead's face she added, "Hey, they stabilized him on the ship ... lost a lot of blood ... but he's going to be fine. I can guarantee he's headed for home, though. No more war for that sailor." She smiled. "Come back in a few hours, Major. I assume he's a friend of yours."

Mead smiled too, and said, "Correct assumption, ma'am."

He had one more thing to check and he had a little time. The taxi still sat out front of the Admin building. Mead slid into the front seat. "Camp Ascot, guvnor," he said with a terrible British accent attempt.

"Found your mate, eh?" the driver replied. "You're a bit more perky than when I dropped ya."

The gravel flew once again.

Mead found Captain Edward Bonfoey at the 5th Replacement Depot located at Camp Ascot, Brisbane, Queensland, Australia. Bonfoey had officially turned his command over to Major Don Drake who had flown down from the States for that purpose. Relieved to hear about Donovan Gochais, he told Mead that the 1st Fighters had lost 10 men killed. Eight by drowning. He also told Mead something that puzzled the Marine—but that he fully understood. Bonfoey had volunteered to stay with the 1st Fighters. He had resigned from the FBI because he wanted to stay and fight. Major Drake quickly made it happen for him.

Probably with a little help from a certain Major General Nielsen, Mead thought.

Amos Mead caught a break. MacArthur's private communications ship, the ocean lighter OL-31, is back in Brisbane and he can get his reporting done verbally before the paper pile began.

The fifteen minutes it took to synchronize the two ends of the SIGSALY call seemed like an eternity. "Chief Wetmore! How're they hanging? Hey, I've got some good news for you ... and for a couple of pretty ladies you know."

 **CHAPTER 27**

Brisbane, Queensland, Australia
1700 hrs, Monday, December 20, 1943

Major Amos Mead, USMC, had a few more days in Brisbane before heading for Washington, DC — and reassignment.

A chance meeting adds a complication to his life that he didn't foresee—but didn't resist either.

Mead stood beneath the red and white canvas awning that marked the entrance to the Lennons Hotel. The clatter of the trolley cars passing by on the George Street tracks caught his ear, their ornate Victorianesque décor captured his eye, reminding him of London. In no particular hurry, he allowed the sights and sounds around him to slowly supersede his thoughts, his unanswered questions.

What's next? Back to London where it all started? Maybe a crack at going into Europe ... get into some real combat with the Germans? Gochais is going home ... beautiful BJ's husband? Going home too ... Me go home? Hell, I don't even know where home is anymore.

The torpedo sinking of the American troopship USAT *Cape San Juan* near Fiji on 11 November, 1943, had abruptly ended Mead's assignment—except for the intense rescue mission that he participated in with the crew of the Pan Am Martin Mariner. Now, cleaning up the loose ends, he at least knew that he'd done all he could to protect the secret radar from falling into Nazi hands. He also knew that during the *Orion's Eye* operation, while his OSS team on the ship had fought and suffered, he'd missed most of the action.

Lieutenant Gochais suffered grievous wounds, and Mead couldn't quite shake the feeling that he'd placed his young friend in harm's way.

His enemies also suffered casualties. Harris, the traitorous American officer, took a fatal bullet and his half-brother, Otto Hauptmann, the Nazi spy and mastermind of the unsuccessful attempt to capture the radar unit, also took a bullet, but survived.

Now Mead is returning to Washington, DC for re-assignment. He stared idly across George Street at the ornate ironwork façade of a red corrugated-steel roofed residence, not fully in focus while his mind slipped and slid around his situation.

Is it the war ... or is it just me? College, a screwed-up marriage ... can't even remember why I married that one. Lust for sure. Love? What the hell is that? Law degree ... do I want to be a lawyer, or was I just hiding out in grad school? Dad made it easy. Thanks, Dad. So I got the Marine Corp commission on my own ... but then Dad got me into the OSS. Thanks, Dad. Which part of all this is me? Why the hell is this stuff buzzing in my head? Maybe it's the heat. Yeah, the heat.

He turned and stepped into the hotel.

It took a moment to adjust his eyes from the bright Queensland sun to the lobby's subdued light. Ceiling fans twirled lazily, only partly dispersing the humid late afternoon air.

"Good afternoon, Major. Joining us for a cocktail are we?"

Mead smiled and acknowledged the greeting from Mrs. Margaret Byrne, the flamboyant manager of the Lennons Hotel. "Yes I am, Margaret. Thank you for asking."

Taking Mead's elbow in a flourish, as if they were about to be announced into a grand ballroom somewhere, she said, "Well then, let me show you to your usual table!"

He'd been staying at the Lennons Hotel for a couple of weeks, and knew well Mrs. Byrne's love of flirtatious behavior with Allied uniformed personnel. He smiled broader and went along with Mrs. Byrne's usual flair for the dramatic. As he took his seat near the window of the Lobby Bar, he said, with only slight exaggeration, "Thank you, my dear Mrs. Byrnes."

She smiled demurely, always enjoying the attention of this handsome Marine, and said, "I'll send Charles over with your usual, Major."

Mrs. Byrnes turned with a princess wave of her hand and the swish of her full skirted flower print dress, and moved to the bar. "Charles, a Chivas Regal on ice for the Major!"

This performance of a pseudo-Edwardian drama is being quietly watched with amusement from a high-backed wicker chair tucked next to a potted palm in the corner of the Lobby Bar. Army Nurse Major Brigit O'Hare waited a moment until Mead had been served his whiskey. She gazed at his chiseled profile and short cropped dark hair, noting slight

261

graying at the temples, and feeling hesitant about approaching him, but for what reason she didn't know. He'd been friendly enough at the hospital on Noumea, and he'd solved the riddle of her patient's identity. She thought, *He won't think I'm too forward, will he?*

When it seemed evident that Mead is not meeting anyone else, Brigit O'Hare stood and moved toward his field of view.

Mead sat relaxed, eased deeply into the cushioned high-backed wicker chair, when he caught a glimpse of the tall, auburn haired beauty moving in his direction. He just focused on the smooth curves of the tailored cotton khaki shirt when she surprised him by speaking. "Hello, Major Mead."

His eyes tracked up to meet the sparkling brown eyes of the speaker. Recognition set in as he carefully placed his drink on the glass topped table. "Hello, yourself ... Major O'Hare, isn't it?"

She smiled and extended her hand. "It is. Call me Brigit."

"Amos," Mead said as he stood and warmly clasped her hand. He glanced back toward the seat she had come from and asked, "Are you alone? Would you join me?" He hadn't waited for the first question to be answered.

Brigit answered with a small curtsey and a flirtatious lowering of her eyes, "Why thank you, kind sir ... let me get my bag."

He watched her walk away from him. The cotton khaki uniform of an Army Nurse did not hide the curves and athletic moves as she shouldered the russet leather handbag that matched her army-issue 1½" heels and turned back toward him. He didn't look away as he pulled out a chair for her at his table.

Brigit O'Hare was Boston born and raised of good Irish Catholic stock. But, at nearly 30 years old— actually just over 25— and not yet married with a sizable brood of kids, her family saw her as the maverick daughter. She had gone to nursing school and earned an RN, which pleased her schoolteacher mother. Then she continued college and finally earned a doctorate in psychology, which didn't please her retired Boston cop father; at least not to her face. But, when he joined his friends down at the JJ Foley's pub in the south end of Boston, he bragged like the Irishman that he was.

Mead waved Charles the bartender over from his station behind the ornate dark wood bar where he stood, carefully polishing the surface with a folded cloth, and then turned back and asked Brigit, "Can I order you one of these? Chivas?"

"No, sir," she said quickly with mock dismay and a richly flirtatious Irish brogue, "Yer spellin' yer whiskey with an *e* ... now, are yah true?"

She turned to Charles who stood at her side, the cloth carefully folded over his crooked left arm. "Sir, I shall have Jameson if you please ... neat and spelled with no Scot's *e*."

Louder than he needed to, and with a broad smile, Charles said, "One Irish whisky coming up, ma'am!"

Mead laughed aloud. "You are full of the blarney, Major!"

"Guilty as charged, Major; and I've been so told. But today I'm feeling relaxed for the first time in this damn war, so maybe I'm gettin' a little sassy."

"First thing, my dear, lose the *Major* ... it's Amos. So how's our Navy pilot, uh, Williamson doing?"

"Improving, *Amos.* He's stable and on his way back home. Or part way home, at least. He's headed for Tripler Hospital in Hawaii day after tomorrow."

Mead perked up and said, "No kidding? So am I. My partner, Gochais, is being medivaced out to Tripler and—"

"Well, well, Major Mead ... you and I are going to be seeing quite a bit of each other! I'm the head flight nurse for that medical transport."

Charles approached the table with a drink laden wooden tray, its worn edges wrapped with rattan. "Your Jameson, ma'am. There's a bit of ice on the side. And here's some little snacks for ya both."

The arrival of the Irish whisky allowed a brief moment for each to collect their thoughts. Mead pulled a half empty pack of Camels out of his jacket pocket. He reached toward Brigit, flipping his wrist so a cigarette emerged from the pack and asked, "Cigarette?"

She raised her hand, palm forward, and said, "No, thank you, I've never developed the habit."

Pulling the loosened cigarette from the pack with his lips and lighting it with his Globe and Anchor Zippo, he replied, "Sorry I did." Exhaling a long stream of bluish smoke toward the ceiling, he looked back at Brigit. "How long have you been in the Army? I mean ... to make rank as Major."

She replied, "Actually, just two years. I came in as a captain." Resting her elbows on the table and holding the glass with both hands in front of her face, she swirled the ice and gazed into the twinkling light show it produced. "You see, nursing is my secondary MOS. I have a doctorate in psychology. That's what I received a commissioned for, but the Army in its

264

wisdom decided they didn't need a lot of shrinks, especially lady shrinks."

She lowered her arms to the table in front of her, leaned back in the chair, and raised her gaze to meet Mead's. "Since I'm already an RN, I volunteered to serve as a nurse. So here I am."

He looked at her and caught her gaze, but he only barely heard her words, totally mesmerized by the lady that sat across from him. *Her dusky, but sparkling clear voice, the thick auburn hair, the limpid brown eyes.* Suddenly aware of his day-dreaming, he stuttered, "Oh, yeah ... So here you are." *That sounded stupid.* "And, and, Tripler ... uh ... will you have some leave, some, er ... time?"

Brigit laughed—a melodic laugh that left a sly smile on her face. "Yup, I'll have time. Tripler's a duty station transfer for me. All of a sudden the Army needs shrinks, and I'm going back to practice my profession. Working the flight is just a good use of resources."

Amos Mead dropped his gaze with a tinge of red in his cheeks. Brigit used the moment to look closer at his short cropped dark hair and broad shoulders. She'd noted when they'd first met at the Army Hospital in Noumea that he's a few inches taller than her 5'8"—*and that's a good thing.* "So, Amos, are you a career jarhead?"

He answered quickly, thankful for the yank back to plain talk, "Far from it. I'm a lawyer. I hope you can forgive me."

"Hah! Forgiven you are, sir. And where are you headed? San Diego?

"Another *far from it* answer, my dear lady. You know that wounded prisoner you've got on the flight? Well I'm going where he's going ... D.C."

"He's a prisoner ... you're a lawyer ... are you defending him or something?"

"Your third *far from it* ... I'm with the OSS, and the POW is a Nazi agent."

He immediately felt that he had said too much. "We'll leave it at that."

His slight change of demeanor cooled the conversation a bit. The flirtatious banter had been pleasant, but Mead felt the need to reconnoiter his feelings.

Leaning back in his chair, he brought the last of the Chivas to his lips, then said, "Do you have plans for dinner?"

"Well, I am meeting some of the girls from the Navy Hospital at Camp Hill. But, kind sir, if that's an invitation, I shall make other plans."

"It's an invitation." *Damn it's getting warm in here.* As warm as the smile he couldn't turn his eyes from.

While complications were developing for Mead and Brigit, even more complications were developing at a much higher level.

In fact, as high a level as he could imagine.

 **CHAPTER 28**

The White House
Washington, DC

"Come in, Bill," the man in the wheelchair said through the cigarette holder gripped tightly in his smiling teeth.

"Thank you, Mr. President," General William 'Wild Bill' Donovan, head of the OSS, replied, extending his hand. "It's always good to see you, Franklin."

The President of the United States waved Donovan to a chair as the liveried butler stood near the sideboard, white gloved hands folded in front, anticipating a request for a libation for the guest

"A Scotch, Bill?"

Donovan responded, "Yes, thank you Franklin." He turned to the butler, "Ice, splash of soda, please."

Addressing the butler by name, the President said, "Mr. Trimble, when Mr. Hoover arrives you may serve dinner … and then see to it that we are not disturbed.

The butler replied, "Yes, Mr. President," and handed the already sweating glass to Donovan, and bowed slightly with practiced grace before slipping out of the small private dining room.

General Donovan began, "Franklin, we have others who know ... or at least suspect our situation with the Vice President." His voice rising, tension beginning to show, he added, "Sir, we cannot allow this to leak. Espionage in war time? Good God, sir—"

Roosevelt interrupted with a wave of his hand, "Okay, Bill, okay ... I'm concerned too, but we'll wait until Edgar arrives to get into this unsavory business. Have you assigned someone to get on the ground out there for us?"

"Yes, Mr. President. I'm sending Marine Major Amos Mead?"

"Ah, yes, the chap who foiled that Nazi plot to steal radar secrets. Amazing ... German submarines in the Pacific. Is Mead in Washington?"

"No, Mr. President, he's on his way home from Australia. He doesn't know it yet, but his team is intercepting him in Hawaii."

"His *team*? Would that include Mr. Wetmore, Bill?" Roosevelt raised his hand, palm forward toward Donovan and answered his own question, "No, no, I know your answer, Bill. If this situation is as bad as we feel it is ... well, who else but Harmon Wetmore would do?"

Butler Trimble entered the room and announced, "Director J. Edgar Hoover, sir. I shall serve dinner."

The President said, "Excellent," as he waved the FBI director into the room and pointed at a chair. "Please join us, Edgar. We have something important to discuss with you concerning the war in southeast Asia.

The FBI director smiled and said, "Thank you, Mr. President. I appreciate the invitation." He slipped into the chair, glanced at General Donovan, and added, "How may I be of service to you?"

At the same time he thought, *What the hell has the President gotten us into now?*

Amos Mead will not know until he reaches Hawaii.

 **EPILOGUE**

Orion's Eye never got into German hands beyond its boat ride on the submarine *U-835*'s whaleboat.

The incredible breakthrough in radar technology went into combat with the 1st Fighter Control Squadron after they reformed and re-equipped in Brisbane, Australia.

The 1st Fighters and their secret weapon participated in the landings at Hollandia, Sarmi and Wadke in New Guinea, then on to Leyte and Mindoro in the Philippines.

Chief Harmon Wetmore ran across a report that he forwarded to Lieutenant Gochais, serving recuperative duty on Catalina Island where he taught navigation to new merchant mariners.

The report read:

1st Fighter Control Squadron

```
A detachment of 66 enlisted men and 11
officers, commanded by Captain Edward M.
Bonfoey, was assigned the mission of
setting up a temporary fighter control
sector at Mindoro, the detachment to
participate in the initial landing on that
```

island and to be operational within a few
hours after setting foot on the beach.
This detachment was composed of two
groups, the D-Day group led by Captain
Bonfoey and the D+1 group led by Captain
J.W.R. Johnson. The two groups together
with their equipment were loaded aboard
separate LSTs, 1036 and 1025, on the 29th
and 30th of November at Leyte.

The German sailors and marines who survived
the sinking of their submarine and the USAT *Cape
San Juan* were officially recognized for their role in
saving American lives and sent to prisoners-of-war
camps in Arizona for the duration of hostilities.

Upon his full recovery in Australia, Otto
Hauptmann is escorted to Washington, DC for
interrogation by the OSS at Fort Hunt in the Virginia
countryside. There Hauptmann learned of his
father's death. The full story of his father's activities
in the United States and Germany is obtained, as well
as the history of Graham Harris's double life. Harris's
body is never recovered.

George Nicolaus was extradited to the U.S. and
tried for his role in the attempts to steal *Orion's Eye*.
He was sent to federal prison, but paroled after the
war and returned to Germany.

An announcement appeared in the Bennington
Banner, Bennington, Vermont:

Lieutenant and Mrs. Phillip J.
Williamson, USNR, are proud to announce
the birth of their son, Amos.

Born September 3, 1944, Amos Nathan
Williamson weighed 9 pounds, 3 ounces.
His godfather, Marine Major Amos N. Mead
is on active duty in the Pacific.

AUTHOR'S NOTES

Code Name: ORION'S EYE is a work of fiction based on actual events. Many of the characters in this book are real people. Some are historical figures and some are *regular Joes*. One thing they have in common is that if they were alive today, and read this book, they would know where they are, but not recognize the words they speak, the actions they engage in or their relationships to each other.

So where does **fact** merge with **fiction**?

Following are a few of the people, places and things mentioned in the book. Fact or fiction?

ORION'S EYE

FACT in its existence, but FICTION in its advanced powers. The book gives this radar special powers from a convergence of four technologies. The four technologies existed, but just not at the same time or place.

The first: '...the invention of the magnetron by a guy named Hull at General Electric.'

Albert Wallace Hull is credited with inventing the first magnetron in 1921. Strangely, it's based on a German concept by Greinacher. (The Japanese were also working on the magnetron in 1943, but never attempted to militarize it.)

The second: '... the klystron that serves as an oscillator in the receivers.'

A klystron is a specialized linear-beam vacuum tube (evacuated electron tube) used in regular radar at the time.

The third: '... developed in Bell Labs by a guy named Schockley ... a transistor.'

Not invented until 1947.

The fourth: '...air-to-ground radio ... Al Gross ... hand-held VHF/UHF ... spectrum above 100 mhz radios.'

The OSS actually recruited Gross, who worked for them throughout World War II. By 1941, Gross designed both a ground unit, called *Joan,* and an airborne unit, *Eleanor,* which communicated with each other via Hertzian radio waves in a manner virtually impossible to monitor—even behind enemy lines.

OSS SAFE HOUSE

The address on Wilshire Boulevard is fiction. However, the house and grounds described are patterned after a house in Claremont, California, previously owned by a dear friend.

OTHER LOCATIONS

The SS headquarters, Goering's offices in Berlin, the hospital in Vienna and the various OSS locations in D.C. are factual. So is the Catalina Island OSS School on Toyan Bay and the Baja, California location for the *Sinarquists* (also factual).

All of the Pacific islands are real and located as in the story. While the Mexican and Chilean sites are used in a fictional setting, their general locations and waypoints are factual.

SIGSALY

Fact! But no way could a couple of spy chasers like Wetmore and Mead be allowed to use it.

SIGSALY (an acronym with no meaning) began operation in World War II as a digital encrypted voice telephone system connecting London and the Pentagon. Bell Labs developed it.

Bell Labs had developed the A-3 telephone scrambler for Roosevelt and Churchill in 1939 using older non-digital technology, but it was not secure and by 1941, broken by Germany.

A Bell Labs contract with the Army in 1942 developed the revolutionary digital SIGSALY 12-channel system by 1943.

The 805th Signal Service Company is the actual unit that manned the real SIGSALY locations.

USAT CAPE SAN JUAN

Fact. The ship is as it is described and pictured in the book. The date and location of the sinking are factual. The rescue, except for Mead's presence, is written as it was recorded in war records.

THE SHIP'S CREW

The captain, chief mate and second mate on the *Cape San Juan* are the real people. My father and mother knew them well. They wouldn't recognize their dialog in the book, but they would certainly tell tales of the sinking. I use their names to honor their memory.

All three of the communications people—Harris, McIntire and Makowski are fictional. However, the names are from real friends of mine who would recognize nothing of their adventure.

1ST FIGHTER CONTROL SQUADRON

Fact. This unit organized and operated in every location cited in the book. Of course time frames are truncated and activities simplified for the story. Command structure is also fictionalized, except for Bonfoey and Donald Drake. Both of their families have graciously provided material for the book.

855TH ENGINEER (AVIATION) BATTALION

Fact. The *colored* unit sailed aboard the ship and quartered in the #2 Hold as described. The casualties and conditions after the explosion are accurate—if understated. The survivors went on to fight in the Philippines and other Pacific battles.

253d ORDINANCE COMPANY (AVIATION)

Fact. They were on the *Cape San Juan* at the sinking. Though I could not find any history of the unit, I have communicated with two veterans of the unit and the sinking who provided me with valuable insights into the experience.

AMERICAN OSS & MILITARY OFFICERS

Mostly Fact. The roles of the officers and government officials are either real names or based on real people.

In Chapter One (London and DC) all of the people mentioned are historical—except of course Amos Mead. Their dialog, jobs and actions are fictional, but based on real history.

GERMAN OFFICERS & SPIES

All of the German spies, Kriegsmarine Officers and SS Officers, except Kapitän Kalbruener and Otto Hauptmann, are historical—real people.

The Velasquez's are fictional. Their dialog and actions are fictional, but in many cases based on real history.

AMOS NATHAN MEAD

Fictional. The name Amos Mead has intrigued me ever since I ran across it in my family tree.

The real Amos is my 5th great grandfather, a 1777 Revolutionary War veteran of the Battle of Bennington and the Battle of Fort Ticonderoga. I'm happy to have found him—his name—a home as Major Amos Mead, USMC, and an agent for the OSS/CIA. Just maybe, he has a future.

CHIEF HARMON WETMORE, USN

Fictional. The Chief is a fictional character. He's based, however, on a composite of a number of friends of mine in the American Legion.

BETTY JEAN (BJ) WILLIAMSON (nee BROWN)

Fictional. Betty Jean and her husband, Phillip, are fictional.

Too bad. She seems like someone you'd want to know.

EDWARD M. BONFOEY

Fact. Born in 1912 in Pennsylvania, Edward Monroe "Munny" Bonfoey is a graduate of the University of Virginia Graduate School in Foreign Languages. As a Lieutenant, then Captain, U.S. Army Air Corp., Bonfoey served with distinction with the 1st Fighter Control Squadron in the Pacific Theater from 1941 to 1946.

The unit history mentions his exploits repeatedly. He participated in five of the Pacific islands assaults. Bonfoey is the scion of a distinguished military family. His son, Ned, served as an Officer in the Special Forces. His grandson, granddaughter and grand son-in-law are all senior Officers in the United Sates Army. I'm proud that he could play "himself" in a fictionalized role in this book.

ARTHUR LEE JETER

Fact. Born in Pennsylvania in 1923, Arthur Lee Jeter enlisted in the U.S. Army in 1942. He served with the 855th Aviation Engineers Battalion, HQ Company, throughout the Pacific campaigns.

His heroism and suffering during the sinking of the Cape San Juan is real. Jeter was discharged in December 1945 and awarded the Purple Heart, the

Philippine Liberation Ribbon with one star, the Asian-Pacific Theater Service Medal with two stars and the WWII Victory Medal. His fictionalized role in this book is not far from fact.

CHESTER W. DRIEST

Fact. Chester Driest is the reason I could write this book. While searching for information on the sinking of the Cape, I discovered Chester. Generous with information about the 1st Fighter Control Squadron (he even made me an honorary member of their group!), Driest is the author of the compilation *From L.A. to Luzon With a Slight Pause Off Fiji.*

Chester Dreist passed away in 1999. Since then I've met Chet's daughter, Edie Driest, who was invaluable in locating other original documents and photographs. She has become a friend, and I'm forever grateful for her help and support.

Based on his communications with me before his death I've included him in the book—with fictionalized dialog and activities—as an honor to his memory and in gratitude for setting me in the right direction to learn about that fateful morning of 11 November 1943.

Oh, one more item:

The GOCHAIS Family

Fact. The Francophiles among you—or those who actually learned something in their high school French class—have already recognized the fact that *Gochais* and *Gauthier* are both pronounced go-chay. So you caught me.

Based on a real family, my family, all of the family names and events in the life of Donovan Ignatius "Gochais" Gauthier are real, except the LAPD and OSS roles.

Donovan did serve in the Navy aboard USS West Virginia; he did serve on Catalina Island (with the Maritime Service); did graduate from the Alameda Maritime Officers School in its first class, and he served as third mate aboard the USAT Cape San Juan. His last voyage with her was the coast-wise trip mentioned in the story. He missed the fateful voyage in this story. After the war, the boys, Bobby and Tommy, were joined by three sisters and Donovan joined the Santa Barbara Police Department, retiring as Chief of Police.

He had a lot of FBI friends.

(photo) The Gauthier Family, early 1944 after the sinking of the USAT Cape San Juan.

(photo) Soldiers from the 855th Aviation Engineers Battalion and the 1st Fighter Control Squadron on the bow of the USAT Cape San Juan as she sails from San Francisco Bay to her destiny 300 miles from Fiji.

U.S. Navy Archives. USAT Cape San Juan just prior to sinking. (USAT designation is U.S. Army Transport)

ACKNOWLEDGEMENTS

As with any endeavor, like the writing of this book, there are many people involved, people to acknowledge and to thank.

First and foremost is my wife, Marlene, who allowed me to chase a dream and reformat my life, spending a year ducking chores, to research and write. Though *Code Name: ORION'S EYE* isn't her preferred style of story, she patiently read the various iterations and proved invaluable as a proof reader and critic. Thank you!

A close runner up for primary colors is my mentor and teacher, Kris Franklin. An accomplished author, teacher and published novelist (*Relentless, Silvercat*), Kris kept me on a tight leash in the early work on the book. I learned and learned—and learned again from this man the skills and craftsmanship that produce a good work. Thank you, Kris.

A book is characters and plot. While this book is a work of fiction there are core events that actually happened and people who actually lived through them woven through the plot. An important part of my motivation in writing this book is to honor and remember them as well as I could. There are three soldiers, honored veterans, who played a great and appreciated role in my work on this book. They are Chester W. Driest, Edward M. Bonfoey and Arthur L. Jeter.

I sincerely thank Tony Jeter, son of Arthur L. Jeter, for not only allowing me to use his father's real name, but also for sending me photographs and documents from the times and places of Technical Sergeant Jeter's honored service in World War II. The experience at sea of Sergeant Jeter and the 855th Engineer (Aviation) Battalion in the story are based on real events. Permission to use his real name provided me with the opportunity to relate the bravery that Sergeant Jeter displayed in rescuing comrades during the sinking of the ship. He is a true hero. Arthur Jeter passed away March 28, 2008.

Deserving equal gratitude is Edward M. "Ned" Bonfoey, Jr., son of Captain Edward Monroe Bonfoey, Sr. Ned also allowed me to use his father's real name in the story, providing photographs and documents that allowed me valuable insights about these heroes in 1943. In truth, Captain Bonfoey didn't really have that much fun on the voyage of the Cape San Juan, and he wasn't an FBI agent. But he did serve as an officer and leader with the 1st Fighter Control Squadron. After surviving the sinking of the ship in real life, Bonfoey went on to serve in the Pacific Theater with the Squadron until 1946, participating in five of the Pacific islands assaults. (The 'report' on pages 251-52 is authentic.) Edward Monroe Bonfoey passed away April 14, 1997.

The last of my personal acknowledgements goes out to Chester W. Driest. Chester is the catalyst that moved this book to reality. Unfortunately, he didn't live to see it happen. Let me digress and tell you the story of our meeting.

I had grown up with my father's stories of the sinking of his ship, the USAT Cape San Juan. After his death in 1992, I had a faint idea about writing about the event and tried repeatedly to find information on the ship and the event. Serendipity lent a hand. I ran across a newspaper article about a reunion of soldiers who had experienced the sinking of the Cape San Juan. Chester Driest was an organizer of the event. My call to him in Florida proved to be the seminal event for creating this book. After I told him of my connection to the ship he made me an honorary member of the 1st Fighter Control Squadron. He sent me a document that he had compiled recording the official reports, photographs and memoirs of the group.

It was one comment that he made that launched the plot. He said, "You know, Tom, a lot of the guys in the unit didn't realize how secret our radar equipment was."

Chester W. Driest passed away in March 1999. His honored memory lives on. Thank you, sir, for helping me with my dream and for adding one more memorial to the memory of your comrades in arms. I know how important that will be to you.

There are many others who directly or indirectly helped in the research for this book, too many to list by name. Through the magic of the internet I 'met' veterans who provided me with the details on radar, radio, ships, locations, aircraft, flying routes and the like.

Thank you one and all for keeping me historically honest and as close to technically accurate as I could. I can't say that I 'met' any of our former enemies, but I can be grateful for the Japanese Imperial Navy records and the histories of the Kriegsmarine U-boats and the Nazi Party for adding the authenticity of facts that I could fictionalize for the book.

(photo) Technical Sergeant Arthur L. Jeter, 855th Engineer (Aviation) Battalion

(Right) Captain Edward M. Bonfoey

Steven Dybas (left) and Chester Driest

ABOUT THE AUTHOR

Dr. Tom Gauthier lives with his wife Marlene in Reno, Nevada. Tom is a retired Human Resources Development executive, having worked for one multinational corporation for over 34 years.

He holds a BS in Management, an MBA and a Doctorate in Psychology. Tom and Marlene have four grown children, thirteen grandchildren and twenty great grandchildren. He has traveled extensively and is an avid student of history.

A veteran of the Army and Air Force Reserve, Tom served in a Combat Intelligence unit and on a C-119 Flight Crew.

Since retiring in 2000, he has been writing novels.

Contact: tomgauthier@gotsky.com

OTHER BOOKS
By
TOM GAUTHIER

Amos Mead Adventure Series

MEAD'S TREK

REVENGE ON THE BLACK SUN

FORCE THREE RISES

Story of Ben "Coach" Wade of CBS Survivor

A VOYAGE BEYOND REASON

Compiled History of the Actual 1st Fighters

The SAGA OF THE 1st FIGHTER CONTROL SQUADRON

Children's Book of Poems and Stories

PUMPKINS To HOLLY

All Available on Amazon.com

The true history of the 1st Fighter Control Squadron from initial formation, through the torpedo sinking of USAT Cape San Juan, and on through their involvement in the battles of the Pacific campaign is told in the book compiled by author Tom Gauthier from the memoirs and histories of the unit.

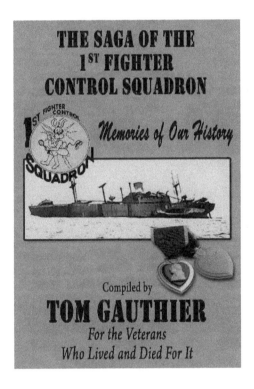

Available on Amazon.com